Praise for the novels

"Sensually delicious. It gives us a glimpse of the train-wreck that can occur when the past meets up with the present in a catastrophic way."
—Tarryn Fisher, *New York Times* bestselling author, on *Such Dark Things*

An authentic, absorbing story of love, friendship, and grief.
—*Library Journal*, starred review, on *I'll Be Watching You*

"Fans of domestic thrillers with an unreliable narrator will gobble this up. Recommended for all thriller suspense collections."
—*Booklist* on *Such Dark Things*

"Written in breathless style, this page-turner relies on quick thrills, surprise twists...[for] readers seeking a fast entertaining tale."
—*Publishers Weekly* on *Such Dark Things*

"Keeps you thinking about it long after you have finished it... *Such Dark Things* is a novel full of suspense that you will love to read!"
—*Fresh Fiction*

COURTNEY EVAN TATE

THE LAST TO SEE HER

mira

mira™

Recycling programs
for this product may
not exist in your area.

ISBN-13: 978-0-7783-0941-3

The Last to See Her

Copyright © 2020 by Lakehouse Press, Inc.

This edition published by arrangement with Harlequin Books S.A.

For questions and comments about the quality of this book, please contact us at
CustomerService@Harlequin.com.

Mira
22 Adelaide St. West, 40th Floor
Toronto, Ontario M5H 4E3, Canada
BookClubbish.com

Printed in U.S.A.

Also by Courtney Evan Tate

Such Dark Things
I'll Be Watching You

THE LAST TO SEE HER

1

GENEVIEVE TIPPED THE courier and set the certified letter on the coffee table.

She knew what it was. She'd been waiting for it for almost a week.

Every day, she'd wondered, *Will it be today?*

And each day it wasn't.

Until today.

Nervous energy buzzed through her fingers and toes, tingling through her veins, like ants scurrying in a thousand directions. She paced for a minute, stopping at the floor-to-ceiling windows, staring at the magnificent cityscape lining the horizon. Buildings burst through the hazy pollution, their tips scraping the clouds.

People far below her were bustling here and there, quick

to walk, slow to linger. They had things to do, places to be, and she didn't.

Not anymore.

She ripped open the envelope, pulling the banded documents out, scanning through the words, hunting for the official stamps and signatures that declared this an official act of the court.

They were all there.

This was real.

It was finally happening.

She focused her gaze on the words before her.

Honestly, they were simple.

The black-and-whiteness of them was stark and startling. There were no gray areas, no areas open to interpretation.

They reduced the last ten years of her life into a handful of legal phrases and technical terms. *Incompatible differences associated with adultery, marriage dissolution* and *absolute divorce.*

She stared at the words.

Soon, she would be *absolutely divorced.* She just had to sign the papers.

It had only taken six months of her life to iron out the details. To separate all of their worldly possessions into two camps, his and hers, to figure out who got what. Divorcing a lawyer was the only thing worse than being married to one. No matter that he was the one in err, because he repeatedly fucked someone else, he was out for blood and it took months to sort it all out.

But thank God no children were involved.

That's what people kept saying, like it was a good thing or a blessing.

But if she'd had a child, she wouldn't be all alone, and someone would still love her.

She felt like she was floundering. For so long, she'd put all of her energy into a man who hadn't deemed her worthy to stay faithful to. That had done something to her self-confidence. Something terrible. It wounded her in places she hadn't known she had, and now she had to figure out who she was without him.

She wasn't Genevieve Thibault anymore, one half of a whole. She was Genevieve McCready again, and what was Genevieve McCready going to do now, now that she had to stand alone?

She pushed herself off the couch and ran water in her coffee cup. It was a habit Thad had taught her. He hated it when the cups developed coffee rings. She stared at the running water, and then set her cup down.

She didn't have to do what he wanted anymore. If she wanted coffee rings or tea rings or any kind of fucking rings, she could have them.

It was an epiphany.

She was her own person again. It had been so long since she was a *me* instead of a *we*.

She looked around, at the condo she had fought so hard for… the marble floors that they couldn't agree on—she'd wanted slate, he'd wanted marble—at the modern light fixtures that he'd gotten his way on, at even the tan wall colors. She'd wanted gray.

Why had she even wanted this place?

It was all Thad, and none of Genevieve.

A sense of exuberance, a strange jubilation, welled up in her as she searched online for a Realtor and then dialed the phone.

Bubbles of excitement swelled in her belly as she arranged a time for the Realtor to come see the place.

And then again, as she stared at a map.

Unlike Thad, someone who had spent years building up his legal practice and honing his networking skills in this one city, she could work from anywhere.

She wrote novels.

She could work in Antarctica if she wanted to.

She *didn't* want to, but she could.

She already had a plan. She knew where she was going, and what she was doing. She just had to have the courage to do it.

She picked up the phone and called her only sister, Meghan.

"Meg, I'm moving home."

Her sister paused. "Home as in…?"

"Cedarburg." There was a long pregnant pause now.

"Um. Why would you want to move back to Wisconsin? You haven't lived there in…"

"In eighteen years. Since I left for college. Yes."

"But…why?"

"I don't know," Gen said honestly. "I just feel a need to get back to my roots. I love Chicago, but the traffic and the noise…" She stared out from her twentieth floor windows again. Even from up here, even though the vehicles looked like Matchbox cars, she could still hear the honking. "This feels like Thad. I want to feel like *me*."

"There's nothing there," Meg said carefully. "Nothing but fields and cold and—"

"And friendly people," Gen interrupted. "And our parents, and familiarity, and open spaces, and distance from Thad."

"But I won't be there," Meg reminded her gently. "I'm not moving back. I think you need to be near me, Gen. You need a support system. Divorce is no joke."

"I know that," Gen said patiently. "I'm the one living it. You're still with your Prince Charming and point five children living the American Dream, and I'm the one sitting in an empty condo."

She fought to keep the bitterness out of her voice, as she compared Meg's bustling, messy home to her own stark and empty condo in her mind's eye.

"I'll tell Joey that you're counting him as a point five," Meg chuckled.

"Well, he's only five, so it's fitting. I mean, honestly. He's not a whole person yet."

They laughed again, and then Meg sobered up.

"Is this really something you want to do?"

Gen nodded. "Yeah. I think so."

Meg took a big breath. "Well, let's do it, then. I'll help you with your condo, and finding a moving company, and looking online for a house there, and hell's bells, we've got a lot to do!"

"You don't have to help with all that..." Gen trailed off, but Meg interrupted with their lifelong pact.

"Sisters forever," she decreed. They'd used that pact since they were kids. Whenever one didn't want to do something, the other would remind them "sisters forever," and they would concede.

Gen realized she wasn't going to get away with not letting Meg get her hands in all the new plans.

"Sisters forever," she agreed.

"But first, you promised to go to my convention with me," Meg reminded her.

Gen hesitated.

"Don't tell me you forgot. New York City? Spa days, shopping—you need a new wardrobe, sis—and nights on the town. *You promised.*"

Gen paused again, and Meghan cajoled, "Pleasssse. We need this. You need this. It can be your divorce party."

"Okay," Gen found herself saying. "Fine. I'll still come."

Her sister squealed and Gen hung up before Meg could get too excited. She was moving away from everything she'd known for over a decade. Even though the world seemed unsettled and uncertain, for the first time in at least five years, she felt at peace.

2

THE AIRPORT WAS busy today, which was fine. Gen was used to *busy*. Chicago teemed with life, with people, with traffic. Soon, though, she'd have to acclimate to rural living again. The slowdown, take-a-minute-and-chat kind of life. So, yeah, it would be an adjustment.

But first... New York City.

She hefted her battered leather laptop bag over her shoulder. She'd packed everything else into a moving truck, and she had one suitcase checked in for the plane, but she would never trust anyone else to transport her laptop. It was the instrument she worked with. It was how she *lived*. It was more precious to her than gold. She'd be leaving directly from NYC to her new home. She already had a farmhouse out in the country bought and paid for, sitting at the end of a little one-lane road in Cedarburg.

She wove in and out among the people crowded in O'Hare's corridors now, and made her way to a bar. Flight delays sucked, but at least she could have a drink while she waited.

She pulled up a stool at the far end of the bar, and ordered a Long Island iced tea, her drink of choice. The bartender didn't even blink.

"Sure thing, little lady." Being five-seven, she wasn't *little*, although she was slender. But she smiled anyway.

She set her laptop at her feet and watched the people.

Being a writer, her favorite game was to make up a story for everyone.

"See that lady over there?" she asked the bartender as he set her drink on a napkin in front of her. She motioned toward a heavily made-up woman standing in the middle of the flow of people, talking on her cell phone. "I think she's breaking up with her boyfriend because she works too much."

He lifted an eyebrow, examining the woman. "Oh, really? What makes you think that?"

Gen examined her, too. "Well, check out her pricey shoes. They indicate that she's not married. Husbands tend to throw fits about shoes that expensive. She's not wearing a wedding ring, and her suit is super expensive. Also, she's been crying."

Her eyes were red, and the bartender nodded. "You could be right."

Gen sipped her drink. "I probably am. But either way, that's what is happening with her in my head."

"Okay, what about him?" the bartender gestured toward an elderly man in the back corner, nursing a beer. "He's been there for at least an hour."

"Him? He's waiting on his mail-order bride, of course," Gen said immediately. "That's still a thing, you know. She's coming in from the Czech Republic and her flight was delayed."

He chuckled, and his eyes crinkled as he laughed. "You've got friendly eyes," Gen observed. "You like your job."

"I do," he agreed.

"You must see all kinds of stories here."

He nodded. "Yeah."

Gen sipped again. "Wanna share? I'm a writer. I can always use new material."

"What do you write?" he asked with interest. "Because I've been working on a sci-fi novel for a couple of years now."

Gen tried not to cringe. That was inevitably something she heard from strangers. *Oh, you're a writer? Awesome, I'm writing a book, too! How do I get it published?*

"I don't know much about sci-fi," she admitted to him. "I write romance."

He looked down at her. "Oh, you're one of *those* writers." She could hear the disapproval in his voice and it made her want to whip out her tax returns from last year and wave them under his nose for validation.

But, of course, she didn't. That was considered socially unacceptable.

Instead, she smirked. "Yeah. I write about sex. They say to write what you know."

Then she winked.

Because fuck him.

He didn't have to know that she hadn't had sex in months.

He seemed intrigued now, at the very least. Mention sex, and you get a man's attention. It wasn't always the attention you wanted, though.

He stared at her. "So, what's your story?"

Gen paused, taking another sip of her drink. It was perfectly mixed with the right amount of sour and liquor. "Me? I'm not that interesting."

"Are you running from something?"

Her head snapped back. "Why would you say that?"

He shrugged. "You've just got the look."

"I most certainly do not," she said, as indignantly as she could. "My sister is a surgeon, and I'm going to spend the weekend with her while she's at a convention."

He nodded. "Uh-huh."

"It's true," Gen insisted. "And then I'm moving to a new life. I'm not running from anything."

He stared, unconvinced.

"Damn, bartenders are intuitive," she said finally, drumming her fingers on the bar top. He grinned at that. She glared. "But I'm not running. I just lost two-hundred pounds of cheating husband. I'm divorcing his ass."

He eyed her up and down. "What kind of idiot would cheat on you?" he asked, and she couldn't decide if she was flattered or unnerved at the way he was looking through her. She shrugged.

"My ex, I guess."

"What did the chick look like?" he asked, still incredulous.

She shrugged again. "Does it matter? I don't even know how many there were. My ex is a lawyer, so he knew all the tricks to avoid a paper trail."

The bartender cocked an eyebrow. "So how did you find out?"

"I saw him with one. From the back. It was entirely by chance. I was in town, and so was he. Only…he was with her."

Gen was sarcastic, so she didn't show her pain from that moment. It still stung.

Seeing him with her was so unexpected. It had sent her

into a literal physical shock. Her mouth had gone dry, her vision blurred, she'd gotten cold and clammy. She hadn't suspected a thing until that moment. She'd been such a fool.

"He was a dumbass," the bartender told her, although he didn't know her or her ex personally.

"Yes," she answered. "And soon, he'll be out of my life for good."

The divorce would be final just a few weeks after she mailed the papers. They were tucked safely in her bag right now.

Her phone buzzed, and she glanced at it to find texts from her sister. Meg was already in the hotel in New York City, anxiously awaiting her.

I hope you packed lightly. We're gonna buy all new clothes for you. I can't wait!!!!!! Hurry up and get here!!!!!

Her sister's excessive use of exclamation points was a direct comparison for her personality. Meggie was a walking exclamation point. Honestly, she was the one who seemed like a romance author, expressive and passionate, and Gen was the one who seemed like a physician, meticulous and careful.

Over the intercom, Gen's flight to LaGuardia was announced.

"Can I get my bill?" she asked. "My plane is boarding."

He shook his head. "Go ahead. It's on me today. Have fun with your sister."

"Oh! Thank you," she said, surprised. "It's been a long time since a man has bought me a drink."

He smiled. "I'm lucky to be your first. Oh, and here's a tip. You might want to take your wedding ring off."

Her head snapped back, and she looked down at her finger. How could she have forgotten that?

She twisted it around and around while she waited to board, and decided to take it off when she reached the hotel. She'd stick it in her suitcase and decide what to do with it later. It was a four-carat diamond.

She slept on the flight, and when she arrived, she actually felt good.

She was energized as she headed for a cab, and the bright lights of the city bounced off her skin in the back seat of the taxi. She texted her sister that she was close.

I'll wait for you in the lobby, she answered. Hurry up!!

The cabdriver let her out, and she hadn't even turned around before Meg grabbed her in a bear hug. "I thought you'd never get here," she exclaimed. "I'm starving!"

Like usual, she was wearing three-inch heels and looked perfect in her highlighted hair, slim suit and red lipstick.

"Let me at least drop my bag off in the room," Gen complained as Meg tried to hail another cab. Her sister grumbled but stepped back, and they walked to the elevator and rode to their two-bedroom suite on the top floor.

"Nice," Gen observed, as they walked in. There were glittering chandeliers, marble counters, a spectacular view.

Meg shrugged. "Nothing but the best for my big sis."

Gen dropped the bag. "I'm hungry, too," she said. "Let's go."

They chattered all the way back to the main floor in the golden elevator, and were still chattering in the cab. As they glided to a stop outside a steak house, Meg's stomach audibly growled and they laughed.

They tipped the driver and got out.

They were seated inside the glittering restaurant within a few minutes, and the waiter knew Meghan by name. After she'd ordered wine, Gen stared at her.

"How often do you come here?" Gen demanded, an eyebrow lifted. "I didn't even know you were in New York that often."

Meg smiled slightly, her fingers wrapped around her water glass. "I'm here a lot ever since I took my new role. It involves a lot of travel. New York is one of the cities I don't actually mind."

Gen rolled her eyes. "That's the price you pay for brilliance, I guess. If you didn't want to hustle, you shouldn't have invented a new method to..." She paused. "What is it again that you figured out?"

Meg sighed. "Using robotics, I figured out a safer method to perform a coronary artery bypass graft. It's literally called the McCready Method." She stared at her sister, and Gen grimaced.

"Sorry. I'm not a doctor, so I don't remember all of that... jargon. Also, I don't know why you kept your maiden name."

"That one's easy," Meg answered. "Meghan McCready sounds like a rock star. Meg Harris sounds like a housewife."

The waiter returned with their wine, took their steak orders, and they were left to drink in peace.

"There's nothing wrong with being a housewife," Gen pointed out.

"Of course there isn't. If that's your thing. It's just not mine. My mind races all of the time. It's hard to explain. I've got to have a challenge, Gennie."

Gen didn't bother pointing out that running a household full of children was probably an incredible challenge. It was one she hadn't had the opportunity to find out. Thad hadn't wanted kids.

Meg lifted her glass. "Sisters forever."

Gen nodded. "Sisters forever." They clinked glasses, then drained them, in an almost identical way, each setting their empty glass down with a thud at the same time.

They chuckled, then poured a second glass.

After their second glasses were empty, Gen's phone buzzed with a text. She glanced at it.

Have you signed the papers yet? They were delivered.

She ignored it, and her sister looked at her questioningly. Gen rolled her eyes with a sigh.

"Thad. He wants to know if I've signed yet."

"Have you?" Meg asked, sipping her third glass of wine. By this time, her lips were starting to have a slight purple hue from the merlot, and her cheeks were flushed.

"Not yet. I will, but I'm gonna make him sweat a little first. He certainly took his time coming to an agreement about them." Gen dripped a bit of wine on the table, and the waiter came immediately to blot at it.

"True," Meg agreed. "But what did you expect? You married a lawyer."

She screwed up her face and then laughed. Her own husband, Joe, her high school sweetheart, was a contractor, and Joe didn't have a contentious bone in his body.

The appetizer and salads they had ordered came, and they stopped talking as they attacked the brie drizzled with pesto and oil with wolfish vigor. By the time the steaks arrived, they had graduated from red wine to Long Island iced teas.

"We probably shouldn't drink anymore," Meg suggested, but they both laughed.

"Aren't we here for my divorce party?" Gen laughed. "Don't kill my buzz. Check out the hottie. Nine o'clock."

Meg looked to the right, and Gen scowled. "Your other nine o'clock."

"That's your nine o'clock," Meg pointed out, peering at

the tall handsome waiter across the room. "But he's delicious."

"I think he's Greek," Gen said, almost falling out of her chair as she leaned to examine him more closely. He glanced at them, and they tittered and righted themselves.

"I am a dignified surgeon," Meg announced to her sister. "I do not get drunk."

"That ship has sailed tonight," Gen answered, her nose pleasantly numb. "This is a nice way to kick off my new life, sis. Thank you for making me come."

"That's what *he* said." Meg laughed hysterically and her sister rolled her eyes, but then got the joke and laughed, too.

They plowed through their steaks with abandon, without regard to calories or even manners.

"That was the best steak I've ever had in my life," Gen announced at the end, when she finally decided to be ladylike and pat at her lips delicately.

Meg agreed. "They do it up right here."

"How *you* doin'?" Gen said, looking up at the waiter, and he smiled as though he handled drunk women every night of his life.

"Quite well, miss. Should I hail you a cab?"

"We're two independent women," Gen slurred. "We've got this."

She paid their bill, signing the check with a flourish. Miraculously, a cab was waiting outside (courtesy of the waiter) and they tumbled in. Gen practically fell into the back seat, and Meg laughed.

"You're so drunk," she giggled.

"You are, too," Gen replied indignantly. In the rearview mirror, Gen saw the cabdriver smile.

"Not as much as you," Meg informed her, prim and proper now, straightening her jacket.

Gen pulled out her phone. "Here. We gotta take a drunk selfie for Mom. She'll be so proud." They leaned together, and Gen snapped the picture, sending it off to their mother. Periodically, on the way back to the hotel, they broke out into uncontrollable laughter fits for no real reason.

When their mother replied to their text with, Oh, my gosh, you two. Don't talk to strangers, they practically howled.

The doorman at the hotel opened the door, and Gen stopped to straighten his tie. To his credit, he didn't even blink.

They laughed in the elevator up to the room, and when they burst into their suite, Gen went straight for her bed and collapsed onto it.

Meg came, too, lying down next to her sister.

"Is the room spinning, or is it just me?" she sighed.

"It's spinning," Gen confirmed.

Meg started to grin, but then she noticed Gen's hand. In particular, the wedding ring.

She narrowed her eyes. "Why are you still wearing that?"

Gen shook her head, subconsciously covering it with her hand. "I forgot about it until earlier today. I haven't taken it off in forever."

"You should." Meg nodded. Her eyes lit up. "Ohhhh, you could give it to me. Mine is small. Joe doesn't like large rings. And yours has that giant diamond." She sniffed as she looked at her own smallish ring. Gen rolled her eyes.

"It's bad luck," she announced, standing up. "Also, this ring has terrible energy."

Her mood shifted into something dark, something angry, and her mirth was long gone. Thoughts of her ex-husband crushed it into the night.

The room swirled into a kaleidoscope of light, but she was

determined. She marched to the balcony and stood by the edge. Suddenly, she wanted nothing more than to be rid of it.

Meg rushed to her, pulling her back. "Don't stand there. You're too close. You're scaring me."

Gen shook her off. "You're just scared of heights. Wait a second.

"I hope that whoever finds this ring will have better luck with it than I have," she said loudly, kissing the ring and then throwing it into the night as hard as she could.

They both peered over the edge, but obviously they couldn't see where it landed.

"Oh, my God. I can't believe you did that," Meg said, staring into the darkness. "That thing was worth like a jillion dollars. I wonder where it landed? Maybe a homeless person will find it."

"That would be nice. They could sell it."

"*You* could've sold it," Meg answered. "It was valuable."

"I don't want anything else from that man. Ever. Fuck him, and his whore."

"Yeah!" Meg agreed. She slumped against the door. "Fuck them. I'm sorry, Gen. You don't deserve any of this." She reached out to rub her sister's back, but Gen hated the sympathy.

The idea of someone feeling sorry for her... It was too much in this moment. She wanted to be alone. Her happy buzz was gone, and anger had replaced it.

"Feel sorry for *him*," she suggested. "He's the one who will be leading the empty life. Not me." Meg nodded, but Gen could tell her sister thought she was just blowing smoke. "I mean it," she insisted. "I hope he ends up with that whore, and she ends up cheating on him. And then they both end up miserable. Because...karma."

"You're right," Meg agreed. "He's an asshole."

"I'm gonna go get some air," Gen decided, her cheeks flushed and hot. She hated feeling like a bitter wench.

"We're standing on a balcony," Meg pointed out.

"Nah. I mean, I'd like some air *alone*," Gen clarified. Away from the sympathetic eyes of someone who knew she was scorned. It was humiliating, even in front of her sister.

Before Meg could protest, Gen backed out the door.

"At least take a jacket," Meg managed to call.

Gen grabbed her sister's coat on the way out the door. She couldn't wait to move away, to a place where they wouldn't know the whole seedy story, or a place where she didn't have to wear her humiliation like a coat. It was a label she didn't want.

For the fourth time today, she took a ride in the elevator. She dropped the coat on the floor, bent to pick it up and stumbled. Annoyed, she tied it around her waist, tugging it hard.

"Mrs. Thibault." The doorman in the lobby nodded, as he opened the door for her. "Can I hail you a cab?"

"No, thank you," she said. "I'm just going for a little walk. And I'm not Thibault anymore. It's McCready, like the Lord intended."

"All right. Be careful, ma'am," he cautioned. "It's dark."

As if she didn't know that.

She thanked him for his concern and set out on the New York City sidewalks…just for a minute. The night air was cool on her face, and it woke her up, clearing away a little of the two stiff Long Islands and countless glasses of wine she'd had at the restaurant.

The streetlights seemed hazy in the night, but the stars… The stars twinkled like beacons of hope.

She stared at the sidewalk, fighting to stay focused, and as she did, she saw a sparkle.

It couldn't be.

She knelt to examine it, and *it was.*

It was her wedding ring.

What were the odds?

She shook her head as she curled her fingers around it and stood up. Maybe she'd never be rid of it.

She walked quickly, her shoes clicking on the pavement, and she stared up at the skyscrapers. She held her arms open wide and twirled drunkenly around. Spinning, spinning, spinning, she laughed at the sensation in her belly, the drunken blurriness, the moment of complete lightness.

Her joy was short-lived, however.

As she turned, someone grabbed her in the night, sharp fingers biting into her soft flesh.

There was a flash of pain in her temple.

Then nothing more.

3

MEGHAN GLANCED AT the clock. It was 8:03 a.m. She'd passed out the night before while she waited for Gen to come back. When she woke up at 7:30 a.m. with a start, she'd realized Gen hadn't returned.

She was jittery now, a sense of foreboding swelling in her heart. For the second time, she picked up the phone and called the front desk.

"Were you able to reach the doorman from last night?" she asked them, her panic growing ever larger in her belly.

"Yes. He saw your sister go out for a walk," the clerk told her. "He did not see her return. Is there a problem?"

Only the fact that Gen wasn't answering her phone.

"It's not like her," she insisted to the clerk. "Something is wrong."

She hung up and walked outside, looking all around. New

York was already moving, trash blowing in the gutters. Her imagination started drifting. Had Gen snapped? She'd flung her ring off the balcony. *Who does that?* Meg felt guilt pull at her. She should've known right then and there that her sister wasn't in her right mind.

Maybe Gen realized her mistake and went to look for it.

Meg paused, looking around at her proximity to the hotel and their balcony. If *she'd* thrown a ring into the night and wanted to find it, where would she go?

She started tracking a path, along the sidewalks, into the bushes. She looked high and low. For a ring, the diamond was huge. But in scale with the size of a city, it was hunting for a needle in a haystack. She paused at a coffee cart, and paid for a cup of coffee, her fingers trembling. She gulped at the bitter liquid, trying to sharpen her fuzzy thoughts.

Why had they drank so much?

Two women alone, one of whom was emotionally shattered. Meg should've known better. Her sister had always been passionate and mercurial. Meg should've known that getting her drunk at a time like this was playing with fire.

"Damn it," she muttered to herself, her fingers wrapped around the hot cup. "Think. *Think.*"

Maybe Gen headed to The Strand…to see if any of her books were displayed in the window. It was the gold standard for authors. She might've needed an ego boost. If Meg were Gen, that's what she would've done.

She pivoted to head in that direction and promptly tripped, her coffee flying out of her hand.

As she scrambled to maintain her balance, she caught sight of something pink.

She froze and then knelt in the gutter to pull the pink coat from the ground.

THE LAST TO SEE HER

It was soiled from being run over, but it was her own. The one Gen had been wearing last night.

Her breath caught in her throat and she whirled in every direction.

"Gen!" she shouted. "Gen!"

No one even glanced at her twice, not even the homeless guy on the bench.

"Did you see a woman last night in this coat?" she asked him. He stared at her with milky eyes and slowly shook his head.

She handed him a ten-dollar bill. "Are you sure?"

He nodded.

"Damn it."

Her hand was shaking as she called 9-1-1.

After she explained the situation, the dispatcher wasn't sympathetic. "Ma'am. This is not an emergency. I'm transferring you to the local precinct."

Before Meg could argue, the call was transferred. She had to explain everything all over again to the man who answered the phone.

He didn't seem concerned.

"She had too much to drink and went for a walk?" he asked, and she could almost hear his pen stop writing. "Lady, this is New York. Your sister wanted to see the sights and dropped her coat. She's probably on a bench somewhere, sleeping it off."

"No, she wouldn't do that," Meg told him. "In fact, it wasn't like her to just get up and go for a walk alone. But she was upset, and..."

"What was she upset about?"

"She's getting divorced," Meg answered. "She threw her ring off the balcony and needed some air. Maybe she wanted to look for it. I have no idea. She was very upset."

There was a pause on the other end. "Is her husband here with her?"

"No, of course not. They're getting divorced. He's in Chicago."

"Is it an amicable divorce?"

Meg stared at the phone. "I know what you're getting at, but Thad wouldn't do anything to her. He's a lawyer. He can be an asshole, but he draws blood on paper and in the courtroom. He doesn't need to in real life."

"Is it an amicable divorce?" the officer asked again calmly.

Meg took a breath. "No."

"Okay, ma'am. It's too early to file a missing person. You'll need to wait twenty-four hours. You can go look for her on your own, and wait for her to call, and if she doesn't, call us back."

"So, my sister is lost and you're not going to do anything?" Meg was incredulous. "What do we pay you for?"

"Call us back in twenty-four hours if she doesn't turn up," the officer said curtly before hanging up.

"Twenty-four hours from when? From now, or from midnight of last night?" Meg asked, but, of course, the officer was already off the phone.

Meg went back upstairs and paced the hotel suite, back and forth. She picked up her phone again, but laid it down. Should she really call and alarm people so soon? She waffled back and forth, trying to think logically. People who are severely emotionally distraught don't act like themselves at times. Perhaps Gen really did just want time to herself.

But Meg didn't think so. Deep in the pit of her belly, she felt like something was wrong. It was an instinct that had served her well in dozens of surgeries gone wrong. She usually listened to it and ended up saving a life that way. In the operating room, Meg was God. She called the shots. She always knew exactly what to do, because she had learned every contingency through a thousand surgeries on a thousand days, in a thousand different ways.

But this was different.

This wasn't something they trained you for, and she didn't have control over it.

Besides, as mercurial as Gen could be, this wasn't in her wheelhouse.

Even still, Meg paced all the way out to the balcony, and though she was afraid, she pressed her belly against the cold railing and looked down. The sidewalks were bustling, and her sister was nowhere in sight.

"Where are you?" Meg whispered. "Come back."

She threw on a heavy sweater, pausing only for a minute to scribble a note to her sister before she went out to look again.

CALL ME IF YOU COME BACK. IMMEDIATELY!!!

She walked for several city blocks, checking every bench, every hidden set of stairs, every shadowy crevice. She checked her phone every few minutes.

Gen didn't call.

She tried to call Gen, but got her voice mail, over and over. *You've reached Genevieve Thibault. Leave a message, and when I find my phone, I'll call you back. Or you could just text me. That would be better.*

"Gen, call me back. Now," Meg demanded. "I mean it. This isn't cool. You're scaring me."

She looked at the picture they'd taken the night before, the one in the cab when their eyes were slightly unfocused and their cheeks were pink from alcohol. They were so happy, so delighted with life in general, in spite of everything. And now Gen was gone.

"What happened?" Meg whispered, as she stood there, her heart pounding.

She ducked inside several twenty-four-hour pharmacies, asking the clerks if they'd seen her sister the night before or early that morning. But they hadn't. At the last one, she bought ibuprofen, and tossed three down her throat. Her head was pounding.

There was another homeless man at the end of the block. She approached him with a photo of Gen on her phone, but he wouldn't talk to her at all. He grunted and turned away with a snarl.

She was growing more frantic and more alarmed by the minute.

She stopped to question the day doorman. "Are you sure you haven't seen my sister since she left around midnight?" she asked firmly, waving a photo of Gen from her phone at him. Her hands were shaking, and she hoped no one noticed.

The solemn man nodded. "I'm quite sure, ma'am. But I talked to Peter—he was the doorman on duty last night. He said he told her to be careful and saw her walk down the street. When he looked again, she was gone. He doesn't know what direction she went after that. I'm sorry."

He did look sorry. He was sympathetic.

"If I text you this picture, can you show it to guests and see if anyone saw anything?"

He started to nod, but the manager at the desk spoke up.

"No, we can't do that, ma'am. I'm sorry. We can't interfere in an investigation until the police instruct us."

"But there's not an investigation yet." She turned, confused. "I can't officially file a report until midnight. Plus, helping to find someone isn't *interfering*."

"After it becomes an investigation, we'll do anything the

police want us to do. In the meantime, we can't disrupt our guests." The manager's face was stoic.

"Gen *is* your guest," she replied slowly. "And she's gone."

"I'm sorry about that," the manager said, but he was still firm. "We don't want to alarm our other guests unnecessarily. We'll be happy to cooperate with the police when they request it."

She was hitting a stone wall here. Annoyed, Meg returned to her room and sat on her bed.

She hadn't seen her sister since 12:30 a.m. It was now 10:04 a.m. The first session of the convention she came here to attend would be well underway. She couldn't imagine sitting through panels about advances in medical devices while Gen was missing. All she could do was sit in the hotel room, and watch the clock, and wait. The time passed from 11:04 a.m. to 12:04 p.m., then 1:04 p.m., to 2:04 p.m., and finally, when it was 4:04 p.m. and her sister hadn't come back, she knew she had to call someone.

Anyone.

She didn't want to worry her parents yet, especially her mother, so she called Gen's husband, Thad.

He answered quickly, his voice sharp.

"Yes?"

"Thad, it's Meg."

"Why are you calling?"

"Gen's gone," she said without hesitating.

There was a pause. "What do you mean, *gone*?" he asked.

"She came to New York with me, and she went out for a walk late last night and she hasn't come back to the hotel."

"How long has she been gone?" he asked calmly.

"Since midnight."

"That's not like her," he admitted.

"No, it's not."

"Did you call the police?"

"Of course. They said they can't do anything for the first twenty-four hours."

"Okay. Well, call them at the twenty-four-hour mark."

"Are you coming? I think something is wrong. I mean, really wrong."

There was silence on the other end.

"No," he replied finally. "She's divorcing me, remember? She doesn't want me involved."

"You don't…" Her voice trailed off, and then she squared her shoulders. "You don't think she…"

"Don't be stupid," he answered.

And he hung up.

Meg stared at the phone in disbelief. How could Gen's husband be so cold? She thought back to what the policeman had asked her. *Is it an amicable divorce?*

Lord. Thad wouldn't do anything to Gen. That was stupid.

She shook the thoughts out of her head and took a shower.

She had skipped the entire first day of her convention because this was so much more important. She felt like if she left the room, something terrible might happen to Genevieve. It was illogical, but her mind was past logic at this point. She couldn't imagine carrying on business as usual until Gen came back. The convention was just not that important.

She paced, and paced some more. Maybe Gen ran away. Maybe the divorce overwhelmed her all at once, and she'd snapped and just run away from it all.

But that train of thought didn't last long.

Gen wasn't that kind of person. She never ran away. She confronted everything head-on. Plus, Gen would never purposely worry her this way.

By the evening, when she hadn't heard anything yet, she finally called their mother.

It wasn't an easy phone call to make.

"I don't understand what is happening," her mother said. "You sent that picture last night. She was so happy. You girls were *drunk*. She probably got lost."

"Mom, I think something might've happened," Meg told her carefully. "This is New York City. It never sleeps, and crime never stops. I don't know…"

"Don't even say something like that," her mother snapped. "She's fine. I know she's fine."

After promising to call when there was any news, Meg hung up. Her arm was limp. Her mind was fuzzy. She collapsed onto the bed, staring at the window. The emotional roller coaster of today hit her in a wave, exhausting her. All of the adrenaline spikes and panic collapsed upon her now.

She didn't even realize that she had fallen asleep until she woke up with a start.

It was dark.

She sat up, and looked around, finding the clock. It was 11:57 p.m.

She grabbed her phone, only to find zero messages.

She rushed through the suite, checking for Gen.

But her sister's bed was unrumpled and the rooms were empty. She hadn't returned, and it had now been twenty-four hours.

Meg decided not to call the police again—instead, she went downstairs and hopped into a taxi and went to the station in person.

"I'm here to file a missing-person report," she told the person at the front desk.

She had to wait for over an hour for a detective to call for her.

"Detective Nate Hawkins," he said as he shook her hand curtly and led her back to his office.

He was around her age, had two-day-old dark scruff on his jawline and eyes that had seen it all. He was unfazed as she answered his questions. *What hotel are you staying at? Why are you here? Has she ever run away from loved ones before?*

But then…then…his questions took a strange turn.

"Had you and Genevieve argued?" he asked, his blue eyes staring a hole in her.

She stared. "Um. No. We'd been to dinner."

"You said you were talking about her divorce," he corrected, glancing at his notes. "On the balcony."

"Well, yes. Afterward. We'd just come back from dinner."

"Were you angry with your sister?" His question was direct.

"Of course not!" she replied indignantly. "I love her. We were having fun. We were tipsy. Drunk, actually."

"But you said that she was planning on leaving Chicago, and you clearly don't agree with that decision."

"That has nothing to do with this. I mentioned that as an aside. It's irrelevant."

"Never assume something is irrelevant," he advised her. "In a situation like this one, any detail could be important."

"Well, here's a good detail: She's my sister, and I love her. I want you to find her."

"I'm sure you do," he said, almost soothingly. "Listen, Miss McCready…"

"*Dr.* McCready," she corrected him haughtily.

"Dr. McCready," he confirmed. "We have to cover all the bases, and I'm sorry if my questions offend you. But here are two very blunt and very important facts about missing-person cases that I want you to know. The first forty-eight hours are crucial."

"I know!" she snapped. "And you made me wait a full twenty-four to file this report."

"And second," he continued, ignoring her, "is that in a high percentage of cases, someone the victim knows is involved."

She froze as she processed his words, and her mouth closed, as though it were on a hinge. He'd just referred to her sister as the *victim*. It suddenly seemed all too real. She stared at him without speaking.

His next words chilled her to the bone.

"You were the last to see her."

4

Gen, Then

GEN PICKED UP her wineglass, and drew a long sip over her lips, glancing at the clock.

Thad was late yet again. A pit had formed in her belly over a week ago when she'd realized it was becoming a pattern.

In the earlier days of their marriage, he'd been late every once in a while. But he'd always called, was always apologetic.

Now there was no such thing. No calls, no apologies. He didn't even seem to care.

She swigged the wine and then poured another glass.

Their wedding portrait mocked her from the mantel. She squinted at it, at the happy smile on her face. Was that all a lie? Thad looked happy, too. He had his arm draped around her, his eyes crinkled as he laughed, and he'd pushed a tendril of her hair away from her face.

He had loved her then.

What the hell had happened?

Gen got up and paced around the condo.

She hated this condo, but she'd conceded on just about everything. She just wanted Thad to seem himself again, and tan wall colors didn't seem a high price to pay.

But they hadn't worked.

Nothing had.

And here she was, pacing around her condo at 10:00 p.m. on a Tuesday night, waiting for her husband.

Her stocking feet slid with ease on the stone, making her skin cold.

As cold as my heart is becoming, she thought sardonically. Thad was making her into a bitch. She felt it, more and more each day, and she resented it with all of her being. It wasn't fair. He was out doing whatever he wanted to do, and she was stuck here, growing suspicious and bitter.

Just as she was pondering what she could do to change that, a key turned in the lock.

Her husband was home.

She quickly dropped onto the couch and pretended she had been casually sitting there all along.

Thad strode in, his shiny leather briefcase slung over his shoulder. His shirt was cleanly tucked in, his tie perfectly knotted. His dark brown hair was just brushing his shoulder, and she noted that he needed a haircut.

He bent quickly and brushed a kiss on the top of her head.

"Sorry I'm late," he mumbled. An apology, but not really.

She cocked her head.

"What was it tonight?" she asked innocently. He shrugged.

"Same old crap. Clients who don't give a shit about my personal life. They want to meet for dinner to discuss their issues, then dinner turns into drinks, and I can't get away, then here I am dragging myself home just in time for bed."

He was definitely making a point to stress how tired he was. How weary.

Gen thought back in her head. When was the last time they'd had sex? A month ago? Two? It was a bad sign that she couldn't remember. She hadn't even shaved her legs in weeks. Why should she? Her husband sure as hell wouldn't notice.

Thad poured a scotch and stood at the window, staring down at the street far below.

"I love this place," he said quietly, and for just a minute, she heard the man she'd married.

"I do, too," she answered, and joined him. She lifted her hand and touched his back.

He didn't react.

She tried again, brushing her hand against his shoulder.

He didn't notice. She cringed. When had this started happening? How had she not realized it?

"Do you still love me?" she asked.

Thad's head snapped around, and he stared at her with wide eyes.

"Of course. Why would you ask such a thing?"

He seemed so startled, so appalled, that her stomach unclenched just a bit. He lifted an eyebrow. "Well?"

"I don't know," she said, and it did seem silly now. "You're just so distant."

"Babe," he said, and he pulled her to him. She inhaled the familiar scent of his skin, his shirt. "I'm just building a life for us. Everything I'm doing is for you. For us."

She nodded, and she truly felt silly now. Of course, he was right. He was a hard worker, an overachiever. He always had been.

"I know," she finally answered. A weight lifted off her

shoulders at the finality in his voice. He meant it. She'd stake her life on it.

"Okay." He nodded. "Now. How about…we go to bed early."

"It's not early," she pointed out with a giggle.

"Details," he announced. "Let's go to bed."

His voice was suggestive, and her belly twinged in response. It'd been a while since they'd made love. This was good. It was a definite good sign.

They went to bed, and for the first time in weeks, Gen didn't doubt her husband's love.

5

Meg, Now

"THIS IS DR. MEGHAN MCCREADY, Jenny," she
spoke quickly into the phone. "I'm away at a convention in
New York City, and I've been delayed. At this point I don't
know exactly when I'll be back in the office."

The office assistant seemed taken aback. "But what should
I do with your consultations and speaking engagements?"

Meg sighed. "Ask Dr. Callahan to handle them. He knows
the material and he can easily cover for me. Lord knows, I've
done it for him. I've got an urgent family emergency. I'll let
you know when I am returning."

She pressed End and tossed the phone on the bed, glancing around the room. It had been forty-eight hours now,
and there had been no sign of her sister. Not anywhere. No
phone calls, no sightings, not a thing.

She showered and blow-dried her hair, letting the bathroom steam up. Something about not having anything specific to do was both frustrating and oddly liberating at the same time. She had no place to be, no surgical maneuver to teach.

But she was anxious. Gen was gone. Things were not okay.

Meg traced on her lipstick and slid her jewelry on. As she glanced at her wedding ring, it looked like there was a missing side-diamond. She examined it closer, but no. It was there. It was just small, unlike her sister's massive rock that she'd simply thrown out.

That ring.

Had Gen gone hunting for it? Was that why she'd disappeared into the night? Had she realized it was silly to throw away something so expensive?

Meghan doubted it. Gen didn't always think about, or care about, those kinds of things. It was why she and Thad were honestly not a good match, and never had been. He was a details person, she was a big picture person, and in their case, opposites did not attract.

She thought about calling him again. He hadn't checked on Gen, which Meghan thought was a dick-ish thing to do. Sure, they were getting divorced, but shouldn't he care that she was missing?

She remembered the detective's question. *Is it an amicable divorce?*

Meghan stared at the wall, at a piece of wallpaper that had been snagged and was curling up at the seam.

No, their divorce was not amicable. But she was sure Thad would never do anything to harm her. Right?

On an impulse, Meg picked up her phone and texted Thad.

Thad, there is still no sign of Gen. There's something really wrong.

He didn't answer immediately. In fact, he didn't answer for over an hour. Meg was down on the street, trying to hail a taxi when he did.

Fine. I'll be there soon.

She winced as she read it. Not exactly the words you would expect from someone's husband. She'd known Thad for years. She didn't think he would be capable of harming anyone, but isn't that the first thing you hear on the news when the reporter interviews a neighbor or a family friend? *I would never have thought.* That's what they always said.

Her stomach churned as she dropped into the yellow cab, and the driver whisked her across town to the police department. She tried not to inhale the musty smell in the car, body odor mixed with the pollution of the city, and instead stared out at the street as they drove. The landscape blurred together, and she found herself scanning it for Gen's face.

It was unlikely Gen would be on this side of town, but then again, she could be anywhere.

She tried to call her sister's number again. This time, it went straight to voice mail. It must be out of battery.

Her stomach sank even further. Gen wouldn't let her phone go dead. She was obsessive about charging it. Meg had told her a hundred times that overcharging was bad for batteries, but Gen never cared, because she never wanted her phone to run down.

Yet now, it had.

And now she was gone and had been for forty-nine hours.

She clutched her purse as the cab lurched to a halt, and she thrust some crumpled bills at the driver. She stepped onto the dirty sidewalk and then climbed the steps to the police station. She could probably find her way in here blindfolded since she'd been here four times in two days.

Make it five times, now.

She stopped at the front desk, and the same guy from the day before yesterday was there again. He glanced at her.

"Still gone?" he asked, and she couldn't imagine how he'd remembered her. He must see hundreds of people a day. But she nodded.

"Yeah. Can I see Detective Hawkins?"

The clerk picked up the phone without answering, calling back for the detective. When he hung up, he nodded to her.

"He'll be right out. Heads up, he's not in a great mood today."

And that was her problem, how?

She didn't say that. Instead, she smiled politely and waited.

It was twenty minutes before the detective graced her with his presence. He strode from behind the double doors, and she glanced at him. It didn't look as though he'd slept. His shirt was wrinkled and the back was untucked. His hair was dark. His teeth were white.

If it weren't for the bags under his eyes, he could really be quite handsome, she decided. Oh, and the scowl.

He scowled at her again, as if he could read her thoughts.

"Ms. McCready," he began, but she glared at him.

"*Dr.* McCready," she corrected. He stopped in front of her and started over.

"Dr. McCready," he said. "Coming here doesn't help. It only slows me down, because I have to stop what I'm doing to come out and see you."

"But there must be something I can do," she insisted. "I can't just sit in the hotel room. I need to go out and knock on doors or something."

"This is New York City," he reminded her, as if she could forget. "I wouldn't recommend that."

"Then what should I do?" she demanded. "I'm telling you truthfully, I'll go insane if I can't do something."

He sighed. "Fine. Come with me."

His broad shoulders swayed as they walked into the back, over the dingy tiled floor. She noticed that his shoes were scuffed. She didn't say anything, just followed him through a bustling room filled with ringing phones and the sounds of metal file cabinets slamming closed. If a place could smell like unsolved crime, it would be this.

They came to a small office in the back, and he gestured for her to sit down in the chair across from his desk. It squeaked when she did. She kept her purse on her lap.

"Detective, I need to know what more I can do."

She stared at him and willed her fingers not to shake.

He stared back, his blue gaze unwavering. He looked at her as though he were inspecting her, as though he could see that she hadn't slept in two days, that coffee was her only sustenance. But even still, he seemed suspicious. He didn't miss a detail. His eyes were tired but still sharp. That annoyed her.

"I feel as though you are wasting time by focusing on me," she added. "I know you called my office and asked for my itinerary. You could've just asked me. I'd have given it to you."

"You might've lied," he suggested simply. He took a drink of coffee out of a chipped blue Superman mug. She stared at the yellow and red S emblem. Did he have an inflated ego? Probably. Did he have kids who had given it to him?

"I could've lied," she admitted. "But I wouldn't. I don't have anything to hide."

He took another drink. "This will sound cliché, but that's what everyone says."

Meg felt her blood boil a bit. "Listen. My sister is missing. I know for a fact that I had nothing to do with it. You are focusing on me, and in doing so, you could be letting the real culprit get away. She could be dead right now because you are fucking around with me. Do you hear me?"

Her voice had escalated to almost a screech, and still, the detective was annoyingly unfazed.

"I hear you," he said calmly. "The cops out in the bullpen heard you, too. And the coffee shop patrons down on the corner. Would you like some coffee, by the way?"

She swallowed hard and clenched her fist in her lap.

"No."

"Are you sure? I'll even get you a clean cup." He almost smiled, and Meg noticed that his face, for a brief minute, got gentler, kinder. It instantly hardened up again when she spoke, like armor.

"Detective. To whom can I speak that will find my sister?"

"You're looking at him." He set his cup down, and his eyes were steely. "I'm assigned to this case and I am very good at my job. I'll find your sister. And if you're involved, I'll find that out, too."

"I'm not," Meg said icily.

"Then you have nothing to worry about," he said, almost pleasantly now. He picked up the paper she had filled out with the details of Gen's disappearance and peered at it. "You still at the same hotel?"

"Yes, of course. I'm staying there in case she comes back."

"You been trying to call her?"

"Her phone goes straight to voice mail. It isn't like her. She hates for her battery to go dead. Can you track her phone?"

"Already done," the detective said, laying the paper back down.

Meg's heartbeat picked up a little.

"And?"

Detective Hawkins opened his desk drawer and pulled out a plastic bag. Meg gasped when she recognized her sister's rose-gold iPhone with the custom case.

"Where was it?" she almost stuttered.

"In the dumpster down the street from your hotel. There are only two sets of prints on it."

He stared at her and she stared back. "And?"

"And, would you mind giving your fingerprints?"

"Seriously?" Meg said. "It's my own sister's phone. My prints are probably all over it."

"Then you won't mind confirming it?"

She sighed. "Sure. But what will that prove? I handled my own sister's phone?"

"Yes," the detective said.

"But why would my sister's phone be in a dumpster?" Meg asked, afraid of the answer.

"That's what we are trying to find out. Possibly whoever abducted her knew that it would track her," he replied simply.

Meg's breath caught in her throat.

"So you think she was abducted?"

"It is a suspicious scenario, and we're treating it as such. Of course, she could have dropped it there intentionally herself."

Meg stood up and the air whooshed out of her lungs. The room spun.

Her sister had a few issues, true, and deep down, Meg did wonder if perhaps Gen *had* just run…if she'd just done some illogical thing just to lash out at the divorce. That is, until this minute, when Hawkins declared it as suspicious. If something *truly* had happened to Gen, then the detective might actually think of her as a suspect.

The room spun faster. The next thing she knew, she was on the floor and the detective was reaching down and handing her a cup of water.

Dizzily, she stared up at him.

"You fainted," Hawkins said calmly.

Meg sat up, trying to shake the fuzziness from her head, and took a gulp of water.

"I can assure you I didn't hurt my sister," she told him.

"Okay," he answered.

Somehow, though, Meg knew he was suspicious of her. He was watching her, analyzing her, was still on guard with her.

"Should I call my attorney?" she asked suddenly.

The detective's head snapped around. "Do you think you need one?"

"I'm starting to fear I do."

"Then by all means," he said. "Be my guest."

Meghan's heart sunk more by the minute. She dialed her attorney's number with shaking fingers. When she got through, she told him about her sister's disappearance and how she was at the police precinct in New York City speaking with the detective in charge. Her lawyer said to keep him abreast of any developments. He was at the other end of the line anytime she needed him.

6

Gen, Then

"MEGHAN DIANE," Gen snapped at her sister through the phone. "Come back to reality."

Her sister paused in her diatribe.

"Yes?"

"Quit complaining about Joe. He's an honest guy, who works hard for you. He does all of the renovating around your place himself. Do you know how much money that saves?"

Meg sighed. "I know. I just wish that he would engage more. He's always out in the garage tinkering on his workbench."

"And you think that's beneath you?" Gen raised an eyebrow.

"Of course not."

"Miss Doctor?"

She snarled a little too harshly to be entirely joking. "Don't act like I'm a snob. I'm not. I knew whom I was marrying. I love that he gets his hands dirty. I just... You wouldn't understand."

"No, because I'm married to someone who would rather hire someone to change a simple light bulb."

"We all have crosses to bear," Meg answered, then giggled.

"We're not suffering," Gen decided aloud, and she agreed.

"No, we're not."

They fell silent, and Gen glanced at the clock.

"You know, I've got to get my words in for the day. Do you have patients to see or something?"

"Or something," her sister sighed. "Too much of what I do is administrative these days. All I do is teach and talk, teach and talk."

"You poor baby," Gen faked some sympathy, and she laughed again.

"Shut up. Okay. I'm going." She hung up and Gen was left alone in her big condo.

With Thad at work, she had silence all day to write all the words she wanted. The silence, though, was sometimes suffocating. Today it felt like loneliness.

She padded lightly down the hall to her office, and overlooking the city, with her feet propped up on the window and her butt planted firmly in the window seat, she tapped determinedly on the laptop keys with the machine balanced against her thighs.

His eyes sparkle like the sun, she wrote. *My heart flutters in response, and I inhale a shaky breath, not sure that my knees will support me as he pulls me close.*

Her fingers paused as she pondered those words and the sentiment behind them.

When was the last time she'd felt like that?

When was the last time Thad had made her knees weak?

When was the last time he'd looked at her and it had taken her breath away?

The fact that she had to ask the question was probably the answer.

She didn't remember.

She glanced down at her T-shirt and yoga pants. She'd washed her hair the day before yesterday. Why exactly did she think he'd want to make her knees weak? She hadn't showered since yesterday morning. Maybe he wasn't putting in extra effort, but she hadn't been, either.

She closed her computer and walked to the bathroom. When she stepped into the hot shower, she let the steam erase her worries, her tension, her stress. She stood with her hands on the wall, and she pictured her husband coming home from work and finding her all dolled up, perfumed and ready. Her belly tightened at the look on his face.

He'd be so happy. So content. So surprised.

It made her so excited that she went out and bought a pretty new black nightgown and matching satin robe.

She spent all afternoon pampering herself...grooming, doing her fingernails and toenails and deep conditioning her hair. Everything she could do to feel sexy. She blew out her hair. She walked through clouds of perfume and sprayed their clean bed linens.

She even dug out an old erotica book, priming herself well ahead of time.

By the time 6:00 p.m. rolled around, she was ready. Her motor was purring, and she was lying in wait.

By seven o'clock, she was antsy.

By eight o'clock, she was tired.

She called his office.

No answer.

She called his cell phone.

"Hi, honey," he answered, and he sounded as tired as she was.

"Where are you?" she asked and she was more snappish than she intended. After all, he didn't know she was trying to surprise him.

"At dinner with the team. Why?"

"I was just hoping to spend some time with you tonight," she said, as she looked at her freshly shaved legs and billowing satin nightgown. "What time will you be home?"

"Don't wait up," he advised. "There's no reason for both of us to be up late."

He hung up, and she sat alone for a moment.

Then she turned off the lamp and went to sleep.

When she woke in the morning, he'd already gone for work.

She'd missed him entirely.

7

Meg, Now

"HONEY, YOU'RE BEING PARANOID," Meg's husband, Joe, murmured into the phone. In the background, their son, Joey, ran through the house, making fire truck noises, high-pitched wails that faded into nothing, only to start all over again. If Meg were there, she'd tell him to hush, but Joe let him get away with everything. "It's a normal part of an investigation, I'm sure."

"Joe, he suggested I call my lawyer," she reminded him. "That doesn't seem routine."

"You would never harm a hair on your sister's head," Joe said. "Anyone who knows you both would know that."

"But this detective doesn't know us," she told him. "Not at all."

"Has Thad gotten there yet?" Joe asked. "He should be there taking care of all of this, not you. I don't give a rat's ass if they're getting divorced. If it were you who was missing, I'd be there. I should be there now, actually. I can get my mom to watch Joey... I'll come."

"No, honey," she said. "I'd rather you hold down the fort there with Joey and act normally, like nothing is wrong. I'm not sure I can do that, but I trust you can, Joe." Her husband acquiesced immediately. Because who wouldn't? It was a good point. It was a terrible situation, one not suitable for a child. "And if Thad is here, he hasn't called me."

"Prick."

Meg agreed. Lord knew, his divorce with her sister was nasty, but that wasn't an excuse to be heartless. This was definitely a side to him she hadn't seen, and she wondered if Gen hadn't told her the worst of him.

"Do you know where she might go? If she were to run away, I mean." Joe was hesitant and with good reason. Meg jumped on him.

"She didn't run away," she snapped. "Have you ever known Gen to run away from something? Especially me. She'd never leave me to worry like that. God, Joe."

"I know," he said, trying to sound soothing. Both Joe and Meg knew that when she got like this, the best thing for Joe to do was back away, to retreat. "What did the detective tell you to do?"

"He said *don't leave town*. He made it sound ominous, like he'd be personally watching me." Meg shuddered.

She slid a finger down her pant leg, adjusting a wrinkle. Joe dismissed her concerns.

"Honey, you didn't do anything wrong. He can watch you all he wants. He won't find anything amiss."

"That's a big word." She chuckled absentmindedly.

"I know some," her husband said wryly.

She was distracted enough not to notice his annoyance.

"Just get some rest, Meggie," he added, softer now.

"Easier said than done. But I'll try."

They hung up and the walls of the room closed in on her. She closed her eyes and squeezed them tight. Her sister's face haunted her there, laughing and witty. She opened them again, staring at the ceiling.

What the hell was she supposed to do now?

How could she help? What could she do?

She sat up, swinging her legs around and setting her feet on the floor.

She didn't come through medical school in the top five of her class to sit here and do nothing while her sister could be dead.

She stood, grabbed her purse and strode out of the room and to the elevators. She jabbed at the button and waited, her thumb tapping against her hip. Waiting wasn't something she enjoyed, and she didn't often have to do it. She was far from her comfort zone now.

Her purse rattled against her arm, and she pulled her vibrating phone out. She glanced at the screen, and it simply said UNKNOWN. She almost didn't answer it... It was probably a robocall or a telemarketer. But something in her gut whispered, and she listened.

"Hello?"

There was breathing on the other end.

"Hello?" she repeated.

No answer, but there was a slight rustle, like paper grazing a piece of clothing. Then breathing.

"Who is this?" she demanded.

The line went dead just as the elevator dinged and the doors opened.

It must've been a wrong number.

But the weird feeling stayed in her gut, and she was still

chewing on it as she erupted into the light outside of the hotel and hailed a taxi.

She climbed inside. Could it possibly have been Gen on the line?

Surely not.

But still.

Was it someone who was holding Gen hostage? Did someone want money?

She quickly told the cabdriver to take her back to the police station, and within fifteen minutes, she found herself in Hawkins's office again. This time he was in a meeting and she had to wait for them to pull him out.

He stared at her, his eyes piercing and intense.

"Someone called me," she announced.

This got his attention.

"And?" He waited.

"They didn't say anything. But it gave me an odd feeling."

Hawkins remained still and then finally lifted an eyebrow.

"You came here and had me pulled out of a squad meeting because you *have an odd feeling*?"

She squirmed in her seat.

"Listen, it seemed strange," she insisted.

"What number was it?" he asked, reaching for a pen.

"It said *Unknown*."

Hawkins laid the pen down and sighed. "Sounds like a telemarketer."

"That's what I thought at first, but it wasn't."

"Tell me, then. Why do you think that and who do you think it was?"

"Don't you think… I mean, is it possible…that someone is holding her against her will? That they want money?"

"Is there money for them to get?"

"Well, Gen's husband is quite well-off. And Gen herself

makes good money with her books. They're probably worth a couple million as a married couple. I've got money. I'm a surgeon."

"And your husband?"

Was Meg imagining the emphasis on that word? She swallowed.

"He's a contractor. But he does well for himself."

"I'm sure. I do well enough for myself. But no one would want to ask me for a ransom," Hawkins pointed out. "However, we can't rule it out, and we won't. If it happens again, call me."

"Don't you want to trace the call?" she demanded. "It could lead us right to my sister. I mean, wouldn't it be worth trying?"

"Haven't you ever seen *NCIS* or *Criminal Minds*? It doesn't work like that." He shook his head.

"You can't believe everything you see on TV," she told him, a bit haughty.

"Well, you can believe *me*," he answered. "Listen, believe it or not, I actually am trying to find your sister."

"No, you're not," she replied. "You're trying to see how you can prove I did something to her."

Hawkins's head actually snapped back. "Why would you say that?"

Meg shrugged. "It's true, isn't it? That's why you told me to stay in the city. You think I did something to my own sister."

Hawkins leveled his shoulders and drew in a breath. "First, the percentage of times when the perpetrator is related to the victim is actually quite high. Second, you were the last to see her. Of course, you can't leave the city, nor should I think you would *want* to, in case you can answer questions that might be helpful."

"You're patronizing. Do you realize?" she asked.

His mouth stretched into a tight smile. "Some have mentioned. You're kinda difficult yourself. Do you realize that?"

She actually smiled without meaning to. "Some have mentioned."

Hawkins stood and poured a cup of coffee. "Want a cup?" He turned to her.

She started to say no but changed her mind.

He poured some into a disposable cup and gave it to her.

She sipped it and coughed. "This tastes like dishwater," she announced.

He raised an eyebrow.

She grimaced. "I mean, this isn't great coffee."

He smiled. "Then let's go get a decent cup."

He grabbed his jacket, and in surprise, she stood up.

"We're going out for coffee," she repeated.

"Yeah. Unless you want to drink dishwater?"

She shook her head and silently followed him out, threading their way through the station and out onto the busy sidewalk.

"There's a place just down the street," Hawkins said, and he walked fast, his long strides stretching out effortlessly. She was determined to keep pace without complaining, and she did. Although she was happy when they reached the coffee shop and were shown to a table.

They ordered, black for him and a macchiato for her. While they waited, Hawkins stared at her, his hand under his chin. She met his gaze with purpose.

"I don't mean to be difficult," she said. "I'm just anxious… and I'm a no-nonsense kind of person, I guess. It must be the surgeon in me. I'm direct. Efficient. But my husband is always saying that it comes across as condescending."

"Trouble in paradise?"

She shook her head. "No. Just normal marriage stuff. We got married young, and we aren't the same as we used to be."

He studied her without answering. When he finally spoke, he changed the subject.

"Tell me about your sister," he directed.

"What do you want to know more about? The books she writes? The life she leads?"

"Yes. But tell me first…what is she like? As a person?"

Meg had to think on that. "Well, she's very capable. And hard. But soft. Moody. And funny. And sarcastic. Creative. Dramatic. Protective."

"You look up to her," he observed.

"She's my big sister. I think that's a given," she answered. "When we were younger, I always wanted to *be* her."

"How so?" Hawkins took a gulp of coffee and studied Meg. "You seem just fine all on your own."

She flushed at that, couldn't help it. All of a sudden, she couldn't ignore that he was attractive. His rolled-up shirt-sleeve displayed his toned forearm, and it was apparent he worked out. He seemed strong, capable.

Focus, Meg, she thought.

"I *am* fine on my own," she agreed, snapping herself back. "But when we were in school, you know how it is. All the teachers who had Gen before me compared us. All I ever heard was, *Well, your big sister Genevieve…* It got a bit annoying. Plus, she and I have always been opposites. She was creative and dreamy and mercurial, and I was the staid, no-nonsense, scientific one. So everyone compared oranges and apples, and that's not fair. Do you have siblings?"

"Just one pain-in-the-ass little sister," he told her. "I wonder, hearing you talk, if she feels the same way about me?"

"Oh, definitely." Meg chuckled. "She may love you to bits, but you also annoy her. Trust me."

"Did Gen annoy you?" The question was casual, but Meg caught the undertone and flinched.

"Yes, of course," she said firmly. "And I annoyed her. But we love each other fiercely. Like only siblings can. I'm sure it's the same with your sister."

"It is," he agreed. "No one better mess with her, or they'll answer to me. And that includes her husband."

She laughed, and he joined in. She sipped her drink, then licked the foam off her lip.

"Are your parents alive and are they still together?" he asked, ever so casual.

Meg was smart enough to know that she was being interrogated now.

"Yes, they are," she answered. "And they'll be stubbornly together till the end."

"Oh, not happily married, then?" Hawkins said.

"Oh, they're happy enough. My father is laid-back, and my mother is uptight. So I guess they balance each other out."

"People do tend to do that," he agreed.

"Have you ever been married?" she asked. She regretted it as soon as the words were out, but it was too late.

He didn't even blink.

"Divorced. Life is too short to be unhappy."

"That's Gen's philosophy, too," she told him.

"Why are your sister and her husband getting divorced?" he asked. "What happened?"

Meg cleared her throat and stared at her hands.

"Thad cheated on her, and she found out."

"That'll do it," Hawkins said stiffly, in a way that made her wonder if his wife had done the same. She didn't ask, of course.

"Who was it?" He pulled out his notebook now, and Meg startled.

"Why? You think…"

"We have to consider every angle."

"I don't know who it was," Meg finally answered. "Thad would never tell Gen. It has really bothered her, as it would anyone."

Hawkins nodded in agreement. "But Gen never had any clue? She never dug around and found out?"

"Not to my knowledge," Meg replied. "And if she had, she would've told me. She told me everything."

"Do you have any suspicions?"

Meg thought. "Thad is a lawyer and has an assistant, but she's a lot younger. I don't know that he'd go for that. He's more into mutual wealth, if you know what I mean."

"Meaning, he wants his partner to be as well-off as he is?"

"Pretty much."

"Was Gen?" Hawkins paused, his pen waiting above the paper.

"I don't know exactly how much money my sister makes. But she's had a few bestsellers, and she didn't appear to be worried about supporting herself."

"But you don't know for sure? I thought you shared everything?"

"We never really talked about money, which is why I assumed she's fine on that front. She's buying a house back in our home state. She would've said if money was tight."

"Is she going to get alimony or any kind of remuneration from her soon-to-be ex-husband?"

Meg cocked her head. "I truly don't know. It never occurred to me to ask that. I doubt it, though. That's not Gen's style. She wouldn't want anything from him. She's done."

"I think I'd like your sister," Hawkins decided aloud.

"Everyone does," Meg agreed. "So it wouldn't be unusual."

"Someone doesn't," Hawkins pointed out, and goose bumps formed along Meg's arms.

"So you definitely think something happened to her? That someone did something to her?"

"It's still early to say. But so far there isn't a body, and if there had been an accident, it would've turned up by now. She either ran away, or she was taken, I think."

"She didn't run." Meg was insistent.

Hawkins flipped his small notebook closed. "I'm treating it as an abduction," he told her. "We will follow every avenue, even if some of them make you uncomfortable."

"Because you have to consider me a suspect." She glanced into his eyes, and he didn't look away.

"I have to consider every possibility."

"Very diplomatic." She smiled tightly.

"I need to talk with her husband next," Hawkins said. "When will he be getting here?"

"I don't know," she answered. "You'll have to call him and ask."

"I can do that." Hawkins stood up, and Meg did the same. "In the meantime, we'll be tracing her credit cards, to see if they've been used recently. If she went somewhere on her own volition, she'd have to pay for it."

"You haven't done that yet?" Meg was surprised.

"I'm waiting on the warrant. It should be approved anytime now."

"There's a lot of red tape involved in an investigation," she observed, frustrated.

"Tell me about it," he agreed.

As they walked toward the door, her phone rang again. She pulled it out of her purse and found *UNKNOWN* on the screen again.

She stopped and answered immediately.

"Hello?"

Silence greeted her.

"Hello?"

Nothing. Hawkins took the phone.

"Who is this?" he asked.

The call ended.

"Now do you believe me?" she asked.

He handed the phone back to her. "In this era of rampant robocalls, it's hard to say. I'll get a warrant to get the call traced so we can see where it came from."

"Why didn't you say so earlier?" she demanded, annoyed.

Hawkins smiled, for the first time since she'd met him. "Because I didn't have cause to believe you then."

She rolled her eyes and sighed as they walked out into the rain.

8

Gen, Then

GEN'S PHONE RANG, and her agent's name displayed on the phone screen. She smiled. She'd been waiting for this call.

"Gen," Karen said, and Gen could tell right away she was pleased. "We have an offer for *Too Much*. You're going to be happy."

She detailed out the amount and the publisher, and she was right. Gen was happy. She wouldn't have to worry about money all year.

"This is the perfect news for today," she said, as they got ready to hang up. "I have a date tonight."

"Ohhhhh, with the lawyer you told me about last week?"

Gen laughed. "Yes. I'll give you the details tomorrow."

"Don't hold anything back. Take notes. Use them in a book."

"I always do," Gen answered, right before she ended the call.

How true that was... Literally everything that happened in her life ended up in a book eventually. She wondered if her readers even knew the extent of it. How everything they read was related to her in some way or another.

She showered and got dressed, and checked her phone.

Right on schedule, there was a text from Thad.

I'll be there in twenty minutes. I can't wait.

She smiled, excitement bubbling up in her belly. He was so charming, so handsome. Normally, she'd never go for a lawyer. But there was something about *this one*. He was funny, smart. Genuine. And like Meg said, maybe he'd keep Gen's feet on the ground.

But that almost made her laugh. *Fat chance.* Her head was always in the clouds, and she didn't care.

Her doorbell rang fifteen minutes later.

"Sorry I'm early," Thad said when she opened the door, his chestnut hair dripping from the rain. But he didn't look sorry, and she certainly wasn't. "I couldn't wait to see you."

He smiled, and her heart fluttered.

"I wanted to go to Navy Pier, but it's raining," he told her, his eyes scanning her face, then her body.

"I won't melt," she informed him. He grinned at that, and they set out. There was something about rain, something about the way it clung to warm skin and cleansed the soul. She felt close to Thad, and he pulled her up next to him while they were waiting to go on the Ferris wheel.

"You smell so good," he said softly into her ear. She leaned into him, and he kissed her.

His lips were soft, and his breath was minty.

They tumbled into the gondola and never looked at the scenery once as the wheel went round and round. They were too invested in each other, in their hands that were on each other's bodies and their heat that was fused together, two lit fireworks, waiting to explode.

The tension was delicious, and they kept it up all day.

They walked in the rain, touching constantly. His arm slung over her shoulders, hers around his waist.

He told her jokes; she laughed.

She spun stories; he listened.

"Look over there." Thad pointed toward the water where a houseboat bobbed on the waves. "Would you like to live on the water?"

She shook her head. "No. I wouldn't want my house to sink."

He raised an eyebrow. "I thought you weren't scared of anything?"

She tossed her head. "I'm not. I just prefer my bed to stay dry."

"Anything else I should know about the way you like your bed?" he asked, his eyes mischievous, and she knew in that very moment that he was the one.

"All in due time," she said with a laugh, as flirtatiously as she could.

He laughed, too, and later that night, under the twinkling stars, he received his first lesson in her bed. He was an apt pupil, checking to see what she wanted, so tentative, then so sure. He licked and touched and stroked, and she arched and moaned and smiled.

In the morning, he leaned up on an elbow.

"Good morning," he said, confident and handsome.

"Morning," she mumbled, burying her face in the covers.

"Not a morning person?" he asked with a laugh.

He swung his legs over the side of her bed. "I'll go get you coffee."

And he did. He jogged down to the corner, and brought back java and bagels. They ate them in bed and laughed together all morning, as he told her stories of difficult clients, and everything he said was witty and entertaining. He was kind and confident, funny and sincere.

Everything she wanted in a man. Everything she thought she'd never find wrapped up in one person.

"You're exceptional," she finally said, drawing him back to her, kissing him with yeasty breath from their breakfast, and he kissed her back, slowly, then with urgency.

They made love again, then again.

She pulled him to the shower, where they made love once more against the stones.

By nightfall, they were spent.

"I don't want to leave," he said softly, his fingers threading through her hair.

"I don't want you to," she admitted.

So he stayed. And then again the next night, and the next, until it was just an assumption that he would never leave.

He went to work every morning, and she curled up in her window seat and wrote all day, funneling the exuberance of new love into the keys, into her stories.

Karen called a week later, having read three chapters.

"This is exquisite, Gen," she raved. "I can feel everything. All of it. He's quite the muse for you."

Gen agreed.

That night, they had their first fight.

It was in the rain, as everything seemed to be.

They stood on the sidewalk, and she'd given money to a homeless man.

Thad shook his head.

"You shouldn't. He'll just use it for liquor or drugs."

Gen shrugged. "That's up to him. It's the spirit of giving

that counts. I give it to him freely. I choose to think he'll use it for food."

"You're too trusting," he told her, and for the first time, she saw displeasure on his face. "You'll be taken advantage of at some point, Gen. Everyone isn't as good as you think they are."

"I know that," she told him, rolling her eyes. "I'm not a child."

"You live in a daily dreamworld," he said, which ruffled her feathers. "In your world, you design the rules, and the dialogue, and everyone is what you think they are because you design them. Reality isn't that way."

She stopped in her tracks, and that's where the fight began.

They fought in the rain over his belief in her gullibility.

They fought hard and fast, and when they made up later, in her bed, it was just as hard and fast.

When they lay spent after, he whispered into her hair, "I love your passion."

"I'm not delusional," she told him. "I know what the world is. I just choose to see the best in it."

He nodded. "I love that, too."

They rested quietly, their limbs intertwined, and she was almost asleep when he spoke next, a whisper that was almost lost in the night.

"I love you."

She smiled, and after that, they were Thad and Genevieve.

9

Meg, Now

"WHY ISN'T THAD THERE?" her mother asked, annoyed. "That girl has given him everything, and he can't be there to help find her?"

Meg couldn't help but agree.

"I don't know, Mom," she said limply. "It's very strange. The detective asked if the divorce was amicable, and I have to admit, that for a minute..."

There was a pause, a pregnant one, as her mother realized where she was going with the comment.

"You don't think..." Her mom trailed off. "No, he wouldn't."

"They didn't have a prenup, did they?" Meg asked. "The detective asked about her income, and I don't even know. That's so pathetic. I never asked."

"Why would you?" her mom said, annoyed. "There was no reason. She's fine with money. It's not our business."

"But right now, it could make a difference," Meg said slowly. "What if she ended up having more money than we knew, and Thad wants it?"

"That's a lot of what-ifs, Meghan." Her mom was stern. "I don't like how things unfolded with them. But I can't jump to the assumption that he's done something...crazy."

"I know."

"I just have to believe that your sister just got worked up, you know how she does that, and she just went off to process. She's done it before."

Meg sat still, staring at the embossed wallpaper on the hotel room walls and thinking of last year when her sister had driven to a bed-and-breakfast after a fight with Thad and had stayed there for an entire weekend without telling anyone where she was.

"I know that she has," Meg said slowly. "But this doesn't feel like that. Thad wasn't even here, and she'd never make me worry like that."

"We don't know that. If something had happened to her, I'd feel it, Meghan. And I *don't* feel it. So I know she's fine."

Her mother was absolute, and Meg couldn't tell if it was delusion or denial that was fueling her.

Either way, she didn't push the issue.

"I'll keep you and Dad posted," she told her mother as she hung up.

Meg went back out onto the streets and continued to show her sister's photo to nearby shops and vendors in the streets, and no one had seen her.

Two hours later, she found herself on a park bench, sipping a hot coffee, staring into the horizon. It was so hard to focus lately. It was the level of anxiety she was feeling. She found herself constantly staring into space, consumed by emotion. She briefly wondered if this was how her sister felt *all* of the time. Gen was so much more emotional than she was. Meg was no-nonsense, even brisk. She always joked that she had an ice heart, the opposite of Gen's bleeding heart.

"It's the writer in me," Gen would always say. "I have to channel my characters, Meg. So I have to feel them."

Meg always rolled her eyes because nothing sounded so miserable to her as to experience twice the emotion of a normal person. It literally turned her stomach, and Gen always laughed at that.

"You're too hard," she'd tell Meg. "You need to be a little softer."

"That's weakness," Meg always replied.

"I'm not weak," Gen would say. "I'm passionate."

"You're *something*," Meg answered with a laugh.

Even as kids, Gen would make up creative stories about any given situation. Bumps in the night, animal tracks at summer camp, people passing by. She'd gotten in a lot of trouble growing up for lying, because she hadn't figured out yet how to channel her creativity. Once she discovered writing, her entire life had opened up into a thousand different worlds.

Meg had been almost envious, but then she found science.

The exact knowing of what was what, and what would be, and how it all added up to a perfect answer. She and Gen were polar opposites, yin to yang, and once they'd found their rhythm, it was perfect.

They balanced each other out.

They kept each other sane.

They were the apples of their parents' eyes, in two separate ways.

And if Meg didn't find her sister, everything would fall apart. Without Gen, she'd be too hard, too rigid. She got up and paced the sidewalks, oblivious to the stares. She continued showing Gen's photo, growing more and more frustrated by the second.

"Someone had to have seen something," she told the last person she spoke to. She was met with a sympathetic stare.

"I'll keep you in my prayers," the lady said.

Even though she knew in her heart that Gen wouldn't answer, Meg kept texting.

Come home.
Answer your phone.
I love you.
I love you.

She knew the detective had the phone, but some strange irrational part of her felt better from trying to communicate with Gen, almost as if Gen would feel the messages, feel the sentiment behind them.

Nothing changed, though.

Gen was still gone, and Meg was still here.

Alone.

Joe called that night to check on her, and she read Joey a bedtime story over FaceTime.

"Mommy, when will you be home?" he asked, a smudge by his mouth. She wanted to reach through the screen and wipe it off, to hug him tight.

"As soon as I can, baby," she answered.

"You haven't found Aunt Nini yet?" he asked, his eyes wide.

Her own filled with tears, and she brushed at them, annoyed. She never cried.

"No, baby. I haven't. But I'm looking."

"You'll find her," Joey said confidently. "She doesn't play hide-and-seek very well. She always gives up."

Meg thought about that—how whenever they played, Gen always pretended Joey was too smart for her, that she couldn't find him, and how he always roared with laughter when she'd conceded. She was such a good aunt.

IS, she corrected mentally. *Gen is a good aunt.*

Joe watched her quietly. "She's okay," he told her softly. "You have to believe that."

"Why do I have to?" she asked. "She's gone, and I can't find her. There's no way to know what happened."

"Sometimes, you just have to have faith," he answered. "She's probably somewhere, licking her wounds. You know how she is."

Her agitation bubbled. "Everyone keeps saying that," she snapped. "But she wouldn't make me worry like this. Maybe Thad, but never me. No one understands that this is serious. That this isn't like her."

Joe hugged Joey, and said, "Hey, buddy, run down to the bathroom. I'll be there in a second to help brush your teeth." When Joey had gone, Joe turned to his wife.

"I know that," he said firmly. "I'm trying to help. I'm not the enemy."

She felt immediately guilty for the wounded look on his face, knowing that she'd put it there. None of this was his fault, far from it.

"I'm sorry," she said quickly. She wasn't an emotional person, but she was always quite aware of when she was in the wrong, and she wasn't afraid to admit it. "I'm sorry."

"You're under a lot of pressure," Joe told her softly. "You need to give yourself some grace."

"And other people, too," she added. He smiled.

"Maybe. Everyone is trying their best," he told her.

"Except for Thad."

"We can't presume to know what Thad's thinking, or why he's not there," Joe finally said. "We don't know what happens behind closed doors, Meg."

"Are you siding with Thad?" she asked incredulously.

"No." Joe shook his head. "I'm just saying we don't know everything. There are always two sides to everything, and we've always only known Gen's."

"Because Thad was being a dick."

"I can't argue with that," Joe said. "But that still doesn't mean that there's not something there that we don't know about."

"Maybe," she said, chewing on her thumbnail. "Maybe I should try to find out his side."

"I didn't say that," Joe answered. "I'm just pointing out that he has one."

"But I need to find out what it is," Meg said. "It might make all the difference."

"You need to be careful," Joe told her. "Don't get too involved in things that might hinder the investigation. Stay in your lane, Meg."

"My sister *is* my lane," she replied before she hung up.

Meg didn't know a lot about what was going on, but she did know that she had every right to try to figure it out.

She reached for her phone to call Thad.

10

Gen, Then

"WHY DON'T YOU ever talk about your past?" Gen asked Thad as they held hands and walked along the lake. The water lapped at their bare toes.

"What's the point?" Thad asked. "It's the past. I only like to focus on the future."

"Very diplomatic," she laughed. "But the past can be learned from."

"Or it can drown us," he pointed out. "If that's all we focus on."

"And everyone says I'm the dramatic one," she rolled her eyes.

They stepped over a piece of driftwood.

"All I'm saying is, we're here at my parents' lake house, and you seem to like the family interaction, but you never invite me over to your family's functions, and you never talk about your past relationships. It's like you're a ghost."

"Oh, my God, Gen. You are the dramatic one." He rolled his eyes now, and she had to laugh.

"Okay. You're not a ghost. But you act like you're an army of one."

"I'm not an army at all. I'm just a man in love with you. And I love your family, too."

He kissed her nose, and they climbed the stairs to the house, where everyone else was gathered around a board game. They squeezed in, and soon, an afternoon-long game of Trivial Pursuit was going.

Thad and her father teamed up and skunked them all, and at dinnertime, her mother heaped food upon Thad's plate. That's when Gen knew he had been accepted into the fold. Her mother showed her love through food, through taking care of everyone, and now Thad was under her wing.

"I like your parents," Thad told her as they huddled under the covers that night at bedtime.

"Shh," she cautioned. "You're not supposed to be in here."

"You really think they're dumb? That they don't know I sneaked in?"

"We have to keep up the charade," she whispered. "It's the respectful thing to do."

From down the hall, they could hear Joe and Meg talking in their room. "Joe and Meg get to sleep together," Thad pointed out.

"Joe and Meg are married," Gen answered. "That's the difference. My dad is old-fashioned."

"Then marry me," Thad said suddenly. "Marry me, Gen. Be with me forever. Never leave me."

Gen sat up, stunned, staring at the man beside her.

"Marry you?" she repeated slowly. "We haven't even discussed that."

"Marry me," he said again, smiling now. "I've never wanted anything more."

"Me, either," she said, sounding surprised.

"Is that a yes?" he asked, studying her face.

She nodded. "Yes."

He let out a whoop that was loud enough to be heard two towns over, and they collapsed together laughing. There was a knock on the door two minutes later, and her dad stood there, stern.

"We're getting married," Gen told him, still laughing. "I said yes."

The entire family came out of their bedrooms, and everyone milled about. It was decided they'd go ring shopping in the morning.

"I can't afford a lot right now," he told her when they went back to bed, this time without her father saying a word about it. "But I'll buy you something bigger someday."

She shook her head. "That doesn't matter, Thad. I don't care."

And she didn't.

The next day, they found a simple small diamond at the jewelry shop in town, the band woven like a vine around her finger. She loved it, and showed it to everyone who would look. Her excitement was infectious, and everyone was smiling.

"This is the best day of my life," she told Thad later in the day, as she still was staring at her ring. He smiled.

"It's the first of a million," he told her. "Each will be better than the last."

"Is that a promise?" she asked.

He nodded. "Absolutely. My mission in life will be to

make you happy. To build you a huge life. To provide you with every possible thing your heart desires."

"I can provide those things myself," she said quietly. "All I need from you…is you."

He nestled his head against her neck. "I need to provide for you. My father never did for my mother. I always said I'd never be him."

It was the first he'd said anything about his family, and she froze, almost scared to prod him.

"They're divorced?" she asked, hesitantly.

"No. They're dead. They died when I was twelve."

She sucked in her breath. No wonder he didn't like to talk about his past.

"Do you want to talk about it?" she finally asked.

"Not right now," he answered, utterly calm. "I don't like to think about it. It was a difficult time."

"I'm sure," she answered, shaken. "That's understandable. Just know that I'm here, whenever you do want to."

"I know," he said. "And that feels amazing. Thank you."

She fell asleep, knowing that she'd given him something he'd never had before—a confidante, and that felt amazing, too.

In the morning, he acted normally, just as he always did, and so she followed his lead. When he wanted to talk about it, he would. She wasn't going to push him.

They'd gone boating on Lake Michigan with her family, and her mother packed a picnic of fried chicken and cheese. He seemed so happy, so impressed with the little things, and now she understood why.

His mother had died when he was so young that he didn't remember what it was like to be cared for. It triggered her maternal instincts, and she vowed he'd never feel that way again.

In the evening, when they returned home, she started the shower for him, and handed him a towel.

He kissed her softly.

"You're so good to me," he told her.

"This is just the beginning," she promised.

And it was.

11

Gen, Now

GEN STIRRED, her head splintering in a thousand different shards of pain.

She blinked, then stared at the ceiling.

She was in a room.

She blinked again, trying to focus it into one room from three.

It hurt to move her head, and she tried to lift her hand. It was bound with her other one, and both feet.

The concrete beneath her was cold.

"Hello?" she called out, her voice throaty.

No one answered.

Her pants were torn and bloody, presumably from her being dragged.

She tried to think but couldn't remember her last conscious moments.

"I need help!" she called. "Help me! Please!"

Her mind was black, an abyss of emptiness. She couldn't remember anything.

Where was she? What had happened? How hard had she hit her head?

The pain was overwhelming, and she succumbed to it, closing her eyes and drifting into unconsciousness yet again.

From behind the door, someone peered in, checking.

She was still breathing.

Thank God.

The figure came in, picked up the sparkling wedding ring from the floor, and slipped away again into the night.

12

Gen, Then

THEY BOXED UP her apartment together, she and Thad, deciding what to throw out and what to keep.

"You're so sentimental," he told her with a laugh.

"You're so *not*," she answered. "I want that oven mitt."

"It's got pineapples on it."

"I know. That's why I want it."

"I'm going to build you a mansion fit for a queen," he told her. "Cartoon pineapples won't fit with the decor."

She giggled, and threw it in the keep pile. "Pineapples go with everything," she decided. After she'd made her way into the bathroom, Thad put it in the discard pile when she wasn't looking.

An hour later, her sister showed up with a pizza from Giordano's.

"Thank God," Gen declared, pulling Meg inside by the hand. "I'm outnumbered here. I need you."

Together, the two women lobbied for knickknacks, while Thad fought for simplicity.

They all bonded together over the pizza, though. Hunger was the great equalizer.

"I don't care what you throw out," Gen finally said, as she chewed. "I just want to marry this pizza."

"Promise?" Thad asked hopefully.

"Promise," Gen nodded. "I don't even care. Except for anything Meg gave me. Obviously."

"Nice save," her sister laughed.

"Thank you." Gen smiled primly. In the end, her most sentimental things were put into a cedar chest and boxed away.

"When you get maudlin, you can pull them out and look at them," Thad said.

"Maudlin?" both Gen and Meg said together.

"Are you from 1760?" Gen asked with a laugh.

They teased him for a while longer, and then finally gave up when he pretended he was beaten.

His phone rang, and he chirped, "Saved by the bell."

He excused himself to take the call, which left the girls alone.

"I like him," Meg told her sister. "I really do."

"Back off. You've got your own," Gen joked. They smiled together, and Meg folded one of Gen's shirts, putting it into a box.

"I'm serious. He's your opposite. Like me. He'll be good for you."

"I'm glad you think so," Gen said. "I do, too."

They chatted for a while about wedding things, and Gen surprised Meg by announcing she wanted to elope in Vegas.

"You're kidding!" Meg replied.

Gen shook her head. "Thad doesn't have any family. I don't want him to feel self-conscious."

"Mom is going to kill you. She wants a big wedding."

"She had that with yours. She doesn't need another. Dad will be relieved that he doesn't have to pony up for one again."

"True," Meg said with a laugh.

And that's how eloping came about, which Thad was in full agreement with.

"You're sure, though?" he asked that night, his eyes so concerned. "I'll have a big wedding, if you want. I don't want you to feel deprived of one single thing."

"I'm sure," she said with certainty. "Walking down the aisle with everyone's eyes on me? Ugh. You know I hate that kind of attention."

He paused, then burst out laughing. "Oh, yes. You repel drama."

She stared at him indignantly. "I get enough drama in my books. I don't need a big wedding. I promise."

"I love you," he said. "So much."

"I know," she answered. "You'd better."

They eloped the next week, and after, she, Meg, Joe and Thad had all tied one on and been hungover for a full day. The memories that were made were priceless, including the tattoo of a bunny on Joe's ankle. None of them remembered how that had come about.

"Gah. At the very least, you could've gotten my name," Meg moaned, examining the pink outline on her husband's leg. "I can't imagine whyyyyyy this happened."

Gen laughed, and Thad looped her fingers in his. "I would've gotten your name," he told her.

"You didn't get one at all," Joe growled at him.

Thad appeared smug but opted not to say anything.

Gen decided it had been the best possible wedding. After all, who else had she really needed besides her sister and her new husband?

That night, Thad got sick after eating all-you-can-eat shrimp, and their intimacy level ratcheted up a few notches as she held his head while he vomited, over and over, pressing a cold cloth to his brow in between.

"You don't have to do this," he groaned to her in the middle of the night, but she waved him off.

"Of course I do. In sickness and health, right?"

He stuck his head in the toilet and vomited yet again, and she grimaced but held him tight.

"I hate Vegas," Thad announced in the morning, when the light of day filled their hotel room. Gen laughed, and he scowled. "I'm serious. I'll never step foot in this dingy place again."

And he didn't.

But the pictures of their wedding still existed, and were pulled out at family dinners quite frequently, including those Gen took of Thad when he was sprawled on the bathroom floor.

Pictures were forever.

Gen slept in the Caesars Palace T-shirt for years, even though they hadn't stayed in Caesars Palace—they'd stayed in The Venetian, where Meg almost fell into the "canal."

None of them knew how Gen had gotten the T-shirt, which added to the entertainment value. It was a trip none of them would forget, even though they could only remember parts of it.

Years later, Joe's tattoo remained intact, although Meg had tried to get him to tattoo over it. As good-natured as he was, Joe wanted it to stay.

"Besides," he told his wife, "my work boot covers it."

Looking back, Gen seemed to recall that Thad was absent for parts of it, going and coming, appearing and disappearing, but she'd been drunk, and her memory couldn't be trusted.

13

Gen, Then

GEN STARED AT the rain through her office window. She had two chapters to finish before she could stop for the day, but she was reluctant. Her creativity didn't want to co-operate and she hated forcing it. Regardless, her agent had emailed yesterday, checking on her progress. This was the first time she'd ever been late on a deadline. She couldn't seem to help her distraction. She kept thinking about Thad and how distant he was, how tired. *How removed.*

He'd worked late the last four nights in a row. He'd come in quietly, and gotten up and left before she'd woken up in the mornings. It all felt very sterile, very detached. They almost seemed like roommates now, not the married couple that they were supposed to be.

It made it particularly hard for her to write about happy couples when she wasn't part of one. She was a lie, typing out her happily-ever-afters and all the while she was a fraud.

She texted her husband. He didn't answer.

She got annoyed and stood up, stretching a long stretch, reaching her fingers toward the ceiling. She looked out the windows, at the cars that seemed like toys and the trees bending toward the pavement in the wind.

"I've got to get out of here," she muttered to no one in particular, since she was alone.

She pulled some jeans and a sweater on and piled her hair on her head. She grabbed her purse and headed out into the brisk Chicago air, and strode down the street. The movement stirred her blood and the circulation should help her creativity. Hopefully, by the time she made it back home, she'd have the next two chapters of her book figured out.

She walked aimlessly, or so she thought, until she found herself standing at her husband's office building. She didn't even know how she'd gotten there, and she'd certainly never intended on walking this far.

She started to open the door, but something, and she didn't really know what, caught her eye. A movement, maybe. She turned and saw Thad sitting across the street on a park bench. She'd recognize him anywhere. She started to walk toward him, but then saw him lift his hand and touch the face of someone sitting next to him.

A woman.

Her back was to Gen, and she couldn't see what the woman looked like, or who she was, but he was touching her face in such a familiar way. *Too* familiar.

Gen's heart slammed into her chest, and she wanted to storm over and confront him, to yell, to see who the woman was, but she couldn't. Her heart kept slamming and slamming, and her breath got shorter and shorter, until she couldn't breathe at all. She somehow managed to make it around the corner of the building so that he couldn't look up and see the disgrace of her panic.

She gasped for air, sliding to the ground and staring at the sky.

How could this be happening?

All of the late nights, her suspicions…her gut instincts…were true.

She should never doubt herself again, which didn't help her pain in this moment.

She wanted to kill him, and her, but first…Gen had to breathe.

She sucked and sucked, and finally, it came. Her lungs filled up, and blessed relief. She wasn't going to die.

She wasn't going to die.

She breathed in and out, evenly and rhythmically, until at last, she felt back to normal.

Her blood boiled in a rage she'd never felt before, though, and she stood, ready now to confront them both.

But when she rounded the edge of the building, they were gone.

She stood still, staring at where they'd been. It had happened so fast, and she tried to visualize what she'd seen. What color of hair did the woman have? She didn't know. How big was she? Gen didn't know. She didn't remember anything. Shock had crippled her.

She focused. He'd been touching the woman's face. Wasn't her hair brown?

She still couldn't be sure.

Her mouth was dry, completely drained of moisture.

She decided she was in shock, since she was actually shivering. She felt like she wasn't inside her body, like she was seeping out of it.

She willed her feet to step back into the sunlight, back toward the park bench. Thad was gone; the bench was empty. She had to find him. She turned toward the building, and there was a familiar pink coat, right in front of her, then a hand on her elbow.

Her sister's familiar perfume.

"Gen?"

She was delighted to see Meg.

"Meg," Gen exhaled. "What are you doing down here?"

"Meeting the chief of surgery for lunch. He's retiring this year, and I'm not sure, but I think he might be angling to make me his replacement."

"Wow. That would be amazing, Meg."

"Don't get overly excited," she muttered, rolling her eyes. "It's only something I've been working for my entire career."

"I'm sorry. I…" Gen's voice broke off and tears started welling, and before she knew it, she was a mess. Meg was alarmed, and together, they sat on the very same bench that Gen had just seen her husband on.

In between sobs and breaths and whimpers, Meg was able to make out Gen's words, and her face was stark as she surveyed her sister.

"Babe, that can't be right," she said, stiltedly. "Thad wouldn't."

"How do you know?" Gen screeched, a wounded bird. "You don't."

"I know that I didn't see him," she said calmly. "I was standing right over there for about ten minutes, talking to a nurse on the phone." She pointed across the street. "I would've seen him. He wasn't here, babe."

Gen stared at her sister, her mascara streaked down her face.

"Think about it," she urged. "Think hard. Was the man you saw wearing the same clothes as Thad was today?"

"I don't know. I wasn't awake when he left this morning."

Meg's face settled into victory. "Gen. It couldn't have been him."

"This is his building," Gen told her. "Of course it was him."

"Call him," Meg said suddenly. "See if he's even here."

Why hadn't Gen thought of that?

With shaking fingers, she dialed his number. He answered.

"Hey, honey," he said, and he was cheerful. "Where are you? I came home to take you to lunch."

"What?" Gen said, uncertain now. "You're home?"

"And you aren't," he pointed out. "The one time you leave the house, and I choose it to surprise you with lunch." He chuckled, and she was stunned.

"I guess so," she finally managed to say.

"Well, I'll make it up to you another day," he said.

"I'm in front of your building right now. Do you want to meet around here for a quick bite?"

"Sorry, honey. I've gotta get back to the office. I'll be late again tonight, so I was just wanting to see you."

Gen's chest tightened. "Okay."

They hung up, and Meg stared at her sister.

"And?"

"He went to the condo to surprise me," Gen said limply.

"So it wasn't him." She didn't say *I told you so*, but her tone did.

"I guess not."

But she'd seen him. She knew she had.

Her sister hugged her briskly goodbye and wiped at her mascara with a tissue from her purse.

"You're okay now, right?" She stared at Gen, concerned, her eyes wide and waiting.

Gen nodded. "Of course."

She had to be, right? Apparently, her eyes had deceived her.

Meg left for her lunch meeting, and Gen went back to the condo. Alone the rest of the day, she replayed the events of the morning in her head.

If that wasn't Thad, then he had a twin out there.

In her mind, she watched that hand, his hand, touch another woman's face.

She couldn't see the woman's face, but she knew, *she knew*, that she'd seen his.

Her gut told her that her husband had a mistress.

Her eyes told her that her husband had a mistress.

But facts… They said otherwise.

She might be losing her mind. Maybe she was alone too much. Maybe it was starting to affect her. Maybe writing books and thinking of crazy story lines was causing her imagination to run overtime.

Her eyes fluttered closed.

14

Meg, Now

MEG AND DETECTIVE HAWKINS sat at the coffee shop table again. They had met several times now, and after he and his team had pored over her hotel room, looking at everything she and Gen had in their suitcases, he suggested that she call him by his nickname, Hawk.

Hawk's notebook was at the ready.

"Do you recall anything strange about Thad over the years?" he asked, his pen poised over the paper.

Meg sipped her hazelnut coffee, thinking.

"Everyone is strange," she finally said. "In their own way."

Hawk rolled his eyes. "Don't be interpretive. Was there anything unusual that stood out? Anything that made you feel uneasy?"

Meg shook her head.

"He was a bit controlling in the later years, but I think it was because Gen hated taking care of mundane things. So Thad took them over."

"Her creative spirit and all?" Hawk asked.

Meg couldn't tell if he was being condescending. "Probably. He didn't mind it, or at least that's what he always said. He said he'd rather make sure the bills were paid than wonder if she'd forgotten."

"Surely, together, they made enough to hire someone to do that," Hawk pointed out.

Meg shrugged. "Being an attorney, Thad never really trusted anyone else with their money. He'd seen people burned like that many times before."

"So he was suspicious by nature?" Hawk asked.

Meg paused. "I guess. But that's also a hazard of his profession. He sees the dregs of society at times. Like you."

"Do you always defend him?" Hawk asked curiously.

Meg stared, wide-eyed. "Am I? Do I sound that way?"

He nodded. "Yeah. Every time I say something that could even slightly be construed as derogatory toward him, you dismiss it. Is it safe to say you like him?"

"Yeah," she said slowly. "I do. I mean, I always did. This divorce made things ugly, and I don't like that. It came out of nowhere, and hit us all like a ton of bricks. My parents were devastated. They'd come to see Thad as part of our family. My dad thought of him as a son."

"Divorce is difficult," Hawk said. "On everyone involved. At least they didn't have children."

"That's what everyone keeps saying," Meg told him. "It annoys Gen to death."

"It's true, though," Hawk said. "Too often, kids wind up paying the price for their parents' actions. I've seen it a million times."

He's felt it, too, Meg decided as she studied his face.

"Are your parents divorced?"

He blinked. "Yes."

Just what she'd thought. But she didn't press.

"When will you bring Thad in?" she asked instead.

"Soon," he answered.

"I miss my son, Joey," she told him. "I can't wait until you find my sister so we can all go home."

"I'm sure," he said.

"Do you think you're intuitive?" Hawk asked her. "Did you sense anything about Gen and Thad's marriage as it was falling apart?"

Meg stared at him. "Before it actually did, you mean? No. I have to admit that I did not. Like I said, it was sudden."

"So he hid his affair well, then?"

Meg nodded. "Very well. It seemed to have been going on for a long time, by the way Gen spoke of it. But like I said, he would never confirm the details, which is part of the problem. She couldn't get past something that he wouldn't even admit to."

"He never admitted it?"

"Not really. But Gen saw proof with her own eyes. His admittance of it was unnecessary."

"I thought she didn't know who it was?" Hawk's eyes were razor sharp.

"She didn't. She doesn't. But she saw them together. Saw the woman from the back. It was unmistakable. She just doesn't have the identity of the woman. Not knowing who it is doesn't change the fact that it was an affair."

"No. You're right. It doesn't. Just...knowing who it is could be helpful."

"Do you think she's involved?" Meg's head snapped up.

"Anything is possible," he answered. "Everyone is a possible suspect."

"I thought you'd ruled me out?" she asked, her eyebrow lifted.

"I said I believe you," he clarified. "I could always be wrong."

Meg's sigh was long and loud.

"You and your opinions are giving me a headache," she complained.

"They're not wavering," he corrected. "But things change in an investigation. It will all be clear in the end."

"Promise?" she asked.

"Hopefully," he answered.

Together, they left the coffeehouse, she for her hotel and he for the police station. When she was halfway down the block, she glanced over her shoulder. He was already out of sight.

15

Now

THE HOODED FIGURE wove through the dark sidewalks, among people, through the shadows.

With hands tucked in pockets, it strode with purpose toward a hotel at the end of the street. Sliding next to the building, it waited until someone approached the door at the back of the building. It slipped inside like a shadow behind the hotel guest, unnoticed by anyone. Hunched in a stairwell, it paused.

It seemed to consider something, waiting on the step.

A black-gloved hand emerged from a pocket, flipping the platinum ring over and over in its fingers.

For an outsider, it would be impossible to tell whether the person was male or female, its face was so far hidden beneath the hood of the jacket. The size wasn't telling—it could be a tall female or an average-sized male. The jacket was boxy, so shape wasn't apparent.

It started walking once again, and seemed to zigzag through the hotel, ambling through one floor after another. Finally, it opened the door to Meg's floor and silently made its way to Meg's hotel room door.

It stood there, silent.

Finally, it rapped its knuckles on the door and set something small on the ground.

Then, it slipped away, back into the stairwell.

Across town, Detective Nate Hawkins pulled open his kitchen drawer, hunting for a bottle opener. Unable to find one, he popped the top of his beer bottle on the edge of the counter. He then tossed the cap into the trash can before he took a gulp.

He stretched his legs, rotating first one ankle, then the other. He'd been at work all day, from before dawn until a few minutes ago. Glancing at the clock, he saw that it was almost 10:00 p.m. Too late for anything but a beer. Food would rest heavy in his belly, making it difficult to sleep.

With a groan, he downed the rest of his beer, tossing his bottle in the recycling bin. It landed with a clink. His feet were numb. God, he hated dress shoes. He kicked them off on the way to his tidy gray-and-blue bedroom. As he rounded the corner, he remembered the look on Meg's face earlier that day, how she'd appeared genuinely pained at her sister's disappearance. He would almost believe that she truly didn't have anything to do with it.

His years of experience contradicted that, however.

She was there that night; it was completely unfeasible to think she wasn't involved on some level. He dropped onto his bed, pulling his shirt off. He lay back, staring at the ceiling.

Meghan had been with Genevieve. She was a younger sister who had always been in Gen's shadow, but that also described two million other women in the country. They didn't usually harm their sisters for that. Meg seemed fresh-faced and innocent, sincerely worried and definitely annoyed with him.

He rolled onto his side and reached for the file on the floor. He examined the timeline, the facts.

Thaddeus Thibault hadn't been to see him yet, and it was time to remedy that. In the morning.

Hawk closed the file and turned out the light.

Sleep didn't come easily.

It felt like he was still tossing and turning when his phone rang. He grabbed at it, glancing at the time. Three in the morning. He'd been asleep—it just didn't feel like it. It was the kind of sleep that made a person feel more tired when they were awake than when they went to bed.

"Hawkins," he muttered into the receiver.

"Detective," Meghan said, and her voice shook. He sat up.

"Dr. McCready," he answered. "What's wrong?"

"There was a knock on the door," she said. "I answered it."

"And?"

"And there wasn't anyone there. But..."

"Yes?" he urged her, impatient.

"My sister's wedding ring was on the ground in front of me. Someone had put it there. She threw it off the balcony the night she disappeared. How did someone find it?"

"And why would they put it at your hotel door in the middle of the night?" Hawk added. "That's interesting. Okay. Did you touch it?"

"I picked it up with the bottom of my shirt."

"Okay. I'll be there soon."

"Wait. There's one more thing. There's a small note with it. It just says *FOR THAD* in big block letters."

"Is it your sister's handwriting?"

"No," Meg said shakily. "It is not."

"I'll be right there."

Hawk hung up and pulled his shirt back on. Who needed sleep anyway?

He arrived at the hotel an hour later. The person at the front desk seemed unconcerned when he inquired, and soon he figured out why, as he stared at the surveillance footage from the lobby.

"No one came or went," he said aloud.

The clerk glanced at him. "It was three a.m. Even here in the city, there's not a lot of activity at that hour."

"Except Dr. McCready had a nocturnal visitor," Hawk reminded the clerk. "Is there a back way?"

"Yes," the man nodded. "But, you have to have a hotel key card to access the back door."

"Did anyone swipe their card?"

The clerk punched the keys on his computer. "A few did."

"I'll need that list," Hawk told him.

"And you can have it," the clerk said. "After you bring a warrant. I'm sorry—it's hotel policy. I'd get into trouble, otherwise."

Hawk scowled but relented. He'd just have to come back.

But for now, he'd go check on Meghan. He took the elevator, and when he knocked on her door, she answered in a robe.

She had dark circles under her eyes, and she looked tired.

"Detective," she greeted him.

"Tell me again what happened."

"Won't you come in," she quipped, as he walked past her. He rolled his eyes and went straight for the console table, where the ring sparkled in the light. He pulled gloves on and looked at the note.

"'For Thad,'" he said out loud, studying the letters. "But you say Gen didn't write this."

"That's not her writing," Meg answered firmly.

Hawk looked at her. "Is it yours?"

Meg sucked in a breath. "Of course not."

Hawk looked at the bedside table, where Meg's notebook was. "Do you mind?" he asked.

She shook her head silently and handed him the notebook.

He looked at the letters Meg had scrawled on the page. "You certainly have a physician's hand," he said wryly. She didn't smile.

"Would you mind writing the words *FOR THAD*?"

He looked her in the eye and didn't blink.

Anger surged through her, but she did as he asked.

He studied the letters. "I'm no handwriting expert, but this doesn't appear to be the same," he finally said.

She sat down on the sofa. "That's because it isn't."

He ignored her waspish tone. "Can you walk me through when you received this again? Just recite everything, even if you don't think it matters. Was there anyone in the hall? Did you notice a cologne in the hall? Anything?"

She went through it again, not remembering any new details, and as she did, he turned the wedding ring over and over in his hand. The lamplight caught the facets of the diamond, and she seemed mesmerized as she spoke.

"I'm not well versed in diamonds, but this seems like a very big one," Hawk said after she finished speaking.

"It is," Meg answered. "It's four carats. In layperson speak, that means it's huge."

"From everything I've read about Gen, it doesn't seem very like her," Hawk offered. "I mean, she was moving to a rural town, somewhere that doesn't seem very glamorous. The pictures I've seen of her don't make her appear very flashy. Why did she want this giant ring?"

Meg actually laughed. "That would be Thad," she answered. "He wanted it. He thought it was a symbol of their social standing, I think. She started out with a smaller ring when they first got married. He bought her this one a few years back."

"So Thad is concerned with appearances?" Hawk asked.

Meg nodded. "Yeah. He's an accident attorney. Public perception is everything to him."

"He's an ambulance chaser?" Hawk lifted his eyebrow. Meg smiled.

"Some call it that."

"Interesting."

In Hawk's book, ambulance chasers were toward the bottom of the slush pile that was attorneys. They were all scum, but especially the ones who profited off despair.

"Don't like lawyers much?" Meg asked.

"Not much," he replied. "So do you have any ideas of who might've found this ring? Who might've returned it to you? I mean, how would someone know that it was Gen's? That this is the hotel room to return it to?"

Meg shook her head. "I have no idea. I don't know many people here."

"Maybe it was Gen herself," Hawk suggested, and Meg burst out laughing.

"You think my sister ran away? For what reason?"

"A prank? Maybe she was trying to find a way to get back at Thad?"

"By scaring the shit out of *me*? I don't think so. This would in no way get at Thad. Gen doesn't have a mean bone in her body. She'd never ever want to scare me like this. Trust me, wherever she is, she doesn't want to be there. And as I said, this is NOT Gen's writing."

She stared at him with disdain, and he shook his head.

"Listen, I've seen weirder," he defended. "I meant no of–fense toward your sister."

"You just don't know her," Meg decided. "If you did, you'd understand."

"Well, all I know is, I'm going to be calling Thad first thing," Hawk declared.

"You mean, in…about three hours?" Meg looked at her watch, and Hawk cringed.

"I guess so. I can sleep when I'm dead, right?"

Meg looked stricken, and Hawk cringed again. "I'm sorry. I didn't mean it that way. It was in poor taste."

"Gen can't be dead," she said firmly. "She's not. She's being held somewhere. There can't be a world where Gen doesn't exist."

Hawk looked at the woman in front of him, slender, tired and worried. She certainly didn't seem like a woman who had hurt her sister.

He swallowed hard. He had ignored his instincts earlier in his career a few times, and each of those times, he'd re–gretted it. Every bone in his body was telling him now that Meg McCready was innocent, yet…

Gen's wedding ring had turned up on her doorstep in the middle of the night.

It didn't make sense.

16

Gen, Then

"DO WE WANT KIDS?" Gen asked her husband, her hand flitting along his chest as they lay in bed. Many might say they should've had this conversation before they'd married, but Gen hadn't thought of it before now, not until her sister had just gotten pregnant.

Thad shook his head.

"I don't want to bring children into this world."

Gen paused, not overly concerned. She wasn't the average woman, someone who had played with dolls as a child. She'd always read books instead.

"Okay," she agreed. "I'm fine with that."

"Just like that?" Thad asked, surprised.

She nodded. "You seem very sure of yourself. Since I'm ambivalent, I'll go along with you on this one. It's called *picking my battles.*"

He chuckled. "You're sure you don't want a long-haired little girl who looks just like you?"

She stared. "Are you trying to talk me into it? Just get on board. I'm on your side. Besides, we could end up with a daughter who looks like you, for all we know, on the genetics carousel."

He shook his head, rolling his eyes. "The kid would have good genes, so I'm not worried about that. It's the rest of the world I don't trust. The crime, the ugliness. I just don't want to have to worry about an innocent child. We've got enough on our plates."

Gen couldn't argue with that. She alone had stacks of ideas for books. Thad was working on his law practice. They simply didn't have time to give to a child right now.

She stroked his arm. "It's fine. I'll be happy as the cool aunt."

"You can spoil that child as much as you want," Thad told her.

She nestled into his side. "I plan on it."

No one anticipated that Meg would miscarry the following week.

Gen spent days at her house, curled up next to her, feeding her ice cream.

"Do you want to watch *Gilmore Girls*?" Gen asked on a particularly hard day. Meg's face was puffy and her eyes were red. Her hand slid over her empty belly, subconsciously protecting a baby that was no longer there.

"Sure," she answered quietly.

Gen queued it up, and soon they were immersed in Stars Hollow and the nonsense that followed Lorelai Gilmore.

"If I could talk as fast as her, I could see twice as many patients," Meg finally said later in the day, her legs tucked beneath a quilt.

Gen laughed, and in that moment, she knew Meg would be okay.

"You're so strong," she told her sister, taking her hand. "You can literally do anything you put your mind to. You can overcome anything and achieve everything. I'm so proud of you, Meggie."

Meg swallowed hard and squeezed Gen's fingers. "Thanks. I don't feel strong right now, so I'll take your word for it."

"I'm your big sister, so I'm always right."

Meg rolled her eyes at that, and Gen was relieved that Meg was still able to joke around. She noticed that Meg had managed to let go, just slightly, of the sadness and grief she'd been carrying around all week. Gen hoped that her sister would understand, with her physician's mind, that her baby had miscarried because something was wrong.

God doesn't make mistakes, her mom had told her, and it was true.

She just had to believe that when the time was right, it would happen for her. Everything that was meant to be would fall into place.

Gen was able to convince Meg to get up and get dressed, and they went shopping that evening. They had their nails done and pedicures, and had a nice meal out at their favorite sushi place.

Gen ate an entire plate of salmon avocado rolls and wasn't even sorry. She primly patted her lips after, and Meg laughed.

"You up for a movie?" Meg said.

Gen glanced at the clock. "Let me just see what Thad is up to tonight."

But he was working late on a job, so they loaded up on buttered popcorn and Junior Mints, and watched a movie in a theater with sticky floors.

Thad texted Gen midway through.

How's she doing?

Gen discreetly answered, her phone halfway in her purse.

She's going to be all right.

And she was.

Meg threw herself into her work, and before long, she rarely thought of her failed pregnancy. She thought of surgical maneuvers, and staffing issues, and trying to make enough time for date nights with Joe, and climbing the ranks at the hospital.

That's why, when she got pregnant a year later, it caught her off guard.

It was a happy surprise, but a surprise all the same.

Her pregnancy was easy, the stuff that all mothers dream about. She glowed, never had a day of morning sickness and only gained twenty pounds.

Joe put together the crib and hauled in his grandmother's rocking chair, the one that had rocked him to sleep on so many nights when he was small. Meg sat in it, her elbows resting on the worn wooden armrests.

"We're really doing this," she observed, her hand on her swollen belly, her skinny legs extended like sticks.

Joe laughed. "It's too late to turn back now."

Meg stared at her hand, which was ever so swollen, and the way her wedding ring cut into her finger. She should have taken it off, but that had felt wrong. She'd be naked without it. It wasn't ostentatious, but it was hers. It was a symbol.

Joe loved her.

She loved him.

And soon, they'd experience a whole new level of love together.

★ ★ ★

In the hospital, the entire family sat anxiously in the waiting room. From down the hall, Gen could hear Meg screaming, and pushing, and shrieking. The labor was long and intense, and seven hours into it, Joe came to get her.

"She's asking for you, Gen," he told her, his face exhausted.

Gen immediately went to her sister's bedside and pushed her sweaty hair out of her face.

"Now, listen," she said. "This baby is like, what? Six pounds? Show it who is boss right now."

Meg snarled as another contraction hit her, but she did have some renewed vigor.

She pushed, and Gen held her leg up as the doctor instructed. Meg's strength, in her overwhelming pain, was astounding, and it took all of Gen's strength to keep Meg's leg in place.

"Push," she told her sister. "You can do this."

Meg pushed, and thirty minutes later, Joseph Matthew McCready-Harris was born.

"Joey," Meg said, already drunk on love as she stared into her son's wrinkled face, his little finger wrapped around her own.

Gen couldn't have been happier for her sister, and even as she held her nephew and inhaled his newborn scent, she wasn't tempted to have one of her own.

"I'm going to be your favorite aunt," she told the baby.

No one pointed out that she was his *only* aunt.

It was a beautiful day as they all huddled around the bed, in awe over the tiny bundle. In a lifetime where good days and bad days were scattered, this one was one for the books.

17

Meg, Now

"MAMA!" JOEY'S FACE was smudged with syrup, and his hair stood up in spikes. Meg smiled.

"Hey, baby," she said into her screen. "Daddy made you pancakes?"

Joey nodded happily. "Yup. With strawberries."

"Nice," she said. "Do you know that you've got one slipper on and one slipper off?"

Joey nodded again. "Yup. I lost my Elmo one. And my dinosaur."

"Oh, no," she sympathized. "Did you look under the couch?"

Joe's head popped into the screen behind their son, and he had the missing slipper in his hand. "Just did. Mystery solved."

He slid the slipper onto Joey's wiggling foot. "They never

tell you that hog-tying should be a prerequisite for parent-hood." He chuckled, holding his hand up in victory when he was done.

Joey wriggled out of his grasp and crawled out of the screen, growling like a triceratops.

Meg's husband sighed and looked at his wife. Even through the screen, he could see she was tired.

"Babe, you're not sleeping," he told her.

"I know. I try. But..."

"I know. Is there any news?"

Meg shook her head. "The waiting is the worst. I feel like I should be doing something, yet there's nothing for me to actually do. I pace around here and the walls close in, so I go out and walk around on the sidewalks, but nothing helps."

Joe didn't know what to say, because who would?

There wasn't a handbook for when a loved one went missing.

There were no rules to follow, no protocol to observe.

"Have we grown apart?" she asked suddenly, her eyes boring a hole through the screen.

Joe's head snapped up.

"What? Why would you ask that?"

Her shoulders slumped. "I don't know. It's just... Thad isn't here. They were married for so long. You'd think he'd care enough to be here. No matter what their issues are now. And their divorce was so sudden it scares me. If it can happen to them, it could happen to us, Joe."

He was already shaking his head. "Sweetheart. Are we newlyweds? No. Have we matured? Yes. But we love each other. We've got a son, a family. We've got a bond."

She nodded but was clearly still bothered.

"Have you been able to sleep without me?" she asked.

Joe paused.

"I've gotten used to it," he finally answered.

"Me, too," she replied simply. "See? Once upon a time, we couldn't sleep apart."

Joe smiled gently. "Meg. You are not your sister. I'm not Thad. We're fine."

"We've had our issues, too, Joe," she pointed out.

He froze, as a painful memory flitted across his face, and then he shook it away.

"Everyone docs," he answered. "People make mistakes. People grow from them. We certainly have. We're good people, Meg. We have to let past issues go and stop borrowing trouble. We're solid. That's all that matters."

"We're not Gen and Thad," Meg stated, as if to clarify.

"We're not Gen and Thad," Joe agreed.

Meg exhaled and seemed to let it go. "Okay."

Her husband grinned. "Now, I have to go wrangle our son into clothes. And you have to take a shower. Unless you're fully embracing the street urchin look."

She laughed. They hung up, and Meg did take a shower.

She hadn't packed many clothes, since she thought she'd only be here for a few days, so she also made her way out to buy a few things and grab lunch.

The sushi reminded her of Gen, and her eyes teared up as she chewed.

No one else in the family liked it aside from the two of them.

She pushed her plate away.

What if they couldn't find her sister? How often did that happen? That someone just disappeared forever?

"Ma'am, are you all right?" the server asked, and Meg nodded, tossing down a handful of bills and fleeing the restaurant before she broke down.

Outside, she leaned against the building and sucked in air, her hands pressed to her eyes, willing them to stop leaking.

This wasn't helping anything, and she knew it.

She gathered herself, placing both hands on the cold bricks, allowing the cold to ground her. She felt it in her fingertips and let it radiate through her palms and to her wrists.

She was here. In this spot. She was safe.

But Genevieve was not.

She swallowed, hard, and put that aside.

As a surgeon, she had learned long ago to compartmentalize.

She literally became quite good at purposely not feeling something. After losing a patient that she'd given her all to, she'd learned to seal those emotions away, not letting them escape.

She had to. Because when she went out to talk to the families, to tell them that she'd done everything she could, but it wasn't enough, she couldn't allow herself to feel that. If she did, she'd fall apart. If she did, it would chip away at her until she wasn't able to cope.

And she'd never let that happen.

So she drew on that strength now, that ability to conceal her feelings, to push down her emotions until she couldn't even see them anymore.

Some people believed that surgeons were unfeeling.

It was a misconception.

Surgeons were just incredibly gifted at putting things away, out of sight. It was something that came in handy so many times in life.

Like right now.

Meg straightened, and smoothed her coat.

She would handle this like the superwoman she was. She had no other choice.

Her phone rang, her assistant calling to nail down some questions for Dr. Callahan to present that evening at a conference. He'd been covering for her like a champ, and she'd remember that. It was always good to remember those who were in your corner no matter what.

She answered the questions, made a few comments and hung up.

It was odd how life went on, even when hers was stopped.

She longed to be back at a convention, back in normalcy, back where she belonged.

She didn't belong in limbo, not knowing what was happening.

You have such a God complex, her sister had told her once. *You can't control every situation, Meggie.*

That was true, but she didn't have to like it.

18

Gen, Then

GEN DIDN'T KNOW when they'd started drifting apart.

Had it taken two years? Three?

She really hadn't even noticed until she watched Joe and Meg teasing each other tonight in front of the Christmas tree. They still liked each other. They still craved each other. She could sense it.

She herself had gotten so immersed in her fictional worlds that she had let the real one slip away.

She glanced at Thad sitting on the sofa, talking with her father over a glass of scotch.

Thad wasn't innocent, either. He had gotten complacent and absorbed in his work, as well. Becoming a partner had been huge for him, and then after that, he had become consumed with ambition, wanting more, more, more.

Greed was something that crept up on a person. It overtook people who would never have suspected they'd succumb. People like Thad.

He'd never much worried about having *things*, until they started having them. Then after that, he worried about buying more, and then more, until their lives were completely different than what they'd started out with.

She caught his eye now, and he nodded, acknowledging her, but went immediately back to talking politics with her father. She felt annoyed, but oddly not concerned.

Shouldn't someone feel concerned when they realized their marriage was so radically different than what they had imagined it would be?

Thad excused himself, tall and slender in his black slacks, and made his way over to her.

"Your dad is a staunch and hopeless democrat," he told her.

"So am I," she reminded her husband.

"I'll forgive that," he announced, refilling his glass. The cubes of ice clinked together as he poured the scotch. She used to love the smell of it on his breath, especially combined with his masculine cologne. It felt so classy, so familiar. So *Thad*.

But now, she was ambivalent.

Unmoved.

What had happened to them?

Their life was picture-perfect. Last year, they'd taken a second honeymoon to Greece, sailing through the Mediterranean on a luxurious yacht. He'd given her a new wedding ring, a huge symbol of his love, but it hadn't really felt that way, she realized now.

It had felt like a symbol of his own prestige. It was a symbol of how far he had come. It didn't really have anything to do with *her*.

They hadn't really had sex in forever, something that they were equally responsible for.

She wasn't interested—she was too immersed in spinning tales of perfect love on her laptop, and he never took the time. How long had it been?

Six months?

A year?

Her head spun when she realized it had actually been a year. That couldn't be healthy, yet she didn't really care.

They'd changed. Grown apart.

And she didn't know when it had started.

"Aunt Nini," Joey squealed, opening a big box. "I wanted this! Thank youuuuu!" He launched himself at her like a cannon, and they almost tumbled backward onto the floor.

Joe helped her up, apologizing, but she laughed.

"It's fine," she insisted. "Wanna play the game, Joey?"

He beamed, and they set up the game console and immediately launched into a video game.

They kept at it for hours, consumed with the fun, and it was evening before Gen realized that Thad wasn't there.

"He had to go to the office," Meg told her. "He said to tell you he'd be back in time for dinner."

"It's dinner now," Gen answered, gesturing at the fully set Christmas table, complete with flickering red candles.

Meg was silent, because what could she say?

Gen tried to call, but Thad didn't pick up.

So she ate a full plate of turkey, cranberries and mashed potatoes.

She had been in bed for a couple of hours when Thad came in. He tried to be quiet, but she was lying in wait, without any intention of falling asleep before she'd spoken with him.

"Where have you been?" she asked, annoyed. "Everyone kept asking."

He examined her. "Are you upset because they asked, or because I had to work on Christmas?"

She turned her head. "That's a stupid question."

"Is it?"

She didn't answer.

"Your silence speaks volumes, Gen."

"Is there someone else?"

He was silent, completely still.

"Would you even care if there were?"

She sucked in a breath.

"That's an outrageous thing to say. I've never shared my things well."

"I'm not a thing," he answered calmly. "Never have been."

"Do you even still love me?" she asked, and he pulled at her resistant arm, trying to get her to lie against his chest. She resisted.

"I will always love you," he said firmly. "We're not newly-weds anymore, Gen. But I love you. Always have."

"I love you, too," she answered, and finally melted in next to him.

She laid her head on his shoulder, and really thought about it. She did love him. It was different, but it was still there. This was surely normal for couples after years of marriage.

He fell asleep a few minutes later, in a way that she always marveled about.

"How do you sleep so fast?" she whispered, watching his face. "Don't you have thoughts?"

Her own sleep was always late in coming, since her mind spun constantly. She was considering a plotline when Thad's phone vibrated on the nightstand, ringing relentlessly.

She glanced at the clock. It was 11:56 p.m. Who would be calling him so late?

She was just reaching for it to check the number when it rang again.

It was a Chicago number.

"Hello?" she answered it quietly.

There was silence.

"Hello?" she said again.

She could hear breathing and some muffled background noise.

But that was it.

"Why are you calling my husband?" she asked.

The line went dead.

There was no way that had been a work call.

She replaced the phone on the nightstand and rolled away from Thad, facing the opposite wall. She always said that she'd never tolerate cheating. That it was a deal breaker. That she couldn't live with it.

Now, though, it looked like it was upon her.

And things are always different when they are in front of you.

19

Meg, Now

MEG PULLED UP Gen's website and scanned through the contents. A blog where she mused about various things, a collection of her books, pictures.

She skimmed the pics. Gen at various book signings, Gen with other authors, one of Gen and Thad, although she tended to keep her private life off her social media. And finally, one of Gen and Meg from two Christmases ago.

Meg stared at the photo, at the empty smile in Gen's eyes, and wondered how she hadn't realized back then that Gen was so unhappy at home.

It was the usual story, she supposed. She was just ensconced in her own life, and hadn't seen outside of her own bubble. It was normal, but that didn't make it any better.

She clicked on the Contact Me page. It was an email form, but it did list the name of her agent, Karen Markus, for book inquiries.

She looked up Karen's contact details and called the agency.

At first, the receptionist wasn't willing to transfer her call to the agent, but once Meg explained, she was put right through.

"Dr. McCready?" Karen came onto the line. "What is my assistant talking about?"

Meg drew in a breath and explained how Gen was missing. Karen listened intently.

"When was the last time you spoke with her?" she asked the agent.

"Last week. She seemed fine," Karen answered. "She was annoyed because she had writer's block, but that's par for the course. Every writer gets it sometimes. I told her to just plow through, to keep writing, and one day soon, she'd feel it again."

"Fake it till you make it?" Meg asked.

"Pretty much. I'm so sorry to hear all of this. Gen is a treasure. I adore her."

"I was wondering if I should post on her social media channels and just… I don't know. Raise the flag for people to watch for her. Or to watch for anything unusual from her accounts."

"You would probably need to see what the police think about that first," Karen said wisely. "Just to be sure."

"Good idea. Listen, if you hear from her…"

"You'll be the first to know."

"Thank you, Karen."

"Keep me posted."

They hung up and Meg immediately called Hawk to pitch the idea.

"I won't particularly need to sign in on her accounts," Meg said. "I can just tag her, and it will show up in her feeds. I can just post and see if anyone has seen anything."

He shrugged. "It can't hurt. But don't get your hopes up. Usually, that type of thing just leads to tons of calls that lead to dead ends."

"Thanks for your optimism."

"I'm just telling you the truth… I'll tell you the truth. No matter what."

"And I appreciate that."

She hung up and immediately looked through her phone for the picture she and Gen had taken the night she disappeared, then posted it on all her social media channels, tagging Gen.

Hey. This is Gen's sister, Meg. My sister and I were having a girls' weekend in NYC, and Gen disappeared. We can't find her. We haven't seen or heard from her since last week. The police are involved, but I wanted to reach out to you, her loyal fans, and ask you to keep your eyes peeled. Any news would be welcome. Thank you so much.

Replies began almost immediately, hundreds, then thousands, well into the rest of the day, as Gen's readers were sympathetic, and some even panicked.

Tell us what we can do, one said.

Is there a reward? That might help.

At first, Meg was repulsed, but then realized that the advice had been given with good intentions. Of course a reward would help—complete strangers are never motivated to do something quite so well as they are when money is involved.

She edited the posts.

There is a $10,000 reward for information that leads to finding my sister.

Hawk called her almost immediately.

"Now you've done it," he said, and she could almost hear him shaking his jaded head. "Every crazy person in the city will be calling the department."

"And it'll be worth it if just one of them has a valid lead," she declared.

"I'll let the desk clerk know you said that," he answered.

But she could tell he wasn't really upset with her. In fact, did she sense a little respect?

She wasn't sure.

"You know, I've seen press conferences on TV before... when someone goes missing. To appeal to the kidnapper. Can we do that?"

Hawk sighed. "We don't know there is a kidnapper. There hasn't been a ransom note."

"But you said you were treating it as suspicious," she answered.

"I am."

There was a pause. And then realization.

"You think she might've been mugged and killed," Meg said slowly. "That wouldn't explain the ring and the note."

"I know," Hawk answered. "But every avenue is still a possibility."

"I'm so tired of talking about the possibilities," she replied tiredly. "I just want to find my sister."

"And we will."

"So you say."

They hung up, and Meg felt slightly ashamed of her snippiness, but he had to give her some latitude.

She sat on the bed and read the influx of comments on the social media posts, and waited for some concrete answers.

20

Gen, Now

GEN WAS CURLED up on the floor when she woke.

Her legs felt tight, her hair felt dirty and there was gunk under her fingernails. She flexed her fingers around the constraints of the duct tape, craning her neck to look around.

It was dimly lit, dirty, public. Almost like a public utility shed.

She thought she could see a mower in the corner, some lawn implements stacked to the side.

It was cold, but not unbearable.

The gag in her mouth made it impossible to scream and difficult to swallow.

She tasted blood but didn't know why. Maybe from when she fell to the ground. She wasn't sure.

She fought to think of the last things she remembered.

She had been with Meg. They had steak. Drinks. The balcony. She'd thrown her ring. Then found it. She flexed her hand again. It was gone now. Someone had hit her in the temple. Blood was dried around her nose. She could smell it.

Her sister must be frantic, and Gen didn't care.

She wondered if Thad felt guilty, and she hoped he did.

When she thought about it, this was all his fault one way or another.

Or was she being overly harsh? Unfair?

Probably.

But she was the one lying on the ground, bound and gagged and dirty. This wasn't how it was meant to be.

She wasn't supposed to be here.

She tried shrieking, but no one came.

She listened intently, and it seemed like she could hear a train in the distance. She felt the slight vibration in the ground, but that was it. She listened for anything else—children, traffic, anything.

The only thing she could hear was birds.

In New York City.

21

Gen, Then

GEN AND THAD sat side by side at the dinner party, the glasses clinking around them, the dimly lit dining room beautifully set.

The woman next to Gen, Stella, leaned over to whisper, "Check out Amy's new rock," she whispered. "Anthony gave it to her when he thought he was making partner."

Gen peered at it. It was almost as big as hers. Too bad Anthony hadn't actually been promoted.

"You should never count your chickens before they're hatched," she whispered back to Stella. "He should've waited."

"He's probably still paying for it," Stella answered, with amusement in her voice.

Gen nodded. "Probably."

She looked around, at the extravagant restaurant, the jewelry dripping from the attorneys' wives, including her own, and it all seemed like such a waste.

The caviar, the lavishness. She suddenly wished for happier times and a happier place, a simpler place, where she didn't have to worry about her husband cheating.

She eyed the long table. Was the woman here?

She went from person to person, but she knew it wasn't likely he would choose a colleague's wife. Maybe it was a paralegal, or someone's assistant. Or maybe even a barista. That would be even less complicated.

She tuned out the mindless chatter and thought once again back to the other day, when her husband had fingered that woman's face.

It had been a caress, of that she was sure.

The woman was a brunette. She was fairly certain.

She was annoyed at her brain's unwillingness to cooperate but she'd done a search online and found that shock can do that to a person. To shield the brain from too much at once. If she was patient, she might remember more details in due time. When her brain decided she could handle it.

"Honey?" Thad asked, and from his tone, Gen could tell that someone had been speaking to her.

She shook her head. "I'm sorry. Yes?"

Melanie, from down the table, had asked about how to publish a book.

Of course.

So many wanted to discuss that.

With a patient smile, Gen talked about how hard it was to get the attention of an agent, then a publisher, and how difficult the entire process was, really.

"Writing the book is the easy part," she finished up.

Melanie looked properly scared. "Then I'm sunk," she announced. "I haven't gotten past the third chapter yet."

Everyone chuckled, and attention was shifted from Gen again.

She excused herself and slipped off to the restroom. When she was washing her hands and reapplying her lipstick, she was joined by Regina, another wife.

"You look beautiful tonight," Regina told her enviously. "You never gain weight."

"I haven't had any children," Gen answered. "That makes a difference."

"True," Regina said ruefully. "Little wretches, they ruined my boobs for good." She laughed, though, and glanced at Gen in the mirror. "You have any plans to have them?"

Gen shook her head. "That ship has probably sailed, and it's fine."

Regina washed her hands. "As much as Thad works, that's probably for the best. I saw him at the office last week at eleven p.m. I told Sam that it was crazy—that he needed to get home. I mean, working hard is great, but he needs to remember he has a life outside of work."

Gen automatically agreed, then paused.

"You go to the office?"

"Sometimes. I usually take Sam lunch or dinner when he's too busy to get it himself, and the other night I went with him when he forgot a file. That's when I saw Thad working so late."

"Was he alone?" Gen asked, before she could stop herself.

Regina stared at her. "I think so. Why?"

"No reason," Gen mumbled. But Regina wasn't convinced.

"Girl, spill it. What's going on?"

Having had three glasses of wine, Gen's judgment wasn't its best, so she wound up on the settee in the ladies' room, telling Regina all of her suspicions. Worse, Regina didn't soothe her fears.

"They always say that he's a flirt," she offered helpfully. "To get things done around the office, he'll charm the girls into doing things his way. Maybe he took it too far. I know he loves you, though."

"If you love someone, you don't cheat on them," Gen pointed out.

Regina shook her head, like she was talking to a child. "Oh, girl. The real world isn't always like that. Just call him on it, and move on."

Gen stared at her. "Are you high? No. That is not acceptable. I deserve more respect than that."

"Of course you do," Regina soothed her. "But your husband is a partner now. All of your struggles from earlier are over. You are set for life. Don't let some girl from the mail room mess it up."

Gen froze. "A girl from the mail room? That's oddly specific."

Regina put a hand over her mouth. "Damn it. I didn't mean to… I mean, I don't know for sure. It's just gossip…" She stood up. "I'm sorry, Gen. Forget I said anything."

As if that were possible.

Gen made her way woodenly back to the table, and she felt like everyone was laughing at her. They all knew about the girl from the mail room, and she'd been little naive Gen… writing alone at home, completely oblivious.

She fumed all through dinner, and by the time they were in the cab for the ride home, she was boiling over.

"Who is the mail girl?" she turned to him and demanded.

She'd had four glasses of wine by this point and couldn't feel her lips. Thad's lips pressed into a line.

"You're drunk. And not making sense."

"Who. Is. The. Mail. Girl?" she asked. "Does that make enough sense for you?"

She saw the cabbie glance back at them and should've felt humiliated but didn't.

"Regina told me," she blurted. "Everyone in your office knows about it. What did you do? How long did it last?"

Thad sighed.

"The *mail girl*'s name is Christy, and there was nothing going on. She helped me with a big mailing and spent a few hours in the evening in my office, and that set the rumor mills going. You know how the office is. It's all gossip, Gen. And why would you listen to Regina? You know she's the most gossipy of them all."

He wasn't wrong about that.

Gen stared at her husband, and he looked straight into her eyes. If he was lying, he was damn good at it. But then again, he was a lawyer.

"On my honor," he said now.

Did he have any left? Gen was immediately aghast at her own thoughts, and then couldn't help but wonder…when did she start feeling that way about her own husband?

For hours, after they went to bed, she thought about that. She came to realize that she'd lost respect for Thad when he decided to become an accident attorney, preying upon people in some of their most difficult moments. It seemed like a field of leeches and it didn't have honor.

She'd lost respect for her husband and hadn't even realized it.

22

Thad, Now

THAD GRABBED HIS bag off the luggage carousel and strode down the airport passage. Coming to New York City to sort this situation out was the last thing he wanted to be doing.

He hailed a cab and ducked inside, his lip curling at the smell of body odor permeated in the seats.

He'd barely had time to settle in when his phone rang with a familiar number.

"Hey," he answered, his entire demeanor shifting, his face almost gentle for a moment.

"Thad," a female voice replied. "You said you would call this morning."

"Oh, man. I'm sorry. Do you remember when I said I had to go to New York City for a few days? I rushed out so quickly that I completely forgot. But let's talk now. I have a few minutes. How's your trip?"

He sat and intently listened to the female chatter on the other end, his fingers drumming on his knee as he did.

"Well," he finally replied. "It sounds like you've been really busy."

"You have no idea," she answered. "We've been doing all kinds of activities. I wish you called when you said you would. I was waiting for it."

She pouted, and he was patient. "Jody, I call when I can. You'll be back from your trip in a few days. I'll see you when I get back."

She paused. "When will that be?"

"I don't know," he replied. "Soon, hopefully."

"Well, call first," she said. "I'm busy."

Thad rolled his eyes and sighed, accustomed to her pouts. "Okay. I'll call first. But it will be soon. There's no reason to be upset."

"I'm not," she protested, but she was.

He knew and she knew it.

She paused for a beat and then continued, "Genevieve isn't worth all this fuss."

Thad bit his lip. He didn't know what he thought anymore.

Gen had seemed to go off the deep end this past year, and even though he was used to her dramatic, even at times mercurial, moods, it had grown thin. He had enough to deal with without his wife adding to his stress.

In all honesty, she hadn't known about *everything*, but still.

He fully believed that spouses should *support* their partner, not add to the worry.

"Jody, you know I don't like to talk about her with you."

He imagined her nodding her head when she sighed. "I know. I'll see you soon."

He hung up, and waited for the cab to finish weaving through traffic and finally pull up to the curb at the hotel. A bellboy rushed out to unload his bag. Thad tipped him handsomely, as he always did. Gen said he was condescending, but he wasn't. Just because he didn't chat with everyone he came in contact with didn't mean that he was rude.

Gen, at least in the past year or so, had found fault with everything that he did, and in fact, everything that he *was*. She felt impossible to please.

But he was the asshole. At least, that's what he was told.

He took the elevator to the third floor and found his room.

He considered calling Meg to tell her he'd arrived and had checked into the hotel, but then thought better of it. He wasn't on the list of her favorite people presently, so he'd wait for her to call him.

Once upon a time, they'd been so close.

And then there was that *one* time…but, of course, that was then. This was now.

Everything had changed.

He picked up the phone and called the detective to let him know that he'd arrived in the city. Voice mail picked up, so he left a message.

Then he reclined on the bed.

Was this room like Gen's had been? He stared at the gray ceiling, the magnificent view. What had she been thinking that night? Had she been upset?

He knew his wife better than anyone. Probably even better than Meg did.

Imagining her last moments before she disappeared wasn't too much of a stretch.

She'd been out with Meg, so they'd had a few drinks.

They'd probably drunk texted their mother to annoy her, and then they'd gone back to the hotel, this hotel, to hang out and relax. Meg had probably tried talking Gen into going shopping earlier in the night. He was sure he'd been a hot topic of conversation, the verbal crucifixion of Thad Thibault.

He closed his eyes to take a short nap.

He should be used to the verbal lashings.

He was an attorney, after all.

23

Gen, Now

GEN SQUIRMED AGAINST the duct tape.

Her arms had lost feeling long ago, and she wondered if that could cause permanent damage. Would she ever be able to feel her fingers again?

The person holding her here hadn't been in for almost a full day, and Gen was thirsty.

She couldn't tell if it was a man or woman, young or old. She couldn't tell if she knew them. It. She'd decided to refer to the person as an *it*, since a real human being wouldn't be able to do this.

She wondered who was looking for her.

Meg, certainly. Was Thad?

Doubtful.

He was probably holed up with one of his whores and hadn't thought twice about her.

She should have been used to that by now.

24

Gen, Then

GEN SPUN HER wedding ring around and around on her finger. She'd never actually liked it despite the size of the diamond, and now, today, it seemed more of an anchor than a promise. She took it off.

"Who is it?" she whispered aloud, staring out the window.

Yesterday, after a few hours of troubled sleep, she'd woken to Thad in her bed. He was asleep, too, his face relaxed in slumber. Her dreams had been filled with him and another woman, a faceless woman. And her gut… It was screaming at her to listen. She'd hovered above him with a pillow in her hands, watching him inhale and exhale. Her anger was beyond rage, and her hands had shaken.

She'd actually considered smothering him in his sleep.

It would have served him right.

In some Middle Eastern countries, she was pretty sure that

women could get stoned to death for adultery. It was only fair that Thad suffer the same fate, right?

But then, then… She lowered the pillow.

That simply wasn't her, and from all appearances, she was wrong. He wasn't unfaithful. He had a good story for the mail girl, and it seemed impossible that he'd been in the park when she thought she'd seen him. Why, then, was her gut screaming so loudly at her?

Something occurred to her.

Thad was smart. Brilliant, actually. Perhaps he'd seen her in the park, too. Perhaps he'd rushed to leave, and so Meg hadn't seen him there? Just because he had said he was at their condo, didn't mean he *was*. Saying something didn't make it true. If he'd known that she was in the park, he could've simply *said* he was at home, assuming full well that she couldn't tell the difference.

She'd investigate.

She'd figure this out.

She'd allow him to think that she wasn't suspicious, and she'd find out the truth. If there was something to find out, she'd discover it.

She could lure him into a trap, where she could capture evidence of his unfaithfulness, and with it, the truth.

Her blood pulsed even now, fueled by that purpose. To discover the identity of her husband's lover, and to find enough evidence so that she could get more in court. He deserved to have everything taken from him. It was only right. It was only fitting.

When Thad had gotten up for work, Gen shuddered at the thought of kissing him goodbye, so she made sure she was in the shower when he left. As soon as the door closed behind him, she was going through his desk, hunting for anything.

There wasn't anything amiss.

She checked the drawers, his pockets, his iPad, his email. Nothing.

She searched his closet and his golf bag.

Nothing.

She searched everywhere she could think of and couldn't find a single thing that indicated there was another woman. Not one thing.

She slid to the floor in the hallway and stared at the wall.

Was it possible that she'd misinterpreted the interaction in the park?

Was it possible that he wasn't seeing anyone?

She went over the memory again in her head. It hadn't changed. He had cupped the woman's face.

With a start, she realized that she hadn't checked the phone bill yet. She pulled it up online and studied it. Nothing amiss, but he did have a business phone he could use. She didn't have access to that bill.

Still, though, despite the absence of compelling evidence here in her hands, she knew without a doubt that her husband had cheated. She felt it down into her bones.

She had such a bad taste in her mouth that she left her wedding ring on the nightstand, and later when Thad finally came home, he didn't even notice. She kept her hand in conspicuous places, and he still didn't even blink.

"What have you been doing lately for lunches?" she asked as casually as she could. Thad didn't even flinch.

"You mean aside from yesterday?" he grinned at her. "I've been working through most of them, or having Angie pick something up when she goes out."

"Is Angie new?" Gen asked. "What happened to Staci?"

"She decided not to come back after her maternity leave," Thad said, and he seemed almost annoyed. *How dare a family get in the way of work?*

"Angie's been there for months. I'm sure I've mentioned her."

But he hadn't. Gen was certain of that.

When Thad was in the shower, she slipped into the bedroom and retrieved his phone. Leaning against the side of the bed, she went through it. Texts, emails, photos. She'd expected to see a selfie of him and a woman, something he'd forgotten to delete.

But there was nothing.

Was he really this good at hiding things? At lying?

Or was she wrong?

She put his phone back and pulled on a long cotton nightgown.

She glanced at her wedding ring and sighed, putting it back on.

She went to bed, turned off the lamp and was asleep long before Thad came to bed.

25

Meg, Now

MEG FLICKED HER hair out of her face as she studied a map of Central Park. Maybe Gen had gotten curious and wanted to explore. Her sister had never been one to think about consequences. It's possible that she had inadvertently wandered into danger in the night.

She narrowed her eyes in concentration. Eight hundred and forty acres that Gen could've gotten lost and abducted in. As she thought, she remembered Gen's cell phone sitting in the detective's desk. She grabbed her own.

He answered on the first ring.

"Yeah?"

"Nice," she said wryly. "Hey. Who were the last phone calls on Gen's phone?"

"You planning a new line of work?" Hawk asked, and she could almost hear the humor in it. "I'm the detective here."

"So you already checked?" she guessed.

"Of course."

"And? Anything interesting?"

"Not really. A few calls to her editor, a few to you, one to her agent and a few to Thad."

"Thad?" Meg asked. "Are you sure? She didn't want anything to do with him. They only spoke through their attorneys."

"I'm quite sure. It's her husband's phone number. Let me see here… Several earlier in the month, and then two in the two weeks leading up to now."

Meg shook her head. "That's not right."

"Meghan, it's right. One call was for seven minutes, and the other was for twelve."

"What the hell? She didn't want to even hear his *name*, much less his *voice*. This is very odd," Meg said slowly.

"Anyway. I already told you more than I should have," Hawk said, bringing the conversation to an end.

"Thank you," Meg replied, and she hung up. Standing, she paced the length of the room, then again before she dialed another number.

Meg let it ring a few times before Thad finally picked up right before she was going to give up.

Meg knew him. Thad was far too intelligent to hurt Genevieve. But what if he'd hired someone?

"To what do I owe this pleasure?" Thad asked, as a greeting, his voice calm and sure. She would soon find out that he was already in the city and had checked into her very hotel.

His greeting annoyed Meg to no end. "My sister is still missing," she snapped.

"I'm aware," he answered.

"Have you always been this much of a dick?" she asked.

"I've been told so quite often lately."

She paused. "Thad, are you somehow involved in this?"

He was silent, the quiet so pregnant that Meg could feel it through the cellular waves.

"No."

"I don't know if I should believe you."

"That's your problem," he pointed out.

"I don't know if I can believe anything you say."

"Why? Have I ever lied to you? Have I ever broken a promise?"

"You're scaring me right now," she whispered. "You don't seem like yourself. You seem so calm. *Too* calm."

It hadn't occurred to Meg before this very moment that he could well and truly be involved.

"Of course I didn't have anything to do with this. I'm not stupid."

She was silent, and he chuckled, his laughter a sharp edge.

"You're right, though. I guess if I did, I wouldn't tell you."

He actually laughed.

The hair on Meg's neck rose up.

"I thought she might be exaggerating about you. About the way you didn't seem to care. We all exaggerate about our spouses."

"We all see things from our own point of view," Thad corrected her. "So whatever she said I'm sure wasn't an exaggeration. It was simply her opinion. I have my own, too. About your sister, and about you."

"Are you really this cruel?" Meg demanded. "I guess I just never saw this side of you."

Thad stayed silent.

Meg was flabbergasted. "You were with her for...how many years? Seven? Surely you are concerned for her."

"I don't know that it's your business what I do or don't

feel," he replied. "And I'm not worrying about Gen. She and I are no longer a part of each other's lives."

She drew in a shaky breath, amazed at his cavalier attitude. "What were you and Gen talking about on the phone? The detective mentioned that you had spoken with her on the phone a couple of times in the last couple of weeks. I didn't know she was talking to you at all."

"I'm not sure that it's your concern," he answered. "But it was simply divorce issues. She was stalling with signing the papers. I wanted to know why. Why do you ask? Do you think we got soft and wanted to stay together? Were you jealous?"

Meg's skin almost crawled, even though she knew he was baiting her. He was trying to get a reaction.

"Thad, I think this goes without saying, but no one can ever know."

He had the audacity to laugh.

"Meghan, your sister and I are divorcing. I have no desire to be caught up in family drama."

"It's more than family drama at this point," she snapped. "My sister is missing. I was the last one with her, and I slept with her husband. I'm not proud of it, and I hate myself for it, but the police won't know that. All they'll see is a motive."

"Then stop calling me," he suggested. "Or can you not help yourself? Do you dream about me, Meggie? You can't help yourself, can you?" His voice had turned silken, the way it had in the night she'd spent with him.

She closed her eyes, trying to forget how she'd loved the firm way he'd handled her, the confident way he'd stroked her thighs and brought her to orgasm. He was so sure about everything he did, so arrogant, almost, and it had sucked her in. Her own husband was so traditional, always missionary style, didn't really know how to please a woman in bed. He was laissez-faire. She had gotten weary of always making the decisions, of always being the strong one.

She'd messed up.

It was one night. One drunken night. And she could never take it back, never erase it.

"Don't say that," she whispered.

"But it's true, isn't it? You want me even still."

"Goodbye, Thad," she said, her words stilted.

She hung up, listening to him laugh as she did, and felt sick to her stomach.

She'd slept with her sister's husband. That made her a monster.

She stepped into the shower, turned the water on hot and scrubbed as long as she could, until her skin was pink and raw.

But no matter what, the guilt remained.

26

Gen, Then

"I NEED TO KNOW," Gen told the man sitting in front of her. "It might sound silly, but I know something is going on, and I need answers."

"I'll find out for you," Jenkins, the private investigator, said, gulping at his coffee. His shirt wasn't crisp, but it was still a button-up, which was sort of professional. Gen stared at him.

"What's the likelihood of getting the truth?" she asked.

He smiled.

"One hundred percent, if you're willing to spend the money to do it."

"I'm willing," she said quickly. "Whatever it takes."

"Don't tip your hand to him," Jenkins told her. "Do not let him know that you suspect. So no questions, no nothing. You got it?"

He was firm, and no-nonsense. He must see this stuff all the time.

"How many cheating husbands have you seen in your lifetime?" she asked, and her belly was heavy.

"Too many to count, and wives, too." He shook his head. "Ain't no one exempt from it. Not a one. But trust me on this, every one of them slips up sometime. And now that you've hired me, I'll be there waiting for it."

It actually made her feel better, in a sick way. She was bringing someone into the most personal areas of their lives, with the sole intention of trapping her husband, of finding out something she really didn't want to know.

But she *had to* know.

And it made her feel better.

"Jenkins, I'll make up a new email account for you to email me things. Pictures, whatever. I don't want him to know about it."

"Smart," he agreed. "And I'll start today. Send me a list of the places you know he likes to go. He probably won't take another woman to them, but you never know. Some of the more ballsier ones do."

"Thad is ballsy," she told him. "Always has been."

Jenkins, with his combed graying hair, leaned forward and put his hand on hers. "Listen, Mrs. Thibault, if he's stepping out on you, I'll find it. And I'll get you the proof. You can take him for everything he has."

Gen knew that wouldn't fix the sense of betrayal she felt, the wide wounded chasm in her heart, but she nodded anyway.

"Thank you," she said simply.

"Now, remember, and this is important," Jenkins said, his faded blue eyes serious. "Act normally. He needs to think that you know nothing. Otherwise, he'll cover his tracks even better."

She nodded and Jenkins left. She paid the check for both of them. She'd better get used to paying his expenses anyway. He was the best at what he did, and his prices reflected it.

She thought about what the private detective had said, and picked up her phone.

I miss you, she sent her husband. She added a heart emoji.

She hadn't sent him a random sweet text for a long time, and she was distracted for a minute, thinking about that, trying to remember *how* long. Maybe she'd given up on their marriage, too. Maybe this wasn't all Thad's fault. After all, she had realized that she'd literally lost some respect for him.

Stop it, she told herself. While it was true that she had maybe been sidetracked with her work, so was he. And no matter what, she hadn't stepped out on him. Adultery was a choice, and if he'd made that decision, he was in the wrong. Not her. He could've come to her at any time, and said he was unhappy, that he felt neglected. She knew herself. She would've been open to working harder at their marriage.

But if he'd cheated, he hadn't given her the chance.

If.

She was so tired of that word.

She just needed to know.

Gen left the restaurant and went back to their condo, and when she crossed the threshold, she actually shuddered. What if she was sharing this home with a man who was betraying her? It was entirely possible that everything she knew as truth was actually a lie.

She shook her head, and before she could change her mind, she backed out of the apartment.

She hailed a cab and instructed the driver to drive to an

apartment complex down the street. The apartment she lived in before she met Thad and the one she'd never let go of after moving in with him. She never knew why she'd held on to it, other than the fact that it was *hers* and she didn't have to compromise anything about it. And, of course, Thad hadn't known. She hadn't been here for years.

Opening the door to her apartment, she breathed in deeply.

It smelled like truth in here, like a place she wouldn't have to hide in, a place she wouldn't have to pretend. It was light, it was open, it was breezy. Exactly how she'd wanted her condo with Thad to be. It had no furniture anymore, but she could remedy that. She wouldn't need much here. A desk, and maybe a bed, just in case. This would all be paid for from her business account. He'd never know about it. She'd write it off as an office space.

She went back home, got her laptop and shopped for a couple of furniture pieces. A desk, a full-size simple bed and a love seat. She had them shipped to her apartment, delivered that afternoon. On her way to wait there, she grabbed a few things for the kitchen, a pitcher for water, some glasses, some wine.

As she walked down Michigan Avenue, she saw the most beautiful painting in an art gallery window.

A woman, hunched over and naked, her hair streaming down her legs. It was painted in grays and browns and violets…hauntingly sad and beautiful. It called to her, and without hesitation, she went in and bought it.

It was five-thousand dollars, but she didn't care.

It spoke to her soul, and right about now, she needed her soul spoken to. She had them wrap it up, and they said they'd deliver it to her new apartment that very afternoon.

Once she was back in her safe haven, she curled up on the

floor with her laptop, next to a window, and she felt at peace here, for the first time in as long as she could remember.

Had her time with Thad always felt confining? Had it always felt fake?

She looked around the room and remembered the afternoons she'd spent here, wrapped around Thad's body, wasting away Sunday afternoons.

No. Their time together wasn't always fake.

Being here felt like it brought some of that time back, that time when all had been right in the world.

She wanted to call Meg and tell her, but then it wouldn't be a secret. She liked the idea that she had this solitude here, in this private place. This was hers, and hers alone.

She worked all afternoon, writing words about a fairy-tale ending, a love story that would withstand time. It tweaked at her heart, because with every minute, she knew hers wasn't a fairy tale. Hers wasn't an enduring love. Even if it turned out that Thad wasn't cheating.

It was something she didn't want to focus on yet.

She'd deal with it later.

For now, she had a den of solitude. A place of her own.

It felt wonderful.

She went out and bought poster board and tape and glue, and a printer.

When she went back to her Safe Haven (which was how she would think of it now), she started printing out pictures. Of Thad, of Thad's office and Thad's car. She pasted them onto a poster board, and tacked it to the wall, just as she did with her storyboards for her books.

She drew a map, of where his office was from their condo and the paths in between. What routes he could take on the L, if he chose to take the train. What restaurants were on the way, which ones were around his office. She felt slightly unhinged as she did it, but it didn't matter.

No one would see it but her.

She was safe here. She was away from prying eyes.

She could obsess as much as she wanted.

And so she did.

27

Meg, Now

"MOMMY MISSES YOU, TOO," Meg told Joey. He had spent fifteen minutes telling her about the fire truck he saw earlier, how the lights were bright and the siren was loud. She missed the days when the world was so simple.

Joey's voice was sweet, and it twinged in her belly.

"Maybe you and Joey could come here for a few days," she suggested to Joe when he took the phone back.

"Joey would feel cooped up in a hotel room, you know that." Joe was doubtful and with good reason. Joey was pure little boy.

"I guess you are right," she said. "I just miss him."

"Have you talked to your parents lately?"

"Oh, yes. My mother is trying to decide whether to come here."

"God help you."

Meg managed to laugh. Her mother would definitely make things more tense. She was an anxious woman anyway, and in this situation, she'd be a nightmare.

"The detective would probably arrest her just to keep her out of the way," she said. Joe laughed.

"How *is* the detective anyway? Still being a dick to you?"

"Depends on the day," she answered honestly. "There are times when I think he's focusing on me as a suspect, and then times when it feels like he believes me. I honestly don't know, to tell you the truth."

"He'll love you when he gets to know you," Joe decided. "Everyone does."

"You know, I'm not sure how I feel about having the kind of personality that people have to get to know in order to love," she pointed out. "With people like Gen, they're just loved automatically."

Joe laughed again. "You're a complicated woman," he clarified. "Driven, beautiful, intelligent. I'd marry you all over again."

"Yeah?"

"Definitely. Now go find your sister so you can come home."

The tone of his voice made her pause. It was almost unconcerned.

"You think she left, don't you? You think she ran away and didn't tell anyone."

Joe paused.

"I don't know. But I think maybe. She wanted to be rid of Thad. And let's be honest. For the last couple of months, she's been erratic."

"That's not true," Meg protested. "She's been distracted."

"She's been gone a lot, and no one has known where to

find her. How many times did Thad call you and ask if you knew where she was?"

Meg considered that. How many times Thad had gotten home from work late and Gen hadn't been home. It was so odd that Thad had called looking for her. It wasn't like her sister at all.

"Has anyone considered the possibility that maybe Gen was having an affair, too?" Joe asked hesitantly.

Meg's head snapped back. "No. That isn't Gen."

"It *wasn't* Gen," Joe pushed back gently. "But then Gen's husband had an affair. I think it wouldn't be so uncommon that she went out and found some solace of her own."

"That's a good word," she answered, without thinking about it, the way she always did with their son.

Joe sighed. "Yeah. I know a few."

"But Gen…she's loyal to the bone. She's been that way since she was born. She would never."

"You don't know that for sure," Joe answered firmly. "You've never seen a cornered animal. I have. A cornered animal will retaliate."

"She's not an animal," Meg replied, rolling her eyes.

"No, but she's wounded," Joe answered, and in that moment, he sounded so wise.

"I guess you could be right," she finally said. "Maybe I'll mention it to Hawkins."

"Have you told him about her odd behavior lately?"

"No. Because I didn't want him to think she'd run away."

"Meghan."

She sighed, and sighed hard.

"Okay, fine. I'll tell him."

"Good girl. I'll talk to you later. I love you, Megs."

"Love you, too."

And she did. She hung up, thinking on that. She did love

her husband. What she'd done with Thad was separate, un-related. She'd stepped out of herself, the way she did in the operating room, and she'd participated in that night while she was separated from her feelings, from her guilt.

In order to not torture herself, she'd have to continue that.

She'd have to bury it and never think of it again.

She sent Hawk a text and asked to see him.

He said he'd meet her for lunch, so she waited and showed up five minutes early.

He was already there, sitting there in gray slacks and a deep blue shirt. It made his eyes stand out, definitely bluer than gray. She could see his strength from beneath the material on his arms, the way the shirt stretched across his chest. She hated that she noticed. First, she'd slept with Thad, and now she was noticing a stranger. What the hell was wrong with her? She was a married woman with a child whom she loved.

"What brings us here?" Hawk asked curiously, as she took a seat.

She inhaled and leveled a gaze at him.

"I haven't been entirely truthful," she admitted. Hawk's eyebrow lifted and she rushed to tell him of her sister's odd behavior in the prior months.

When she was done, the detective was unrattled. "So, she stayed out late and didn't offer explanations," he said. "Maybe she was sleeping with someone."

"That's what my husband said," she sighed. "I can't fathom it."

"Because you're seeing her through the lens you've al-ways viewed her in," he offered. "You're seeing her as your sister, not a woman. Think of your own life. Surely, there have been times you have kept things from her, things you wouldn't want her to know?"

Meg startled. Surely, he didn't know. Thad certainly wouldn't have told him.

"Of course. I mean, sometimes."

Hawk nodded. "As I'm sure she did the same to you. No one reveals all of their secrets. Not to anyone."

"I guess."

"I've requested a warrant for all of Gen's things," Hawk added. "Her bank accounts, her condo, everything."

"The condo is being sold," Meg told him. "I don't know when the closing date is."

"If Gen's not there to sign, then that will be put on hold," Hawk pointed out.

"Crap. I didn't think of that. I'll ask Thad if he's told their Realtor."

"Good idea. But in the meantime, I'll be getting a warrant to search through her things. All of it. And if there was someone else, I'll find him. I'll figure out a motive, Meg."

He meant to reassure her, but deep down, it unsettled her.

He'd find out about her and Thad. And when he did… not only would it cast suspicion on her, but he'd stop looking at her in the way he had been lately. And that bothered her more than she wanted to admit.

What is wrong with me? she wondered, as she tried to hail a cab. She had a perfectly respectable husband at home, a son, a career. Why did she even care how this man looked at her?

She only knew that she wasn't the woman everyone thought she was.

She was flawed.

Her heart heavy, she climbed into the cab.

28

Gen, Then

GEN LAY ON her back on the cream-colored carpet. It was soft, unlike the marble floors in the condo she shared with Thad. This suited her better, she decided. She stared at the ceiling, intent on the plot of her book.

She'd written here in this apartment more than she had in months.

Her work was good, inspired. Her agent would be happy.

Sitting up, she peered out the window. It wasn't as high as her condo, so she could see people's faces as they passed by on the sidewalk. They hurried, as people in Chicago do. The wind blew, and she was above it all, up here in her sanctuary.

She glanced at the woman on the wall, the beautiful painting.

What was the woman crying about? She didn't know, but she knew the story would come to her. The woman had been her muse for a week, sparking her creativity to write. That was enough for now.

Her cell phone rang, and she recognized Jenkins's number. She answered immediately.

"Hello."

"Gen, I may have found something. Can you meet me?"

She agreed, and he gave her the address of a restaurant on the edge of town. They met there an hour later.

Gen was dressed in jeans and a sweater, and Jenkins was in another wrinkled shirt.

He'd already ordered her a drink, a glass of whiskey.

"I don't drink whiskey," she said as she sat down and sniffed at it.

"You will today," he said knowingly.

She stared at him, and heaviness settled in her belly at the look on his face.

"Why?"

"Drink," he instructed. Obediently, she took a gulp.

"Talk," she instructed.

"I've found records of an apartment that your husband has been keeping. He's had it for years."

Gen stared at him. For a minute, she was outraged, but then she remembered her own. She'd literally kept her own, and her motivations were not nefarious.

"Where is it? Maybe it's his apartment from before we got together."

But Jenkins rattled off an address that was a mere block from Thad's office.

"Oh, my God," Gen breathed. "Isn't that convenient for him?"

"I spoke with the doorman, and while he was very tight-lipped and loyal to Thad, I did learn from him that Ms. Thibault is there quite often."

"I'm Ms. Thibault. And I didn't know anything about it."

He pushed a manila envelope across the table. "You're *a* Ms. Thibault. The *real* Ms. Thibault. But someone else is calling herself Ms. Thibault. Isn't *that* convenient? And there's this. This isn't from the apartment, but I followed him last night."

Her fingers shook as she opened the envelope.

There were pictures inside, of her husband.

Thad was standing outside of a hotel, and there was a woman with him. It was night, and so a bit difficult to see, and Gen couldn't see the woman's face. But she could see her coat.

It was pink and had a bow on the back.

Her breath halted and her heart seemed to stop.

"Drink," Jenkins urged again.

Without hesitation, Gen knocked back the rest of the whiskey and signaled for another from the bartender.

Jenkins nodded.

"That's it," he soothed. He had a crusty exterior, but he'd been here before, with a betrayed spouse when he'd had to deliver the news. He knew what to do.

Gen gulped the second tumbler of Jack Daniels down in one drink, then slammed the glass on the table.

"Is my sister sharing that apartment with him?" she asked, stiltedly.

"I don't know. But I'll find out. It seems odd that they'd meet at a hotel instead of the apartment if that were the case, but there could be a hundred reasons."

Her eyes were wide, like a startled doe, and Jenkins didn't take his eyes off hers.

"I'll need to get more pictures," he told her. "Ones where your sister's face shows."

"Why?" Gen asked, feeling empty. "I know who she is."

"You'll need them in court," he said simply. "To completely wreck him, to get everything, you'll need to show what an asshole he is."

"What about her?" Gen asked. "It will wreck her life."

Jenkins's face was impassive. "I think she made that choice on her own when she got involved with your husband," he said flatly. "You didn't do this. She did."

"Why would she?" Gen asked, and her stomach was quivering. "Why would she want my husband? He's an asshole. Joe is so sweet, so hardworking, so loyal. I can't fathom why she'd want Thad, of all people. Why would she do that to me?"

"Maybe she knew what I've known from the beginning… that you don't love him anymore," Jenkins suggested. And that snapped Gen's head up.

"What do you mean? Of course I love him."

"No, you don't," he answered simply. "I've known it from the first time I met you. You probably did once. But not anymore."

Gen thought about it, about that absence of feeling in her heart, the raw void. She couldn't deny it, and so she didn't try.

"But that doesn't excuse her," she said stoutly. "My own sister is sleeping with my husband."

"I don't know for sure yet if they actually had sex," he clarified. "But they walked into that hotel together, and they left separately about an hour later."

"When was this?"

"Last night. Ten o'clock."

"I'd just gone to bed. He texted me and told me he'd be working late, and not to wait up."

"I bet," Jenkins answered.

Damn it. Even if she didn't feel the same about her husband as she once had, the feeling of betrayal was immense. It was all-consuming, because not only had her husband screwed her over but her flesh and blood, her very best friend in the world, had, too.

"Don't tell them you know," Jenkins reminded her. "I want more proof."

"I don't know if *I* do," she answered honestly.

"Trust me, you may not *want* it, but you need it. I'll get it for you."

She was woozy from the whiskey, since she wasn't used to it. Jenkins got into the cab with her.

"I'll ride with you to your condo," he said in explanation.

For a PI, he was protective, she decided.

She sat stoically in the cab until one red light when, against her will, her head slid down to Jenkins's shoulder. She remained that way until the cab stopped in front of her building.

Jenkins let her out and hugged her briefly.

"You'll get through this," he said awkwardly. "I know you will."

She nodded, and he got back into the cab. She watched it drive away.

Shouldn't she feel more pain about Thad? But she didn't. All she felt was deep betrayal at her sister's actions. Her sister was the one who had shattered her heart.

She couldn't just stand here and allow it, no matter what Jenkins said.

Rage boiled in her blood, pulsing through her heart.

Joe should know about this.

She couldn't outright tell him, not now, but she could figure something else out.

Instead of going up to the condo, she hailed another cab and rode the few blocks to her apartment. She tacked the pictures of Thad and Meg onto the wall and stared at them.

The wheels of her brain turned and turned, and a plan began to form.

She smiled.

29

Meg, Now

DETECTIVE HAWKINS STARED at the pad on his desk, at the notes he'd scribbled. He checked his email again, waiting to see that his warrant had been granted.

His phone rang.

"Hawk," he answered.

"Detective, this is Marion Keoghe from the Aristotle Hotel. We've pulled the video surveillance that you asked for—from the night Mrs. Thibault disappeared, and from the following night when the ring was left in front of Dr. McCready's room."

"Can you email me the files, or do I need to come there to view it?"

"I can email it now."

Hawk spelled out his email address and clicked refresh on his inbox.

The files showed up.

He'd watched it at the hotel once already, but it was always different when he watched them alone at his desk.

"Thanks," he said curtly, and hung up. He pressed Play and watched the grainy image.

On the first video, Gen Thibault could clearly be seen exiting the hotel, alone and drunk. He shook his head at the naivete in that. She was old enough to know better. She was from Chicago, for God's sake.

He pushed Play on the second video.

According to the note accompanying the files, Meg's room was beyond the reach of the camera, so there wasn't footage from in front of her door. But they'd sent the lobby and elevator footage from the two-hour window that the ring was delivered.

He spent the next two hours scouring it.

At one point, there was a slight figure in a hooded sweater who entered the lobby. The person's face was obscured, but he felt it was a woman. He watched the figure as it purposely walked straight to the elevators. But didn't recognize the person.

The figure was too short to be Gen.

Its chest was too small to be Meg's.

He was almost sheepish that he had noticed that, but then shrugged it away.

He was supposed to notice those things. It was his job.

This tape gave him nothing. He didn't recognize a single person on it. He sighed and rubbed his temples. For some reason, telling Meg that he didn't have any new information was making him unsettled.

He hated the sad look on her face.

That annoyed him. He was from the Bronx, jaded and no-nonsense. He shouldn't have been allowing her to influence him at all, much less feel unsettled. Yet, in unguarded moments, he'd caught himself thinking about her. The haunted look in her eyes made him feel melancholy, and made him yearn to fix everything that troubled her. She was ambitious yet warm, smart yet still soft. It was an intoxicating combination, or it would be to someone else.

He told himself that it was of no consequence to him.

Whether or not that was a lie was also of no consequence to him.

She's married, he reminded himself, and that did, in fact, make a difference.

For Hawkins, marriage was sacred. He'd never tread on its sanctity.

Never mind the fact that she rarely spoke of her husband, and when she did, it seemed perfunctory. She didn't sound the same as when she spoke of her son, or her sister. During those times, she lit up, she glowed, her eyes melted. Not so when she spoke about Joe.

That doesn't matter, he told himself. He looked at the computer again and refreshed his email. Lo and behold, the search warrant had landed in his box.

He was lightning fast to print it out, and the first call he made was to her bank.

The second, to the condo offices.

The third, to her sister.

He ignored the way her relieved voice affected him. He ignored how his heart rate picked up when she said she'd meet him in twenty minutes. It didn't matter. He was a professional. He headed for the coffee shop.

She was five minutes late, but he didn't mind. She came through the door, flushed and in a black turtleneck sweater. Some women might seem frumpy, but Meg looked graceful and classy. She sat in front of him, and he caught a whiff of her perfume. Clean, yet sweet and sophisticated.

"What did you find out?" she asked quickly, after she ordered a cup of coffee. He told her of striking out with the surveillance but then showed her the warrant.

"Are you going there?" she asked, staring at him.

"Maybe," he answered. "I'll ask someone from the Chicago PD to go first, and if needed, I'll follow."

"You mean, if you find something there," she pressed. When he nodded, she continued, "You won't find anything. I feel it. She wanted nothing more than to be finished with Chicago. With all of it."

"I'm also going to touch base with the police in Cedarburg," he said. "Maybe her stuff has arrived from the movers, maybe there will be a storage unit there. You never know."

"Because you really think my sister had something going on that none of us know about."

"Well, unless you or her husband had something to do with her disappearance, it's the only other logical answer. Have you changed your mind about Thad?"

Meg was quiet, drumming her fingers lightly on the table, remembering how staunchly she'd defended Thad to Hawk in earlier interviews. The way he'd been this week was so radically different than anything she'd seen from him that she couldn't help but second-guess.

"I don't know," she said finally. "Maybe there's more to him than I knew."

"As I've said from the beginning." Hawk nodded. "No one knows everything about someone else. And you were only his sister-in-law. You only knew what Gen knew, or what Gen wanted you to know."

Meg was determined not to tell him otherwise, that she

did in fact have firsthand experience with Thad. She found that she didn't want Hawk to think badly of her.

God, you're stupid, she berated herself. But it didn't change the way she felt as Hawk observed her with those eyes. She swallowed hard.

"That's true," she agreed instead. "So, that's why I'm changing my mind. You were right. I don't know what Thad is capable of."

She thought about that night in his bed, and how he'd been a good lover, generous and determined to bring her pleasure. Was that because he'd actually cared, or because he was a perfectionist? She didn't know.

"Well, I'm going to get on this. I just wanted to let you know that things will be moving. I knew you were worried." His voice was gruff.

"Thank you. I appreciate that." She swallowed the rest of her coffee and said goodbye to the detective. Somehow, as she walked away, she felt as though he were watching her go, but she didn't turn around to check.

She continued walking for blocks and blocks, lost in her thoughts and thinking of her sister.

Poor Gen. Meg loved her so much, yet she had completely screwed her over in the worst possible way. Regardless of the way she'd separated herself from her behavior at the time, Meg couldn't excuse it away. She'd been reprehensible.

Selfishly, she found herself hoping that her transgression with Thad wouldn't be uncovered, so that when they found Gen, she'd never have to know. It would hurt her so much.

Meg picked up her phone and dialed Thad's number.

"Hi," she greeted him softly. "Can we talk?"

"Okay," he answered, his voice flat.

"Listen, I'm sorry for everything. I don't even remember now if it was you or me, at first, who made the first move.

It doesn't matter. All that matters is that I shouldn't have done it. I shouldn't have slept with you. I risked my relationship with my sister over one night, and it was so, so, so stupid. Please, can we agree not to tell anyone? Not even the detective?"

"If we don't tell them, we could get charged with obstruction if they ever find out," Thad pointed out, and he didn't have any reason to care. His relationship with Gen was over. "Besides, it's hurtful that you'd dismiss it as one night."

Meg rolled her eyes, and the bile rose in her stomach. "We were both out of our minds."

"You know the chemistry between us was there long before that night," he said, and he sounded almost bothered. Meg flinched at that.

"Thad, you didn't love me. I didn't love you. We needed something more out of life, you and Gen were…what you were, and it was a perfect storm of bad excuses. I'm as much to blame, so I'm not blaming you. I'm just saying, let's never tell anyone."

"I still don't know why you won't talk to me about it," he snapped, and she knew, in that instant, why he'd been such a dick lately.

It wasn't about Gen at all.

It was about *her*.

Did he… Could he possibly have feelings for her?

"You know why. Because you cheated on her, and she found out, and it would've killed her to think that you were carrying on an affair with me."

"If you'd ever bothered to ask me yourself, I would've told you that Gen was wrong. I wasn't having an affair."

Meg rolled her eyes. "As someone you did in fact sleep with, I know you're not averse to it."

"I made love with you," he said slowly. "A woman I had

admired for years. A woman who I know felt connected to me, too. I did not have an affair with anyone. Not when all I could think about was you."

"Oh, my God. Don't talk like that," she answered quickly, her head spinning. "I didn't know you felt that way."

"You never asked," he said simply. "Your sister doesn't love me anymore, and you know it."

"That doesn't excuse anything," she said limply.

"You sound so ashamed," Thad replied, and it surprised him that he cared. But he did.

"I'm ashamed of my behavior," she agreed. "And you should be ashamed of yours. When are you arriving here?"

"I'm already at the hotel."

"*The* hotel? As in, my hotel?"

"Yeah. I'm in room 302."

"You have to stay someplace else," she told him quickly.

"Don't trust yourself around me?" he answered.

"Just stay somewhere else."

"I think that would look suspicious," he replied. "I mean, if there wasn't anything between us, surely we would be adult enough to join forces to look for Gen."

Meg thought on that, and he wasn't wrong.

"Okay, fine. You can stay here, but don't get any ideas. We're still finished, Thad."

"No promises."

He hung up before she could protest. Bewildered, she paused. There was no possible way he felt anything for her. She'd been a distraction for him, a seedy sense of excitement. Nothing more.

But she remembered the tone in his voice for the rest of the night, and it wasn't one of indifference. She didn't want to take the time to think of the implications of that. She had too much to deal with right now, too many balls in the air.

30

Gen, Then

LATELY, GEN WAS at her apartment more than she wasn't.

Further, she liked it that way. She started to view her condo with Thad as a hotel stay, and when she was able to return to her apartment, she was going *home*. She had added more furnishings, more art, more soft blankets, more journals, more of everything. It was a fully stocked home with a desk for her writing.

It was *her* home.

It wasn't like Thad noticed. He almost always texted that he would be late, not to wait up. So Gen rarely returned to the condo before 10:00 p.m.

When Jenkins had something to tell her, he came to her apartment, just as he was doing today. He knocked on her door with two short raps, and she answered. He went inside, as he had several other times, and sat himself on the end of her couch. She brought him an iced tea.

"I have more," he said simply, turning his phone to her.

There, on his screen, she saw Thad walking with his arm around a woman's shoulders, his head leaned in as he talked with her.

"That's not my sister," Gen pointed out.

"No, it isn't. Apparently, he's spreading himself around."

"Do you know her name?"

"I'm working on it."

Gen nodded. She should feel something.

But at this point, all she felt was steady. Determined. Focused.

After Jenkins left, she called her sister.

When Meg answered, it was all Gen could do to sound normal, to not rail and scream at her sister, because above all else, they were blood. They had shared a room until Gen had left for college. They had shared clothing, parents, a life. And then Meg had shared Gen's husband. Only she didn't know that Gen knew. And now Thad was stepping out on her, too. Karma was such a delightful bitch.

"Hey, sis," Meg said, cheerfully unaware of Gen's thoughts.

"Hey," Gen replied. "I was thinking of coming over to hang out tonight to play with Joey. I haven't seen him in weeks."

"I've got an eight p.m. surgery tonight, but you can head over and hang out. I'll let Joe know—Joey will flip."

Gen smiled. "That would be perfect. Have a good surgery."

"Always," Meg answered confidently. And she was. Confident. She did everything in her life with 110 percent. Apparently, even Gen's husband.

Gen cringed.

She chose her outfit carefully.

Meg deserves this, she thought to herself as she got ready and dabbed perfume behind each ear. It was like when they were little, and Meg would get so jealous of Gen for every little thing Gen did. It wasn't Gen's fault she was older. It wasn't her fault Meg had to live in her shadow when she was in school. Was that what this was about?

Did Meg have to prove herself by trying to take Gen's husband?

She shook her head and grabbed a cab, relaxing during the ride across town. When she rang the doorbell, Joe answered. He looked at her in surprise, and he was wearing sweats and a T-shirt.

He was clearly relaxing.

"I've interrupted your evening," she said. "I'm so sorry, Joe."

He shook his head and laughed, opening the door wider. "Of course not. I just didn't expect you."

"Meg didn't call? She said she would. I wanted to come hang out with Joey."

"*Ahhh*. Meg always gets distracted, and rarely remembers to call." He rolled his eyes, good-natured, as he closed the door behind them. "Joey's in his room. Want something to drink?"

"Whatcha got?"

"Beer."

"Okay. I guess, then…I'll have a beer," she chose. He laughed again.

"Your sister has some Blue Moon. I'll get you one."

Gen rambled down the hall to Joey's room, an ocean of blues and turquoises, with army men on the floor and trucks rounding the corners of the bed. Joey, hunkered down in a "fort" behind the bed, peered up at her, his blond hair unruly.

His eyes widened. "Aunt Nini!"

Why he'd always called her that, no one knew. But it was endearing, and so was the way he catapulted himself into her arms.

"Come play army." He pulled on her hand.

She eyed the battlefield below.

"Hmm. Did aliens take over the Earth?" she guessed. He shook his head. "Okay. Did the apocalypse happen, and the military is the only thing left?" Joey narrowed his eyes.

"What's an acopalis?"

She shook her head. "Never mind. What started this war?"

She knelt on her knees and pushed one green man forward.

"The world split into two sides, and they argued forever after."

"Wow, that's a long time," Gen told him. He nodded.

"That's how all the stories Mommy reads me end. Ever after."

"That sounds about right," Gen agreed. "So why are they arguing?"

Joey seemed surprised by that and thought on it. "I guess they just grew apart," he said, shrugging. It seemed like such an adult thing to say, that Gen burst out laughing, causing Joey to grimace at her.

"You know, like what Mommy said happened to you and Uncle Thad."

That stopped her laughing.

"Mommy said that?" she asked quietly, and Joey was nodding as his father walked in the room. She looked up, and Joe's cheeks were red. He'd heard.

"I'm sure she's just speculating," Joe told Gen. "Or Joey heard wrong."

But Gen knew he was lying.

"Meg thinks we've grown apart?" She held her hand out

for the bottle of beer, and Joe obliged, pressing it into her palm.

"Maybe. I dunno. You know how she thinks everything is her business." He tried to dismiss it, but Gen wouldn't have it.

"We're fine," she insisted to him. "Thad and me. He's been busy, but that happens to everyone. I mean, look at you and Meg. She's always at work. And you guys are fine."

She peeked at him as she said it, and he almost seemed to flinch.

"Schedules do make it hard," Joe agreed with her. "So I get it. Your sister is a very driven person. Thad is, too."

"So am I," Gen told him indignantly. "I work just as hard. I just don't make my family suffer for it."

"To be fair, you're a writer," Joe said gently. "You can make your own hours. They can't."

"My mom always said you'd defend Meg over anything, even murder," Gen told him, but she smiled a little. She admired the loyalty, now more than ever.

"She doesn't usually need defending," Joe answered.

"She doesn't now," Gen said, deciding to hide her annoyance. "I'm just surprised she'd say that."

"She didn't mean it," Joe added.

"Do you think it's true?" she asked, studying him. He was fit, muscular, good-natured, handsome. Why in the world had her sister been unfaithful to him?

"Do I think that you and Thad are growing apart?" He lifted an eyebrow. "I don't know, Gen. I don't get to see you guys enough."

But he did. Enough to have an opinion on this.

He reached around her to pick up an army man. He smelled like cedar, and she liked it. It was manly. She'd never liked Thad's cologne. It was so much like a sea breeze it was almost flowery. Too feminine for her taste. In her opinion, and in all of her romance books, men should be rugged. At the very least, manly.

She watched Joe play with Joey, watched their innocent and wholesome interactions, and her heart pulled a little. When had she gotten so jaded? Was she willing to ruin this picture in front of her, just to get back at her sister?

But it wasn't her fault, she thought to herself.

Meg did this. Not her.

Even still.

She was the older sister. She should be the bigger person, the more mature. She demonstrated her maturity by having her army man blow up Joey's dugout filled with his plastic battalion. He crowed and tackled her, unable to contain himself. Little boys were so rambunctious, she decided, after wrestling for five minutes and almost getting a black eye.

"Okay, okay." Joe finally called it, putting his hands up. "Aunt Nini is fragile. You could break her." He laughed as Gen glared at him, but she didn't hesitate to stand up, out of Joey's range.

The little boy giggled like an imp, and announced that he needed a snack.

"No, not a snack," Joe told him. "Dinner." Joe glanced at Gen. "You stayin'?"

"If you'll have me."

He chuckled, and told her she'd have to help, and they went to the kitchen to make spaghetti. Meg's kitchen was something straight out of an interior-design magazine, and it was almost intimidating.

"I don't want to splatter marinara all over the white stone," she told Joe as she stirred. He laughed.

"Trust me, if this kitchen can live through me, it can live through anything."

"You built this yourself, didn't you?" she asked, looking

around at the stone, the white cabinets, the floor-to-ceiling windows. She knew he had—all of it. "It's impressive."

"Well, I'm not the doctor in the family." He dismissed the compliment, and she could tell he wasn't used to getting them.

"I hope Meg knows how good she has it," she announced. "Thad hires someone to do the littlest of things."

Joe laughed, and so did she, and they settled into an easy partnership of preparing dinner. She sliced the garlic bread. He browned the meat. When the house was pleasantly filled with dinner smells, Gen's stomach was growling, and Joe had set three places at the table.

Joe poured Joey cold apple juice and got beers for himself and Gen. Then they sat and ate together.

"I like having you here," Joey told her. "Can you come every night? Want to help me with my bath? Ohhh, you can read me a story."

Gen's stomach tightened at the hopeful look in his wide eyes. "Mommy doesn't get to be here at bedtime much, does she?" she asked him, ruffling his hair.

Joe shook his head, answering for his son. "Not really. When she started a private practice, the theory was that she'd have fewer hours. But then the hospital asked her to still be on-call, and it was extra money, and that just became habit. And now she mainly speaks at conferences, so she's gone for days at a time."

"Money isn't everything," Gen told her brother-in-law. He nodded.

"I agree."

With that, Gen knew that it was all Meg's choice. And she couldn't help but wonder how many of these nights were actually spent consulting, in surgery or preparing her lectures and slides, and how many were with Thad. Maybe they were fucking right this minute. That thought caused her blood to boil again.

She smiled at Joe. "What do you guys normally do in the evenings?"

"Well, usually I take Joey to the park down the street. Burns off some of his energy so he's ready for bed," he replied wryly.

"Let's do it," Gen said, smiling at her nephew. "Go get your shoes on."

He whooped and hollered as he ran for his room, and Joe turned to her.

"He's eating this up."

"I love it," she replied. "I should come more often."

"You're always welcome."

Joe grabbed his shoes and she grabbed hers, and together, the three of them walked down to the park. Gen pushed Joey in the swings and followed him down the slide.

An hour later, she and Joe got texts at almost the same exact time, his from Meg, hers from Thad—both saying essentially the same thing.

Running late, don't wait up.

Gen shrugged, as if to say, *What can we do?* and pretended that it wasn't an all-too-convenient coincidence. If Joe thought it was strange, he didn't say, but Gen didn't think he noticed.

"So you come here every night after dinner?" Gen asked Joe on the way home.

He nodded. "Yeah. It's been our thing—Joey's and mine—for forever." He didn't have to add that Meg rarely came. Gen already knew.

"Meghan really doesn't like being outdoors," she said instead. "She's always been that way."

Joe rolled his eyes.

After Gen had read Joey two stories, turned on his night-light and tucked him in, Gen gave Joe a platonic hug and headed home. When she was in the cab, she looked through her phone for a phone number, finally finding it.

Her friend Kennedy.

She lived nearby, had a little four-year-old daughter and was divorced. She was the world's sweetest person and deserved someone like Joe. And Meg deserved to see what it felt like if her husband cheated. She swallowed the anger and dialed Kennedy's number.

She and Kennedy chatted for a bit, and she casually dropped the information that her brother-in-law was practically a single father, and that little Joey could sure use a friend to play with. She told Kennedy how they went to the park every night, and Kennedy was surprised to hear it was just down the street from her house, too.

"I'll have to take Isabel down there soon," Kennedy told her before they hung up. "Maybe we'll bump into them. Isabel could use a new friend, too."

Perfect.

Gen smiled. She was only setting up the pieces. If Meg didn't make more of an effort to get home in the evenings, and if things started happening between Kennedy and Joe, that would be on Meg. Gen was simply trying to find a playmate for Joey, not to take revenge on her sister.

She was a good aunt.

The fun aunt.

She leaned her forehead on the window for the rest of the ride.

31

Meg, Now

MEG WAITED WHILE Thad talked to Hawk back in the bullpen. She was restless, for some reason. Having Thad and Hawk in the same room was stressful, even though she recognized that standing side by side, they were night and day.

Thad was polished and smooth, while Hawk was rugged and masculine.

She thought of Joe, sitting at home, patiently waiting on her, and felt guilty. She'd always choose *Joe*, she told herself, although she wasn't sure if she still believed it. Joe was sweet and docile, a golden retriever. Somehow, for some reason, Meg came to realize she preferred Dobermans...a fierce man who could protect his woman.

God, that was so Neanderthal, but nonetheless, it was true. Maybe the entire reason she had...transgressed with Thad was because Joe simply wasn't what she needed in a man. Everyone was different, and someone would love Joe for who he is. *She* loved him, for God's sake. She just needed something different. She blinked the thoughts away. She'd deal with those later.

Thad was with Hawk for twenty minutes or so.

When he came out, Hawk was behind him.

"I'll have my assistant send you my itinerary," Thad was telling him. "I'm staying at the Aristotle Hotel."

"The same hotel as Meg," Hawk said, scribbling it down on a notebook.

"Yeah."

Meg's neck bristled. She didn't like the way it sounded, but Thad had been right. It would look odd if they weren't civil, if they weren't working together. A crisis should bring people together.

The men looked at her as they walked out, then she turned toward Hawk.

He smiled, short and efficient.

Thad said to her, "Do you want to share a cab back to the hotel?"

She almost physically recoiled.

Hawk noticed.

"She still has to talk to me," Hawk told him. "I don't know how long it will be."

"It was only twenty minutes for me," Thad said, glancing from the detective to Meg.

Hawk shrugged.

"She usually has more to say than you did."

That made Meg want to laugh, but she didn't. She had never had a problem speaking her mind. It amused her that Hawk had noticed.

Thad seemed disgruntled by it, but he left.

When he was gone, Hawk turned to her.

"You okay?"

She wasn't sure what he meant. Surely, he didn't know about her and Thad. Surely, Thad hadn't said.

"I mean, there seems to be some tension between you two." He shrugged again.

"Yes. He's revealed his true colors," Meg said in explanation. "He's turned out to be more of a dick than I ever thought. He doesn't even seem to care that Gen is gone. It's unsettling."

"Well, they *are* in the middle of a divorce," Hawk pointed out. "I'm not saying he's not a dick, but it's not uncommon for an ex-spouse to not feel that lovingly toward their ex."

"Yeah, but he doesn't seem to care at all," she argued. "It's not right."

"Not everyone is a good person," Hawk said, and he seemed to be dismissing it now.

"Did he say anything that implicated himself at all?" Meg couldn't help but ask.

Hawk stared at her.

"You know I can't say anything."

She studied his face. It was impassive, unyielding. He wasn't going to say anything. Sometimes, he seemed friendly, then other times, like now, he seemed closed off.

"Why do you have to be so professional?" she grumbled.

He laughed and looked at her.

"Come on back. Let me catch you up."

"Oh, so you can tell me *some* things," she said, trying to be clever, but he just shook his head.

She followed him to his desk and sat down. He handed her a soda.

"Do you have diet?" she asked.

"It causes cancer, Dr. McCready."

She rolled her eyes. "Everything does. What have you found out?"

"Well, I've gotten access to your sister's bank records. Did you know that she has her own separate apartment in Chicago?"

Meg's head snapped back, and Hawk nodded.

"I'll take that as a no."

"No," she confirmed. "Where is it?"

"Just down the street from the condo she shares with Thad."

"Maybe she kept the place she had when she was single years ago? But why would she?"

"I don't know yet. I have to have it added to the warrant. That should happen tomorrow."

"I don't know why she'd still have it," Meg said, confused. "That just doesn't make sense. Why didn't she tell me she kept it?"

"She spent quite a lot of money on it, from what I can tell," Hawk added. "Furniture, art. I asked Thad if the charges were for their condo, and he said no. So they must be for her apartment."

"Was there anything else unusual about her bank account?"

"Well, there was one thing," he said, and paused.

"Yes?"

"She hired a private detective. She's paid him almost fifteen-thousand dollars so far. I've got a call in to him so I can find out why."

"A private investigator?"

"Yeah. Probably to find out who her husband was sleeping with, but I can't assume anything. We'll find out soon enough."

Meg swallowed hard. Had Gen known about her and Thad? Had her PI figured it all out? She stared at the wall, at her hands. Anywhere but Hawk. *God, please don't let anyone find out.*

"So after you get the warrant for her apartment, how long until you get someone in there to look at it?"

"Actually, I'm thinking now that I'll fly to Chicago myself to investigate that. I want to make sure nothing gets contaminated."

"And you can only trust yourself for that?"

"It's a good rule of thumb in life," he answered.

He wasn't wrong.

"I want to go back, too," she told him. "I can see my son—you told me not to leave the city, so I didn't, but I miss him, Detective. My Joey."

He noted that she didn't say she missed her husband, but he didn't say anything.

"That's understandable. Why don't you fly back with me. I'm leaving later tonight. You can come over to the apartment tomorrow after I check it out."

"You want to see it first?" she asked.

"Of course."

She sat still for a second. "Because I'm still a suspect?"

He didn't answer.

He didn't have to.

She squared her shoulders. "When are we leaving?"

"Well, I'm leaving on an eleven p.m. flight. You are free to come whenever you'd like."

"Do I need to come back here to the city after?" she asked.

"Don't you want to be here if your sister is found or comes back?"

"If it was within her power, I know she already would be here," Meg told him. "But I'll ask Thad if he will stay in the hotel room while I'm gone. Just in case."

"I'm sure she'd *love* coming back and finding him there," Hawk said wryly.

"Like I said. If she could've come back, she already would've."

"You sound so sure," Hawk replied, studying her. "We don't know that yet."

"I do."

As they were leaving and she was hailing a cab, she realized that she might've implicated herself by saying that, to sound so certain. But she *did* know that about her sister, that Gen wouldn't torture her family like this, and Meg wasn't going to hide that fact. Meg knew she was innocent, and truth would out. That's the way things worked. This was America, for God's sake.

32

Gen, Then

GEN STARED AT her wall, at the pictures of Meg and Thad, the myriad of pictures with the other woman who called herself Ms. Thibault, at the maps, at the pictures of Thad and Angie.

After the call to Jenkins, she asked him to take some additional pictures…of Thad with Angie. She had come and gone from "Ms. Thibault's" apartment, and why? Was it some sort of love nest that he used for all of his lovers? How many did he have?

Her wall was growing larger, and it had outgrown the poster board she had originally bought for this purpose. She'd wanted Jenkins to get more pictures of Thad and Meg, but he hadn't been able to capture any. Her husband was wily. She sat still and contemplated sending Meg the photos of Thad with Angie.

It would have to be anonymous, of course, and it would send a dagger right through Meg's heart. But if she did that, then Meg would probably call it off with him, and that didn't suit Gen's plans. Not at this stage.

No, Gen had set the ball in motion, and it was already rolling.

She couldn't change things now.

Then again, no matter what Meg chose to do at this point, it wouldn't change what she'd already done.

Gen could basically proceed with whatever plans she wanted, and it still wouldn't change the fact that her only sister had slept with her husband.

Her fingers sifted through the large pile, the ammunition that she'd acquired.

Gen had so much of it now, so much proof. There was so much deception here, so much darkness. She'd never have thought it of her sister, and she was sure Joe hadn't, either. Should Gen tell him?

She pictured his face and Joey's, both so loving and kind. It would crush them, and she didn't want to be the one to do that. She'd rather let Meg handle that business on her own.

Today was a Friday, and she wanted to mess with Thad. She knew he probably had plans with Meg for that evening… Wasn't that what people in relationships did on the weekends?

So she texted him.

Hey. I thought we could have a date tonight? What do you think?

The thought honestly turned her stomach, but she didn't have to sleep with him. In fact, she would never have sex with him again. But messing with him was much different.

Far different.

He answered an hour later.

I wish I could, honey. But I've got to work late.

She narrowed her eyes.

No. Listen, I've been patient for weeks. I need time, too.

It took him another hour before he texted back in agreement, and she could feel his resentment. He probably had to cancel something romantic with Meg, and that brought her immense satisfaction.

She returned to their condo, intent on playing with his mind. It was only fair.

She buffed and shaved and perfumed. She lit candles and ordered takeout, and set it up as a picnic on the living room floor overlooking the city. It was the perfect romantic setting.

Thad would be horrified.

She smiled.

When he finally came home at 8:00 p.m., she was sure he expected her to have given up, to have put on sweats and be lounging on the couch. But she hadn't.

She was standing on the balcony, facing the door, her sheer nightgown fluttering in the wind around her. She felt wild, she felt free, and Thad was intrigued. She saw it in his eyes as he approached her, as he took in the entire setting.

"This is new," he observed, stopping next to her. He put his hand on hers, and she didn't even recoil.

"I thought we needed a nice night," she answered. "I haven't seen you very much lately."

"I know. Work has been so insane," he agreed, and she knew he was lying. His phone buzzed in his pocket, and he glanced at it.

"Speaking of, it's Angie. We're working on a case, and it's taking so much time."

"Don't answer," Gen told him. "Take tonight off. Just tonight."

Thad's eyes glinted, wondering what he could be in store for, what carnal delights. He obliged, sliding his phone back into his pocket.

"Okay. I'm all yours."

Lies, she thought.

But she wrapped her body around his anyway, nuzzling his neck, her legs interwined with his. He grabbed her, and kissed her hard, thinking he would fuck her right here on the balcony.

She pushed him away and laughed.

"Not yet," she told him. "You've got to wait."

Thad smiled, thinking that she meant only a few minutes or an hour, and he was inclined to play along, to make the reward worth it.

She led him to the living room floor, and they sat down. She draped her soft, smooth legs over his, and fed him olives and crackers and cheese. They drank wine, and she was as charming as she could be, and treated him like a king. He ate it up and asked for seconds, his hand on her back, on her arm, on her neck.

He thought she was seducing him, and maybe she was.

She wanted to crush him.

She wanted to deny him.

And she would.

She took his shirt off and nuzzled his chest, trailing her fingers lightly over his skin. His nipples puckered and she sucked at them, working them into hard tips. His breathing fractured, because she knew this was what he liked best, and she knew exactly how to do it.

He reached for her. She pulled back.

"Not yet," she said with a smile.

He smiled, too, because he still thought it was temporary.

They had more wine, more cheese, more teasing.

He slid his hand up her thigh, she twisted and laughed, and he smiled.

"I haven't seen this Gen in a long time," he said, and he was mesmerized by her tonight.

"Was it worth the wait?" she practically purred, her hand rubbing his back. He nodded and pulled her closer.

She kissed his neck, skimming her lips along the arch, and then pulled away.

"I just had an idea," she announced, as though it had just come to her. Thad seemed excited, waiting for what he assumed would be a particularly naughty fantasy. She was happy to disappoint him.

"We'll wait," she said, and she stood up, hovering above him. Her nightgown blew around her legs, like Marilyn Monroe over the street grate.

"What?" he asked, confused. His eyes were glazed over with desire, and he couldn't quite shake it enough to understand.

"We just worked ourselves up to the edge," she explained, like she was talking to a child. "Now, we'll stop. When we do it next time, our orgasms should be amazing! It's called edging. It's a real thing."

She laughed at the look on his face. He was crushed, just as she'd wanted.

"I don't want to wait," he growled, reaching for her, but she was insistent, and ultimately, she had the say.

He couldn't have sex with her if she didn't want to.

"I can't believe we're doing this," he grumbled, as he helped her pick up the picnic and carry the things to the kitchen.

"I've read that it makes your orgasms out of this world," she told him, scraping food into the trash.

"That doesn't help me tonight," he said, and she laughed.

"Honey, we've been married a million years. How many nights do you go without sex at a time? I think you'll live," she said, and she looked to see if his lies would show on his face.

He never went a night without sex—it just wasn't usually with her.

His face didn't betray him. He just laughed and rolled his eyes.

"You're right," he replied. "I haven't died yet."

Gen smiled.

Ten minutes later, he tried to tell her that he really needed to go back to the office, that he had to work on closing arguments, that it was dire.

She was staunch in saying no.

"No. I want to spend time with you," she told him. "I want to hold your hand. I want to snuggle on the couch. It's been so long, Thad."

He stayed with her on the couch all night. Gen pretended not to notice his phone continually buzzing in his pocket. She knew that it was Meg or Angie, or maybe both. She also knew that once a man started blowing off a woman for any reason, the woman on the other end started questioning his devotion.

She wondered how long before Meg left him… How many weekends of Gen's time it would take to find out. Then she wondered if it was worth it.

33

Meg, Now

LAGUARDIA WAS BUSY, even at midnight.

"God, I hate late flights," Meg complained as they walked through security.

"Suck it up, Doc," Hawk answered. Meg smiled at the name and put her purse on the scanner belt.

"Do you sleep on flights?" she asked him. "Because that's annoying."

"Sleeping is annoying?" he asked. He picked her purse up and handed it to her.

"No. Sleeping on a plane is annoying. You probably snore."

"I do," he answered cheerfully. "You probably do, too."

Meg glared at him. "Then you will pretend not to notice. It's the gentlemanlike thing to do."

"What if I'm not a gentleman?" he asked, with a grin.

"You are," she answered. "I can tell."

He seemed pleased with that, though she didn't know why. They waited for the flight to be called, and while they did, she glanced through a magazine. The overhead lights were unflattering, but weren't they in all airports? She bounced her foot on the floor, something she always did. Hawk stared at it.

"You're a nervous person," he remarked. "I wouldn't have thought that."

"I just have restless energy," she replied. "Always have. I don't like to sit still."

"I see that. But you decided to be confined in an airplane with me," he pointed out.

"My sister has a secret apartment there," she answered. "Of course I'm on a flight with you. I just keep wondering about it. Why does she have it? Does she have a secret family, too? I'm just stymied."

"That's an interesting word choice," he said. "Kinda snobbish."

"Snobbish? Because I used an unusual word?"

"Yeah. Sometimes, it's like you try to wear your education like a garment," he observed. "You want people to know you are intelligent, sometimes at the cost of their pride, even."

"Why? Did you not know what it meant?" She lifted an eyebrow.

"No. I just wouldn't want to ever purposely make someone feel dumb. Life is good enough at that. We don't have to help."

Meg was a bit stunned. She'd never considered herself an intellectual snob, but then she remembered how she always judged Joe's simplistic word choices, and how she always pointed it out when he used a better word. It had never occurred to her that it made him feel dumb, or annoyed him.

"I don't mean to make people feel dumb," she said honestly.

"I know," he agreed. "I can tell. But it doesn't mean that

you don't. Just be more understanding that some people don't like to sound stiff."

"You think I sound stiff now? Yikes, I'm sounding pretty bad right about now."

He laughed. "Don't fish for compliments. It doesn't suit you."

"Really?" Meg sat back in her seat, folding her magazine. "What *does* suit me?"

Hawk didn't hesitate. "Well, you like to feel smarter than everyone, as we've established. But, you also are very kind. You notice the things around you, and you help those you can help."

"That sounds better," she acknowledged. "Thank you."

"But I also sense a mean streak in you, when you're provoked," he added. She stared at him.

"Why do you say that?"

He shrugged. "I don't have proof. I just feel it in my gut. That's why I'm good at my job."

"You know, that could just be your stomach growling or something," she offered. He rolled his eyes.

"Keep laughing," he advised. "I'll find out all of your secrets soon enough." He laughed since he was joking, but she didn't, in case he was right.

"Speaking of secrets," he said a few minutes later. "What do you know about Thad's past?"

Meg shrugged. "Not much. He never did like to talk about it. His parents have been dead for a long time, and it was always painful for him. Gen never pushed."

"So Gen didn't know a lot about it, either?"

Meg shook her head. "No. They always just said they were focusing on the present, not the past."

"So Gen didn't know that Thad was driving the car that killed his parents?"

Meg froze. "That's impossible. He was like twelve when they died."

"They were apparently drunk, and had asked him to drive home. They were just a mile from home. They didn't think it would be a big deal."

"How do you know this?"

Hawk blinked. "It's my job."

"So he essentially killed his parents? He was in the car," she repeated.

"Yes. And so was his sister."

Meg's head snapped up at that. "He had a sister?"

"*Has* a sister. She sustained brain damage in the accident. She'll never be able to support herself."

"Wait. You're telling me that Thad has a sister," Meg repeated, stunned.

"Yes. I'm going to assume from your tone that Gen didn't know?"

Meg shook her head. "None of us knew. Are they estranged?"

"No. He pays her bills. She lives in an apartment near his law office."

"What?" Meg was beyond shocked. "She lives in Chicago?"

"Yes. I plan to pay a visit to her while we're there."

Meg leaned back in her seat, trying to absorb everything. "When you said her brain was damaged... How bad?"

Hawk shrugged. "Bad enough that she'll never be able to work, but she is able to live alone, with supervision. She has the mentality of a ten-year-old."

"What's her name?"

"Jody."

Meg remained stunned for the rest of the two-hour flight, and after forty minutes, she discovered she'd been wrong.

Hawk didn't snore. At least, not on airplanes. She let him sleep, and only woke him when the plane landed.

"That was a nice flight," Hawk remarked as they deplaned. She rolled her eyes.

"Want to share a cab?" she asked.

He nodded, then hailed one, and she inhaled her adopted city.

"It's good to be home," she said, breathing in the night air.

"Your family will be happy to see you," he said.

She smiled. "I can't wait to see my son."

They climbed into the cab, and as they rode toward downtown, Hawk eyed her.

"What is going on with you and your husband?" he asked curiously. "Have you grown apart?"

She thought on that. "Maybe so. I just think maybe we aren't suited to each other. I love him, but he feels like a friend. I wonder if it's the same for him."

"Do you have a good sex life?" Hawk asked simply.

Meg eyed him sharply.

"What?" he defended. "I wasn't being smarmy. I was just pointing out that if you have a good sex life, he probably doesn't think of himself as your *friend*."

"Smarmy is a good word," she said.

"You're doing it again."

She smiled.

"What will you do, then?" Hawk asked. "Will you ride it out, living a perfectly acceptable life in a marriage of mediocrity?"

"Or will I get divorced?" she added for him. "I don't know. I wonder if everyone just settles into mediocrity. I mean, I could get remarried, and have it be a firecracker at the beginning, but settle into kindling after a few years. Maybe it's just the way it works."

"I don't think so," Hawk argued. "I've seen people have stellar marriages. I, for one, won't settle."

"No?"

"No," he shook his head. "I won't settle for mediocrity, and I will never cheat. It's the most cruel thing you could do to someone. You marry them, and think you can trust them, and then they cut you off at the knees. A spouse is someone who is supposed to protect your heart, not destroy it."

Meg was astounded that he was being so open, so vulnerable about this, and it showed. Hawk laughed softly.

"I guess I get introspective on flights."

"Your wife did a number on you," Meg said quietly.

Hawk didn't answer, so she knew it was true.

"Who was it?" she asked. "You don't have to tell me if you don't want to."

"My partner," he said, and his voice was cold. "When I was still a beat cop."

"Jesus," she breathed, appalled.

She immediately recognized the irony, however. She was appalled at his partner betraying him when she had betrayed her own sister. She swallowed hard.

Hawk nodded. "Yep. So, needless to say, I won't be going through that again. I've made sure of it."

"Well, for one thing, you don't have a partner anymore," Meg pointed out, trying to lighten the mood, and he shook his head.

She laughed. He didn't.

"So this is your city," he said, turning his attention to the scenery. They were passing over a bridge, looking at industrial smokestacks. "It's charming. Kinda small, though."

The lights of the vast cityscape were blinding, and Meg laughed.

"Yeah, it's cramped."

"All I'm saying as a New Yorker is…mine is bigger than yours."

"I should hope," Meg laughed. She liked this side of him, hadn't even known it existed. It was so witty, so soft, so genuine. She had a sense that few got to see it.

They were pulling up to the hotel now, and Meg surprised him by getting out, too.

"Aren't you going home?"

Meg looked at her watch. "It's one thirty. I know you don't have children, but trust me, if I woke Joey up at this hour, we'd be hating life tomorrow."

"Ah, understood," he said, although he couldn't possibly.

"So I'll just get a room here, and go look at the apartment with you in the morning, then go home."

She booked a room and he checked into his, and as they rode the elevator up, Meg found she wasn't tired despite the late hour. She wanted to ask him to have a drink with her, to talk more about Thad's past, but the bar was closed. She could invite him in and raid the minibar, but she knew he wouldn't accept her invite. He was too professional to come into her hotel room.

Their rooms were side by side, and they awkwardly said good-night.

As Meg lay in her bed, she envisioned Hawk on the other side of the wall.

Did he sleep in underwear, or did he sleep naked? Did he sleep with the covers, or did he sleep exposed?

Why was she wondering this at all?

She tossed and turned.

What she didn't know was that on the other side of the wall, Hawk was doing the same thing.

34

Gen, Then

GEN WANTED TO do something so outrageous that she forgot about her life. It was such a mess that it deserved to be forgotten. She wanted to set sail for a tropical island, sailing until she didn't remember.

But her current life wasn't one easily forgotten.

She sat in her sister's home, watching *Finding Nemo* with Joey. His hair was snuggled beneath her chin, and he smelled like puppies and sunshine.

"Look, Aunt Nini." He pointed. "His fin is different."

"Yeah, it is," she agreed. "But he didn't let that get to him, did he?"

Joey shook his head, and she glanced at the clock. Eight thirty, and Meg still wasn't home. She knew that Thad actually was. He'd texted her and wondered why *she* wasn't. If her sister wasn't with him, was she really at work?

Did normal people have to wonder so much?

Joe yawned from his chair across the room. His hands were long and slender, and although some of his fingers were calloused, she still thought he had good hands. Good manly hands.

"Listen, kiddo." He stood up and stretched. "You gotta go to bed. You know how this one ends."

"Does Nemo find his dad?" Gen asked, helping Joey stand up. Joey looked up at her.

"Yes, Aunt Nini. Parents always find their kids." He was so serious that she smiled. His babyish cheeks were adorable, and she kissed one of them.

"Get to bed, babycakes," she told him. He took off running.

"He has two speeds," Joe told her. "Full-throttle and off."

Gen laughed, because it was true.

"You want some wine?" he asked, and she swiveled her head.

"You've got wine? Since when?"

He laughed. "Since Meg mentioned that you liked it. You've been coming over, so I thought it was only fair."

"Awwww, Joe! You bought wine just for me? I'm touched!" And she was.

He got her a glass and poured it halfway full, but she waved him on.

"Fill it up, bartender," she chanted. She took a gulp and then accompanied him to Joey's room. He read him a story, then she did.

"You do the voices better," Joey told her.

She looked at Joe triumphantly, and he laughed.

They turned off Joey's light and cracked his door, then went back to sit in the living room.

Gen sipped at her wine, and Joe got a beer.

"You're not really like your sister," he told her. "Maybe a little, but not in the big ways."

"Oh? What makes you say that?" Gen wasn't surprised. She'd purposely been trying to draw subtle parallels for the past two weeks.

"You enjoy family. Your sister feels trapped by it." Joe sounded so miserable in the moment that Gen's heart pinched.

"Oh, Joe. That's not true. She's just blinded by her own ambition right now."

"I used to think so. But sometimes, the way she looks at us… It's not right," he said, so very quiet now. Gen studied him. His eyes, crinkled by laugh lines, were solemn and tired. "I don't think I'm enough for her."

"You are, too. Of course you are," she replied, because he seemed so very wounded.

"Can I tell you a secret?" he asked and she immediately obliged. He took a deep breath.

"The other day at the park, we met a really nice mom and daughter. She was so interested in me… She listened to me talk, she made jokes. She asked me out for coffee, and I almost went."

He held his breath and waited.

Gen stared at him.

Kennedy.

She needed to act surprised, so she tried to feign it, but then she wanted to comfort him, too. Because he deserved it.

"Joe, you're a very good man," she told him. "You are neglected. Yes, I'm saying this. Yes, I'm Meghan's sister. But I'm not blind, and I see what is happening. She's taking you for granted, and she's going to lose everything if she doesn't watch herself."

"We're just going through a rough patch," Joe said, even though he didn't sound convinced. "But while she was working long hours, I almost went for coffee with another woman, Gen. *Who does that?"*

Your wife, Gen thought. But, of course, she didn't say it.

"You're being too hard on yourself," she said instead. "I'm sure Meg has men coming on to her all the time. She's a surgeon, and she's not an angel. She likes her ego stroked as much as the next person. So quit beating yourself up."

"She's not an angel… Do you know something I don't?" he asked slowly, searching her face for an answer.

"Of course not," she lied. "I was just saying that someone came on to you and that it's not your fault. I'm sure it happens to Meg, too. The important thing is that you said no."

"Men watch her wherever we go," he said matter-of-factly. "It's just the way she is. She owns a room. She lights it up. You do the same thing, you know."

He said it so kindly that she almost blushed.

"Thank you. That's nice to hear. Thad is gone so much that I rarely hear those things anymore. It's nice to know people still think so."

"Surely women like you and Meg know that about yourselves, right? You know what effect you have on people?" Joe was being honestly curious. So, Gen answered him honestly.

"Sometimes we know it," she confided. "But sometimes we forget. When it's been too long since we've been reminded. Egos are fragile things, Joe."

"Want to know one of my favorite things?" he asked quietly. Gen nodded, sipping her wine.

"I love it when we have something we have to attend, one of her fundraisers for the hospital or something. We both have to get dressed up, and I'll watch her getting ready. She sits at her vanity, and so carefully does up her hair and makeup. She looks so beautiful, and I know that even though everyone else gets to see her, I'm the only one going home with her. I get to take her hair down at the end of the night."

It was such a sweet thing to say, it was almost painful, and Gen had a lump in her throat.

"Lord, it would be nice to have someone feel that way about me," she said, and it was the truth.

"Thad does," Joe said confidently, but Gen shook her head.

"No, he doesn't."

"Then why do you stay?" he asked. "You could have anyone you want."

She suddenly found that she wanted to tell him the truth, to spill her guts, to tell him everything. Her tongue started to move, but his face was so sweet…and she couldn't.

She couldn't hurt him that way.

So instead, she shrugged. "I don't know. Because it's not a bad life, it's just not necessarily a good one."

"I don't think that's enough," Joe said hesitantly. "And you don't have any kids. So you don't have a reason to stay."

She shrugged again. "Maybe I won't, someday. For now, I don't want the hassle."

She couldn't tell him that she was plotting out revenge, and she needed time for that.

"Well, you're welcome over here anytime," he told her. "You're our family. Come here, kid." He pulled her into a hug, and she inhaled the scent of cedar.

She'd forgotten how much she liked it.

35

Jody, Then

JODY WRAPPED HER fuzzy robe around her body and turned on an episode of *Gossip Girl*.

She texted her brother.

Thaddie, come see me. I'm lonely.

She had made it through three episodes before he answered.

I can't tonight, punkin. Gen made dinner.

Jody threw her phone down. It was always Gen this, Gen that. Yet, Thad would never tell Gen about her.

I can't, Dee-dee, he'd said. *I can't live with what I did to Mom and Dad. Or what I did to you. You understand, don't you?*

But she didn't. What did he do to *her*? She was fine, the same as she always was. She had her Barbies and her television shows. She was a good girl for her brother, and so why couldn't she just go live with him?

His secretary, Angie, had told her not too long ago that thinking about what he did to Jody made him sad, that he felt so guilty he could barely stand it.

"He has something called PTSD," Angie told her. "It makes him panicky when he thinks about what he did." Jody didn't understand.

The accident that had killed their parents was an accident. She shouldn't have to pay for it. She was always alone, just because Thad didn't want anyone to know, and didn't want to talk about it. It wasn't fair.

She told him so once, and he had been so hurt.

"Dee, do I not provide you with the best possible life?" he'd asked, his tone wounded. "Do I not make sure that you have everything you could ever want?"

"I want a friend," she'd told him. "I don't like being alone. I just want to be with you."

"I don't think Gen would understand," he'd told her. "I'm so sorry, Dee. Maybe someday."

Genevieve sounded like a terrible person, at least to Jody. What kind of person wouldn't approve of someone's sister?

"Can you tell me a story about Mama? I can't remember her face."

Thad looked uncomfortable, like he did every time she asked. "It makes my heart hurt," he told her yet again. "I don't want to talk about it. Besides, I have to get home, punkin."

He'd left her alone, night after night. He sent Angie a couple of times a week to buy her groceries, but she never stayed long because she was busy. They were *all* busy.

Jody wasn't supposed to leave the building alone, but she wanted to get a glimpse of this Gen, the person who kept her brother from her.

So, one day, she slipped out of her own building and waited outside of her brother's. She felt so invisible. If something happened to her, no one would even notice. It was a bad, bad feeling.

She began a pattern of sneaking out of her own home and watching Thad's. She watched Gen come and go, and soon she had learned quite a bit about her brother's wife.

She got her hair styled at an expensive place, she had a huge collection of purses, but most importantly, she had two homes.

And Jody couldn't imagine why.

Was she lying to Thad about something? Because that wasn't acceptable.

No one could ever hurt her brother. He was the most important person in the world.

The next night, Thad came to visit. He brought Chinese food and cupcakes, her two favorites.

When Gen texted and asked him where he was, he replied, Sorry honey. I have to work late.

Jody tried not to let that sting, but it did.

She wasn't work. She was a person. She was his family.

He let her snuggle up against him while they watched *Beauty and the Beast*, and he tucked her into bed before he left for the night.

"I love you, munchkin," he told her, as he kissed her forehead.

"Then tell Gen about me," she couldn't help but say. He frowned.

"Someday. But see, at this point, she'll be angry that I didn't tell her before now. And who could blame her? It was stupid to lie. But lies beget lies, Dee-dee. Once we start, it's hard to stop."

"Just choose to stop," she said helplessly, staring at the night-light that moved around the room in shapes like the moon and stars.

"One day," he agreed. "One day, I will."

"And then I can move in with you?" she asked hopefully.

He nodded. "Yes. Then you can move in with us."

She fell asleep with that wish in her heart.

It was difficult for her to comprehend the passage of days sometimes, but she used a calendar and marked them off.

She kept following Gen, and even Thad. She watched him and Angie shuffling into the courthouse, their hands full of files. She watched him working late, and she watched the lights turn out in his condo long before he got home. Gen didn't even wait up for him.

Jody got very good at evading her own doorman, since she wasn't supposed to be out and about. Thad worried about her wandering.

She counted the days and was surprised when one day, Thad showed up on her doorstep with a suitcase.

"What's wrong?" she asked him, as she stood in front of him in her Cinderella T-shirt.

"Gen and I are splitting up," he told her with a sigh. "I'm going to stay with you for now."

"Does Gen know about me yet?" she asked hopefully.

"No. And now it doesn't matter, punkin. I'll stay here with you, and it will be you and me."

Her heart leaped, and it was true. Thad stayed with her— he moved into the second bedroom, and she wasn't lonely at all. She knew that every night, no matter how late he had to work, Thad would come home and sleep under the same roof as she did.

It was wonderful.

Until the night when she was up getting a drink of water, and she overheard Thad talking in his sleep.

"Gen," he muttered. "I'm sorry. Gen."

She froze, her hand on her glass.

Her brother didn't want to get back together with Gen, did he? If he did, she'd be pushed aside once again, and all alone. There was no way she could go back to living like that.

It struck such a fear in her heart that she started following Gen again.

She started to keep tabs.

She started to plan.

Her mind wasn't what it used to be, but surely...she could do this.

36

Meg, Now

MEG AND HAWK met at the coffee shop in the lobby at 9:00 a.m.

Meg already had a coffee in her hand, and she put one into Hawk's, too.

"Thanks," he told her. "You ready?"

She nodded and they piled into a cab. They went to Thad's sister's first.

He rapped on the door, then rang the bell. But no one answered.

They went down to the desk, and the concierge confirmed that Jody hadn't been home in at least a week.

"I can give her your card, though, when she returns?" He lifted an eyebrow. "But you should know, she's got brain damage. You were aware, weren't you?"

Hawk nodded. "Yeah. How bad is it?"

The clerk shrugged. "She comprehends more than people assume, I think. She's like a little kid. But a smart kid."

Hawk handed him a card. "Then please, give her this and ask her to call me."

They got back in the cab, and Meg shook her head. "This is still crazy to me," she said. "I can't believe he has living family. And that he never told any of us. It's insane."

"When you've been around as many people as I have, you learn that you never truly know someone. There are always secrets, always facets of them that you won't discover. It keeps things interesting," he added.

"If you say so," she muttered.

They pulled up in front of Gen's old apartment, and Hawk helped Meg from the cab to the street.

"You know I have to go in first, and you have to wait outside," he reminded her.

She nodded.

"Yes, I remember that you don't trust me," she said, and he smiled at that.

"Something like that."

She had been aware that their shoulders were touching in the cab. Last night, it had taken her hours to get to sleep, and the reason was sitting right beside her. Something about him attracted her, even though this was the worst possible time.

I'm a monster, she decided.

They both looked up at the higher floors of the building.

Up there, Meg thought, *Gen held a secret.*

"Wait in the lobby, not out here," Hawk told her, glancing around.

Meg smiled. "This is just a sleepy little bedroom community, remember?"

He rolled his eyes. "Best to wait in the lobby."

So she did. She watched him disappear into the elevator, and while he rose high in the sky, her stomach sank. She knew, she just knew, that nothing good was going to come from this.

She paced the lobby, minute after minute, waiting for a call from Hawk telling her it was clear for her to go up. She watched the traffic through the front doors, she watched people passing by on the sidewalks. She waited for the call that didn't come for half an hour.

When she answered, he was terse.

"You can come up."

The floors passed slowly in the elevator, but when she stepped off at the once familiar floor, he was standing there, waiting for her.

"What did you find?" she asked, as they walked down the hallway together.

He didn't answer. He led her through the door she recognized from years ago into the apartment, and she stopped still at a massive photo collage assembled on the living room wall in front of her.

The photos of her and Thad outside of the hotel where they'd met that night were the largest. They were right in the center, surrounded by separate photos of Thad and another woman, positioned as though she'd been following them all.

To see the photos all there in one place made her feel sick to her stomach; it also made her question her sister's sanity. Who would paste all of this on her own wall? It looked like something a serial killer might do.

The pictures were damning, for certain. It made it quite apparent that she and Thad had something to hide.

Her cheeks flared hot and red, and she glanced at Hawk.

He stared sharply back at her, his feet planted wide.

"Well?" he asked. He was waiting for an explanation.

She didn't know what to say.

"I…"

"Don't lie," he told her. "You are considered a suspect in the disappearance of your sister, and you should not lie right now."

She felt like she could hardly breathe as she realized the implications, what this looked like.

"This was not a *motive*," she said slowly. "This was a *mistake*. There's a big difference."

"I can see making a mistake like this," Hawk said, sweeping his hand toward the pictures. "I can even see not wanting to tell me. But what I can't see…and I mean this genuinely… I just can't see how you could pretend to be utterly devastated by your sister's disappearance when you're having an affair with her husband."

"I'm not pretending," she protested. "I *am* devastated. I'm terrified. I love my sister. What happened with Thad really had nothing to do with her. We're not having an affair. And whatever it was, I can assure you it's over."

"I'd beg to differ since Thad is her husband," Hawk replied dryly. "I have to say…I didn't expect this turn of events, and from you. You seemed more sincere."

"I am sincere," Meg argued. "This right here… This is the worst of me. You haven't seen me at my best."

"The worst is enough," he said, and the disappointment in his eyes was unbearable.

Meg physically flinched.

"Now, I've got work to do. You should leave now."

Because he still suspected her. She dropped her head.

"I'm sorry I didn't tell you. I couldn't."

He didn't answer. He just turned away.

When she had her hand on the door, he asked her one last question without turning around.

"Is it really over?"

"Yes. It was just one time."

He didn't say anything else, and neither did she. She just slipped out the apartment door in shame.

She stood on the street in front of the building, stunned. She tried to compose herself. Then she hailed a cab and went home to see her husband and son.

Hawk knelt on the living room floor and looked through a trunk that was next to the chair.

Inside was a journal and more photos.

It was clear that the amount of surveillance the PI had done for Gen was stunning. No wonder she'd had to pay him fifteen thousand. This was clear evidence to support a case of adultery, most certainly. But he wondered if this evidence was enough for someone to want to kill her. And if so, who?

When Gen found out, did she decide to confront Meg at the hotel? Had things gotten out of hand? Or perhaps it had been Thad? Or the two of them together?

He would check if Thad and Gen had any kind of prenup that included stipulations about adultery. Usually people didn't have the foresight, but Thad was a lawyer.

Hawk tried to ignore his disappointment in Meg. He didn't have any right. He barely knew her.

Yet, even still, it churned in his belly. His radar was usually spot-on. But surprisingly not in this instance. He'd almost felt protective over her, and now he felt ridiculous. He was too good of a detective to have fallen for this.

Next, he went into the bedroom and found it neat and tidy, and minimal in its decoration. Just a bed, bedding and a few items of clothing in the closet. He noted the absence of her laptop. As a writer, it should have been here. And it wasn't anywhere that he had found.

There was a large painting on the wall.

He stepped closer to examine it better. It was a weeping

willow, bent in the wind and rain. Every single painting in the apartment was sad and soulful and full of emotion. The one in the kitchen looked slightly crazed. Hawk wondered if the artwork was a good indicator of her state of mind.

Finding out your husband was having an affair with your sister would shock the sanest of people. He had no reason to think Genevieve was any different other than the excess of the massive collage.

He noticed that the bedroom smelled faintly of vanilla; the source was on the nightstand, a thick vanilla candle, half-used.

The perfume sitting on the bathroom counter was also vanilla. He made a mental note.

His cell phone rang and he answered it.

"Is this Detective Hawkins?" an older male voice asked.

"Yes."

"This is Simon Jenkins. Private investigator. You left me a message about Genevieve Thibault."

"Thank you for calling me back. Were you aware that she has a secret apartment?"

"Yessir. I've been there many times."

"Good, so you know the address. Would you have time to come over here and meet me right now?"

"On my way."

Hawk hung up and returned to the living room. He continued to look through the journal he had taken from the trunk. It seemed as though she'd been writing in it for a couple of months, at least. He read passages.

Thad is so distant. He comes home later and later and acts like I shouldn't notice or care. It's so odd. What's happened to us? I'm doing everything I've always done—I'm not doing anything differently. Is this what it's like when a couple falls out of love? I don't get it.

He skipped forward a few days.

*I've been trying to get his attention. He's not really having it.
It's like I don't exist to him anymore, and I don't know what to do
about it. What would make a husband act like that? It's someone
else. I'm sure of it.*

Even the journal pages smelled like vanilla. Hawk held it
to his nose and inhaled. She'd perfumed the page. She clearly
liked the scent. She liked to be surrounded by it.

Perhaps she was seeking to be consumed by her environ-
ment.

He knew Gen was a writer and wondered about how that
affected her mind. Does a writer create pure fiction, or do they
absorb their surroundings and channel that? Did they really
make it all up in their head? Or is there always a grain of truth?

He heard a quick rap on the door, and got up and opened
the apartment door to find a graying man in a shabby shirt
on the other side.

"Jenkins?" he asked.

The man nodded yes.

"Have you found Genevieve?" he asked Hawk anxiously.

Hawk stared at him.

"Not yet…"

Jenkins froze.

"She's still missing, but we will find her," Hawk told him.
"She went to New York to meet her sister who was there
for a convention, and she didn't come home from a walk the
first night."

"I knew she was going," Jenkins said. "She'd told me that
much. Then I saw on the news…"

"I know. I wanted to keep it out of the press, but her parents got them involved."

"I should probably get you up to speed," Jenkins said to
Hawk, as he entered the living room. "You got time now?"

"All the time in the world." Hawk sat down on the sofa.

37

Gen, Then

GENEVIEVE SAT ON the steps of the Field Museum. The breeze was chilly, although the sunshine on her shoulders was warm. Thad and a woman had just left.

She shook her head in disgust. She'd tried for years to get Thad to do artsy, cultured things with her, and he never would. Yet, here he was doing whatever this woman wanted him to do. They were so brazen about it, too. Didn't he worry even a little that someone would recognize him?

Her anger was scaring her lately. It bubbled up so fiercely and so often that she worried it wasn't normal. What *was* normal in a circumstance like this? What was a scorned wife supposed to feel like, particularly when the other woman was her sister?

She'd taken to following them herself. She'd wait in the shadows by his office building and watch him leave. Sometimes, he met work colleagues and clients. But more often than not, he met this woman. At the very least, they didn't display their affection in public, but it didn't really matter. She could imagine what went on behind closed doors. In fact, oddly enough, he seemed to treat her like a child.

"Jody, come back here," Thad called after her one day. "You left your coat. It's cold." He held it out, and Jody reluctantly came back to get it, their fingers barely touching as she took it from his hand.

Maybe that was the issue. He wanted to feel like the man, the caretaker. Maybe being with Gen didn't fill that need since she was self-reliant.

When was it time to confront them, she wondered as she watched Jody put on her coat. Now? Tomorrow? Next month?

She had all the evidence she needed for the divorce, but she found herself wanting more. She wanted a reason. She wanted to know *why*. What was lacking about her that Thad wanted someone else? How long had it continued with Meg before Thad had dumped her for this woman?

Meghan had always been a good sister. Everyone said so. Everyone knew it. She remembered every birthday, every anniversary, every occasion. She was loving, she was funny, she was Gen's best friend.

What changed? Why had Meg betrayed her with Thad?

Gen had to know.

But first, she looked up a therapist's phone number, a woman named Lila, and was able to get an appointment for that very afternoon. On the way, she grabbed a hot dog from a street vendor, piled it with sauerkraut and mustard, and ate it en route.

The therapist's office was tidy and had a diffuser running in the corner with something tranquil. Was it lavender and mint? When Lila came out to call Gen's name, she was dressed neatly in a pencil skirt and a sweater with tiny buttons. She looked about Gen's age, and that put Gen instantly at ease. Maybe this person would understand.

Gen followed her back to a room, where chairs and a couch were arranged cozily. There was another diffuser running in this room as well, and Gen smiled.

"I guess you've got to keep the inmates calm," Gen said, motioning toward it.

Lila, the therapist, smiled. "You're funny. I like funny."

"Me, too," Gen agreed.

Lila settled into her chair. "Is that what you like about your husband?"

"Wow, so we're diving right in," Gen answered.

Lila smiled again. "Well, you sounded so upset on the phone, and you told me the gist. So I'm aware of what's going on. I'd like to help you as much as possible. We'll have to delve into it deeper, of course, as the sessions go on, but I want to help today, too."

"I'd like that," Gen agreed. "And yeah, I guess I like that about Thad. He used to be funnier around me, years ago. But lately, I've noticed that he doesn't really try. Not like he used to."

"Have you tried?" Lila's pen paused on her notepad.

"Maybe not," Gen told her. "I guess we settled into routines."

"That happens," the therapist said. "To pretty much everyone. The key is in realizing it, and in changing things up."

"I think it's too late for that," Gen replied. "On the phone, I told you my husband was being unfaithful. What I didn't say is that the other woman is my sister."

Lila's face said it all. Her mouth formed an O before she could stop herself and Gen nodded.

"Exactly."

"So you and your sister aren't close?"

"No, she's actually my best friend. I don't know what started this. I don't know why she'd do it."

"Have you confronted them?"

"Not yet. My own anger is scaring me. So I called you."

Lila nodded, and they spent the next few minutes discussing what was happening, how Gen had found out and what she'd done to date.

"So you still have your own apartment besides the one you live in with your husband?" Lila asked when Gen was finished.

"Oh, yes. I love it there."

"Why did you keep it?"

"I've just always liked the idea of having my own space. It felt too confining to give it up. To close that door to my own identity."

"I would suggest that you keep it, then. If you decide to leave Thad, you'll want someplace to go."

"I'll be leaving Thad," Gen said decisively.

"Okay. Do you have a plan?"

"Not yet. But I'm not staying. How could I?"

"Well, many women do decide to stay, if their partner wants to work on his issues and recommit. However, I can see where the circumstances here would prohibit that, or at the very least, make family gatherings awkward."

Gen wished she felt like smiling.

"I don't know what I should be feeling," she told Lila. "Some days, I feel unhinged. Some days, I feel nothing. Some days, I seethe with such anger that I frighten myself."

Lila nodded. "There's no normal," she replied. "Every woman in your situation has different feelings, and I'd just tell you that whatever you're feeling is normal for you."

Gen laughed at that. "That's kind of a cop-out," she observed.

"No, it's the truth," Lila insisted. "Every single person handles things differently. We see them differently. We process them differently. And that truly is normal."

"If you say so," Gen offered.

"I do. So, tell me how you are feeling today," Lila instructed.

"Today, I feel murderous. I have a million questions. I want to confront my sister, to ask her how she could do this to me."

"Are you angrier with Meg than with Thad?" Lila paused.

Gen thought on that. "Maybe so," she decided. "Meg is my flesh and blood. I would never, ever, in a thousand years, have thought she'd do this."

"You feel very betrayed," Lila said.

Gen nodded.

"By both of them."

"Of course."

"You've hired a private investigator, and you've gathered evidence. You have enough now. When do you think you want to confront them?" Lila asked.

Gen didn't know that answer.

"I know that when I do, I'll lose my sister," she said simply, finally. Lila stared at her.

"Are you still talking to your sister?"

"Not as much, but yes."

"And you both act as though nothing is out of the ordinary?"

"Yes."

Lila was quiet. "You're not dealing with your anger," she pointed out. "You're pretending all is fine, but keeping all of your rage pent-up. I can tell you that that's not healthy. Have you spoken to anyone at all?"

"That's why I'm here," Gen replied.

Lila nodded. "Okay. Well, we're going to have to think of a way for you to handle this, because honestly, keeping it inside will backfire on you. I would recommend coming clean to them—getting it off your chest. You have what you need for a divorce."

"But I don't have the thing I need for closure," Gen said firmly. "And that's *why*."

"You may never get that," Lila told her gently. "So often, the excuses offered are lies. You may never find out the truth. You need to be prepared for that."

"That sounds so bleak."

Lila nodded. "It's just the truth. However, there are times when the unfaithful spouse wants to work on their own issues, and on the marriage, and in those times, it is more hopeful. Although often, you still won't get the complete truth. They lie to protect themselves. They lie because they don't want the world to know their dark secrets."

"I can get another husband, if I ever want one. But I can't get another sister."

Lila nodded. "I agree. Have you told your mother?"

"Oh, no. She wouldn't believe it. She never can believe something bad about one of us."

"What do you think of telling Meg's husband?" The therapist cocked her head.

Gen thought of her brother-in-law's kind face, his trusting eyes, and her stomach clenched. "Her husband is such a good guy," she said.

"You don't want to hurt him," Lila observed.

Gen shook her head. "I know that Meg is the one who

did this, but if *I'm* the one to tell him, I'll be the one holding the knife."

"To play devil's advocate, if he found out that you knew
and didn't tell him, will he feel betrayed by you?"

Gen blinked. "I didn't think of it like that."

"It's just a thought," Lila said. "And pragmatically speaking, he's the father of your nephew, so you'll want to keep
your relationship with him. So that you can see your nephew
as often as you like."

"True," Gen agreed. "I love that kid. It will be terrible if
his parents split up."

"That probably plays into your decision not to want to
tell Joe," Lila pointed out. "Keep in mind that children in
a very unhappy home don't have it any easier than children
of divorce."

"But they aren't *un*happy," Gen said. "Which is the strang-
est part. Thad and I weren't *unhappy*. She and Joe aren't *unhappy*. So none of it makes sense."

"Different factors play into infidelity," Lila said. "Some
get into a rut and want excitement. Some want variety. Some
develop feelings for someone else."

Gen froze. "You don't think they grew actual feelings for
each other over the years, behind my back? While my father
sliced the turkey on Thanksgiving, they were playing foot-
sie under the table?"

Lila was quick to reply. "Not necessarily. I'm just saying
that there are multiple reasons it could've happened. They
may or may not have feelings for each other."

The thought that they could have real feelings for each
other hadn't really occurred to Gen. For whatever reason, she
had simply assumed that it was a physical attraction. What if
they actually loved each other? That would mean that she'd

be exposed to Thad for the rest of her life, at every family function her parents held, if Meg intended to stay with him.

That wasn't a future she wanted.

"Jesus," she whispered.

"Somehow," Lila said, "you have to figure out a way to work through your feelings, whether you decide to confront them right now or not. If you don't, if you keep suppressing them, it could lead toward you exploding in the future. Bad things happen from too much suppression."

Aloud, Gen agreed. But she didn't explain how she was secretly setting up Meg's marriage to fail, or how she would get revenge on Thad, too.

"Journaling works well," Lila told her. "It helps work through emotions and feelings. You can say whatever you'd like, without fear of judgment. You can even burn it after you're finished, so that no one will ever see. It could be very cleansing."

Gen didn't commit, but on her way home, she did stop at a greeting-card shop and bought a couple of journals.

38

Jenkins, Now

"**HOW DID YOU** meet Mrs. Thibault?" Hawk asked Jenkins. The older man cocked his head. Hawk found himself thinking that a cowboy hat would suit the other man's demeanor.

"I met Gen when she called me and asked me to work for her. She just searched online for a PI to catch an unfaithful husband in Chicago. My assistant set it up on Google somehow, so that my name would pop up when someone used those search words. Pretty smart."

Hawk wasn't in the mood to discuss SEO or other marketing tactics with the man in front of him.

"How long did you work for her?"

"I figure you already know that," Jenkins said. "You've found the bank statements—you already counted the monthly payments."

"There were eleven payments," Hawk said evenly. Jenkins smiled.

"What did you do for those eleven months?" Hawk asked.

"I gathered evidence for her. Pictures, hotel receipts, whatnot."

"For eleven months?"

"She wanted as much as she could get," Jenkins answered. "I suggested to her after about four months that she had enough. She didn't want to stop."

"Did she say why?"

"She said she needed a reason."

"A reason?"

"She needed to see why they did it."

"Did she find out?"

Jenkins shook his head. "Probably not. They never really do."

"How did Genevieve seem to you throughout that time?" Hawk kept glancing at the door, not entirely unsure that Meg wasn't listening outside.

"She varied. She wasn't even-keeled, if that's what you are asking," Jenkins answered, and he looked down his nose at the detective. "But, she was always kind. She's a lady, that one."

"How so?"

"You can just tell by being around her. She was cool and collected, and always nice to people. I saw her give money to homeless people many, many times. She always paid me right on time, didn't cause any hassle at all. She even helped me write a help-wanted ad for my new assistant, and brought us muffins once."

"Sounds like Mother Teresa. Did she ever seem angry?"

"At times," Jenkins admitted. "But wouldn't anyone?"

Hawk couldn't argue that.

"How angry?" he pressed.

Jenkins seemed to think about it. "Well, one time she had a nice painting over there." He gestured toward the wall where a moonscape hung now. "And when I came, she had slashed it all up."

Hawk stared at him. "What was the painting?"

"It appeared to be a man and a woman. It was hard to tell after she destroyed it. But like I said, none of this is abnormal in her situation."

"Anything else?"

Jenkins paused. Hawk stared at him, waiting.

"She learned to shoot a gun," Jenkins finally said. "She was taking shooting lessons. I think she bought a handgun."

That *was* a surprise. Hawk sat forward in his seat. "Did she say anything? Like, why she bought it?"

"She said she always wanted to learn."

"And didn't that make you a little wary? Her husband just cheated on her, and she bought a gun?"

"Well, as far as I know, we're here because something happened to Gen. Nothing happened to her husband," Jenkins pointed out. "So she didn't do a thing with that gun."

"But why did she think she needed it? Did Thad ever get physical with her? Perhaps when she confronted him and wanted a divorce?"

"Not that I know of. I never saw any bruises, and I did watch for them. The day after she confronted him, she called me and checked in. I'd asked her to."

"Do you usually do that with your clients?" Hawk asked.

Jenkins shook his head. "Not usually, but sometimes. I think I already said Gen was a good gal. I felt bad for her. With it being her sister and all, it was a double whammy. She didn't think she had anyone to talk to."

"She didn't have any friends?"

"From what she said, Meg was her best friend. After this happened, she withdrew a little. I think she was afraid to trust anyone."

"She trusted you," Hawk pointed out.

"Yeah. I guess she did." Jenkins looked down, almost pained. "It looks like I let her down, though."

"Have you had personal interaction with either Thad or Meg?"

Jenkins thought about it. "I may have bumped into them while I was staking them out, but they never knew what I was doing. It was just real casual."

"Do you have a take on the situation?"

Jenkins shrugged. "They did her dirty, for sure. She didn't deserve it. What do you think happened to her? Do you think it's him?"

"We don't know."

"She asked me if she should get a restraining order."

"She was afraid of him?"

"She felt like she didn't know him like she thought, like he was cold and emotionless. He got kinda detached there at the end. She felt like he wasn't who she married. And she asked me if she should file an order. She was concerned about doing things the *right way*."

"Did she file that restraining order?"

"I don't know."

"Did she ever confront Meg?"

"That, I don't know. I kept asking her, and she kept saying she wasn't ready. Thad had taken up with that other gal, and Gen had gotten a bit of validation from that...like some satisfaction that Thad had cheated on her sister, too. Maybe she finally confronted her in New York City, and this is how it's turned out." His face looked pained.

"So you think it could be Meg?"

"I don't know, Detective. I don't have anything to base that on. I've just seen it all, and probably you have, too."

Hawk couldn't argue with that, either.

"Have you ever had an occasion to speak to her parents, or do you know about her background?"

"Her parents are older, obviously, but they are still together, I know that much. She went to see them in Wisconsin once while I was working for her. They sounded like a normal family. Her mom liked to cook. Gen was going to help her with some pies or somethin' like that. Just her and Meg, no other siblings. I'll tell you somethin', though. Meg seemed like a decent person, too, just like Gen. I don't know how she got wrapped up with someone like Thad, but probably was reeled in the same way as her sister. Either way, that man gives me a bad feeling. Always did."

"Gut feeling?"

Jenkins nodded. "Yep. You know the one."

Hawk did. He'd had it many times himself in the past.

"Okay. Well, can I call you with any other questions?" Hawk asked. Jenkins nodded.

"Hell yes. I've got a soft spot in my heart for Gen. Like I said, she didn't deserve this. I want her found. If you need any help, I'm happy to do it."

"Noted," Hawk said. He didn't anticipate the need, but it was a nice offer.

"One last thing," Jenkins said, pausing at the door. "You'll probably get a lot more info out of her pink journal. So look for that."

Hawk stooped and picked up the journal in the trunk. It was brown, but he showed it to Jenkins anyway.

"No. That's not the one. Like I said, it's pink. And smaller than that. Purse-sized. She took all kinds of notes in it."

"Did you think her behavior was normal?" Hawk asked him. "Seems to me that she was pretty obsessed."

"She was definitely obsessed," Jenkins agreed. "But you know as well as I do that people act in all kinds of ways when their spouse steps out on 'em."

Hawk nodded, and closed the door behind the man.

Jenkins was certainly soft on Gen. Hawk wondered if it made him biased. On the other hand, the man did have decades of experience. He probably had a good feel for the situation.

Sitting by the window, Hawk stared down at the street. This apartment had spectacular views of the city. He watched the people rushing along, and something surprised him.

Meg was sitting on a bench.

Her head was bent, and to his surprise, it appeared as though her shoulders were shaking.

She was crying.

He kept watching her as he called the department to make sure there hadn't been any sign of Gen back in New York.

There hadn't.

39

Gen, Now

"I HATE YOU," the woman said to Gen, and it was hard to call her an *it* when she pulled down her hood and dark curls fell out.

Gen stared up at her, sitting in her urine-soaked pants and dirty shirt. "Why?" she asked simply. "I don't even know you. I saw you with my husband. That's all I know of you."

"You took him from me," the woman said. "You took him. I was all alone. Do you know what that feels like?"

Gen swallowed hard. "I didn't take anyone," she croaked. Her throat was so dry. "Can I have a drink of water, please?"

The woman grabbed a bottle, tore off the lid and dumped it on Gen's face. Gen licked at it, trying to get as much as she could.

"You took my brother," the woman whimpered, and Gen froze.

"Your brother?" she asked, confused. Was this all a mistake?

Jody glared. "My brother. I had him a long time before you did. And you ruined everything. He stayed away because of you. But I have him back now, and you're not getting him. You can't have him back."

"Your *brother*?" Gen asked, everything coming together in her muddled head. "Thad is your brother?"

Jody nodded. "Of course."

Gen's head spun. Why hadn't he ever told her?

"Where do you live?" she asked Jody, the woman she'd thought was sleeping with her husband, but clearly she was completely mistaken.

"In Chicago, USA," Jody answered, proud that she could recite her address. "I know the door code, too, but I'm not supposed to share it."

Something was off about Jody, but Gen couldn't put her finger on it. She was almost childlike.

"Of course not," Gen agreed, shifting on the ground. "You should never share something like that. Not with anyone. Not even your sister."

"I don't have a sister," Jody told her. "Only Thad."

"But I'm married to Thad," Gen pointed out. "So technically, I'm your sister. It's nice to meet you. I wish I'd met you long ago. Why didn't I?"

"Because. Thad said you wouldn't understand," Jody said uncertainly. "You seem smart, though. I bet you would've."

"Of course I would've," Gen answered kindly. "I always wanted another sister anyway."

"You did?" Jody couldn't help asking.

Gen nodded. "I only have one. Two would be nice."

She knew something clearly wasn't right with this woman. She just didn't know what.

"Does Thad take care of you?" she asked politely, trying hard to lull Jody into feeling that she could trust her. Jody sat down, out of reach, and stared at her almost in wonder.

"Yes. He pays for my apartment. And he came to see me a lot. And now he lives with me. And I won't let you take him away again."

"Oh, sweetie, I don't want to," Gen assured her. "I promise. Your brother is a good man, a good person, and I used to love him very much. But we don't want the same things out of life anymore. I want to move away to a farm. Thad wants to stay in Chicago."

"He wants to stay with me!" Jody lifted her chin. "He'd never let you take him away."

"No, he wouldn't," Gen rushed to agree. She was stunned, and looking at Jody, she could see the family resemblance. She and Thad shared the same eyes, the same nose, the same dark hair.

"How did you know where to find me the other night?" Gen asked curiously. "You took me, right?"

Jody nodded proudly. "I followed you."

"How did you get to New York?" Gen asked, because it didn't seem possible that she traveled alone.

"I have Thad's credit card," Jody answered. "He thinks I'm on a school trip."

"You go to school?"

"I go to a special school, for special people. I have friends there."

"Good. Everyone needs friends. So Thad thinks you're on a trip?"

"Yes. And I didn't lie. I *am* on a trip."

"By yourself, though. He doesn't know *that*."

Jody immediately looked guilty. "I had to."

"Of course you did. Because you thought I was going to

take him away. But I won't. You can let me go, because I'll never take him away."

"I don't know what to do with you now," Jody told her. "I hadn't thought that far ahead."

"You'll have to let me go," Gen answered her calmly. "There's nothing else to do."

"That's not what happens in movies," Jody said. "Because then everyone would find out. Thad can't know, Genevieve."

"I will never tell him," Gen swore. "Let me go, and I'll never tell a soul."

"I don't think that's a smart thing to do," Jody answered thoughtfully, as though she were considering the odds. "I found your ring. And I gave it back to your sister so she can give it to Thad. It wasn't nice to throw it out, Gen. It cost a lot of money."

"You saw my sister?" Hope rushed through Gen.

Jody shook her head. "No. I left it in her hotel." Gen deflated.

"You're a smart girl," Gen told her. "You know that it's smart to not get into trouble for taking me. If you let me go, no one will know."

"I'm not smart," Jody confided. "I hurt my head a long time ago. My mama and daddy died, and my head got hurt. But Thad was fine and he takes care of me now."

Gen quickly put two and two together. The accident that killed their parents had injured Jody. It was tragic, and even more tragic that Thad thought he had to hide it.

But that didn't help her now.

"You are smart," Gen told her. "I think everyone is smart in their own way."

"Could I get into trouble for taking you?" Jody asked, doubtful now. "Are you lying? It's not nice to lie."

"It's against the law to take me," Gen explained. "Do you know what a law is?"

Jody nodded. "Yes. There are too many laws. That's what Thad says."

"Sometimes. But one big law is that you can't hurt anyone else. And keeping me here is against the law. But see, I understand that you didn't know that. So I'm not mad. Just let me go. Take off this tape, and I'll leave, and you'll never get into trouble. I'll even help you get back home, and Thad won't have to know."

Gen lied as well as she could, hoping that Jody wouldn't be able to tell.

Jody seemed to consider it.

"That bad man that was there the other night. I saved you from him," Jody said proudly. "He was going to hurt you. But he didn't. Because of me."

Gen froze. She'd forgotten. She was dazed, and dehydrated, and not thinking clearly. She'd forgotten about that man. The man she'd hired. The man who would make sure that Meg wasn't safe.

She screamed as loud as she could, writhing against her restraints, as Jody watched, appalled.

40

Gen, Then

GEN CHEWED ON the end of her pen.

It's time. I've got to do it. I can't stand to see his cheating face every night. I've got so many photos that I can use to prove it…yet I haven't gotten a single answer yet that will explain WHY. I guess he's the only one who can tell me that. Well, he and Meg.

I haven't decided how I'll confront her, or when. I'm not going to do it yet. I want to wait for the ideal moment.

She drew stick figures of a man and woman holding hands, and then scribbled through them so hard her pen tip broke. She closed the journal and went to the gym. She'd been going for weeks now. Not so that she could look better for Thad— in fact, that thought made her laugh. She liked the feeling of control, of being badass. She couldn't control what her husband had done to their marriage, but she could control herself. She got fit, was getting stronger by the day.

Kickboxing classes were her favorite. She could use all of her pent-up rage and legally hit someone over and over. She pictured Thad or Meg as the face of her opponent and then no one stood a chance. She tapped into her inner fury, and it was a well that ran deep.

The funny part was that Thad hadn't even noticed. He hadn't noticed her muscles firming up. He hadn't noticed exercise clothing in the hamper. He hadn't noticed her burgeoning self-confidence. Why? Because he didn't notice her at all. More and more, as the days went by, he was buried in his phone whenever he was at home. Gen assumed he was texting Meg.

Sometimes, to amuse herself, when he was buried in his texts, she'd blow her sister's phone up with random texts and memes, just to slow down Meg's response time to Thad. He hated to be kept waiting.

Interestingly, Meg was able to act completely normal with her. Gen couldn't fathom it. What kind of person was capable of that? They hadn't been brought up that way.

She called her now.

"Hey, sis," Meg answered. "I've only got a second."

"A second is all I need." Gen forced a laugh. "I just wanted to see if you and the boys wanted to come over tonight for dinner."

There was a pause.

"You never host dinner," Meg said.

"That's because I rarely cook," Gen answered. "But I'm cooking tonight. Be here at seven. It's like a comet—the occasion only comes around every ten years."

"Fine," Meg replied. "Because this I've gotta see."

They hung up, and Gen took a cab back home to shower off her sweat. She texted her husband.

Be here at 7 please. Having Meg and fam over.

Thad answered almost immediately, something he rarely did.

Can't. I've got to work late again.

Thad, you need to be here. I don't ask for much. Besides, I'm going to cook.

I need a terrified-emoji, he answered, adding a crying-laughing emoji.

Just be here.

Okay. I'll make it happen.

Of course you will, Gen thought. You can't resist seeing Meghan and flaunting it beneath our noses. Her blood boiled at the thought, and she clenched her fist. She chose a simple black wrap dress, and pulled her hair out of her face with a black and ballerina-pink ribbon. She only applied lip gloss. As she smacked her lips, she examined herself. Her skin was still good, she noted. Her hair was shiny. She looked very youthful, actually. She didn't need makeup.

She went down to the living room, then called in a food order from a nearby restaurant. When it was delivered, she put it into serving dishes and set the table, making sure she hid the boxes deep in the trash. She set the food in the oven to keep it warm.

She'd forgotten perfume, so she went back to her bedroom and dabbed some behind her ears, knees and neck. The scent of vanilla calmed her, and she breathed it in deeply now. This would be the first time she'd have both of them in the room with her at the same time since she'd found out.

She lit a candle, and turned just in time for a knock on the door.

Meg's family burst in, little Joey barreling for Gen's arms.

"Aunt Nini!" he hollered, and her heart warmed in spite of the circumstances of the evening. He was such a sweet little thing.

"Let go of your aunt," Meg exhaled as she came in holding wine. "You'll smash her. I bear gifts," she said, thrusting it at her sister.

"Thanks," Gen answered. "Did you think I wouldn't have any?"

Meg's head cocked toward Gen. "Of course not. I was just being nice, weirdo."

"I'm happy you made it," Gen told her. "I was worried you'd get held up at the hospital."

Meg stared at her sister again. "It was my pleasure." There was stiffness there—Gen could hear it.

"Come in, Joe," she looked past Meg, and hugged Joe. He felt the same as last time, solid, muscular and smelled like cedar. He smiled down at her.

"I'm starving, kid," he told her. "Whatcha gonna feed me?"

"Italian," she told them. "Go ahead and sit. We can start with bread while we wait for Thad. Meg, pour the wine."

They all sat, and Joey, of course, was next to his Nini. Meg poured them all glasses of red, and Gen passed around the garlic-bread basket. While she chewed a piece, she turned to Joe.

"How are things going at work?" she asked. He shrugged.

"Good enough."

Meg rolled her eyes. "He's being modest. He's doubled his construction crews this year. He's doing amazing."

One thing Gen had always noticed about Meg: she always wanted to point out Joe's accomplishments when they all got together. Was she embarrassed of his profession, so she tried to make him sound better?

Maybe Thad appealed to Meg's ambitious side. He had worked his way up the ladder in his profession, and that attracted her. Joe, however, did well as a contractor. Perhaps it just wasn't white-collar enough for her physician sister.

Gen didn't know.

"Well, thanks, honey," Joe said, graceful as always when Meg gushed about him. If he thought his wife looked down on him, he didn't show it.

"What time is Thad getting here?" Meg asked. "The food will get cold."

"You want to text him and ask?" Gen suggested, standing up. "I'll go bring the food."

"I'll help," Joe said, jumping up to help. Gen smiled at him.

"Thanks."

Meg was already texting Thad. She didn't stop and think that it might look odd that Gen had asked her to do it instead of simply doing it herself.

He answered her immediately.

"He'll be here in ten minutes," Meg called from the table.

Gen handed Joe the manicotti while she grabbed the salad, and then walked back into the dining room.

"Good," Gen said, sitting down. "Let's just go ahead and start."

Meg served up the manicotti and chatted about the tumor she'd removed that afternoon.

"Yum," Gen answered, grimacing a little.

"Baby," Meg answered. "You couldn't deal with half the stuff I see on a daily basis."

"I'm sure I couldn't," Gen answered, but she was thinking of seeing Thad's penis. She wouldn't want to see it now, and Meg saw it every damn day. "I'll just do my thing, you do your thing."

Thad chose just that moment to enter. *The thing Meg was doing.*

"Hey, all," he greeted everyone at once, and dropped into the seat at the end of the table. He looked at his wife first. "How was your day, honey?"

Smart. He was playing the husband role perfectly.

"It was fine." She shrugged. "Worked out, got some words in. How about you?"

"Worked out?" Meg laughed, scooping salad delicately onto a piece of bread to eat. "Since when?"

"A while back," Gen answered. "Living my best life, and all that."

"God, I wish I had time to work out," Meg sighed. "It seems like a luxury at this point."

She and Thad laughed, the two "professionals" in the room, while the writer and the contractor shrugged. Gen had the ass of a twenty-year-old at this point, so she figured they could laugh all they wanted.

"Tell us about your day," Gen urged her husband. "Where did you have lunch?"

She was pretty sure Meg froze at that question.

"A deli by the office," Thad answered. "How about you?"

"I grabbed a yogurt at the gym."

"And I had a salad in the cafeteria," Meg piped up. "Moving on from the mundane, Sherry said she saw you buying a beautiful painting last week. Can I see? Where did you hang it? She went on and on about how pretty it was."

"Sherry, your neighbor?" Gen asked. "She didn't come up and say anything to me."

"No, she said you were filling out paperwork and didn't want to interrupt. But she raved and raved about the art. Where did you hang it?"

"I didn't know we got anything new," Thad said, twisting to look around.

"It isn't delivered yet," Gen scrambled to say.

"From last week?" Meg lifted an eyebrow. "Good Lord, you could've walked it home faster."

"I know," Gen answered. "I don't know what's taking so long. I'd better check on it."

"Well, just show me when it gets here," Meg told her.

"Me, too," Thad said dryly, and Joe laughed.

"Oh, the things our wives drag in, right?" Joe quipped. Gen almost choked.

You have no idea, she thought, and sipped at her wine.

After dinner, she and Meg cleaned up, while the men had a beer in the living room. After, Gen curled up on the couch and read a book with Joey, while Joe excused himself to make a call, and Thad stood on the balcony.

She glanced up from the book after a few minutes and saw that Meg had joined Thad out there. They didn't know she'd noticed, and their heads were bent together. They were whispering. For one scant moment, Thad's hand brushed her back in an intimate way and the way they looked at each other... if she hadn't known it before, she knew it now.

She felt the pulse pound in her head, and she tried to keep reading to Joey.

How long had this been going on without her even knowing about it?

She felt like such a fool.

After everyone had left, and she and Thad were climbing into bed, he reached for her for the first time in a long time.

She was stiff.

"Tonight was a good idea," he told her, kissing her forehead. "It was fun."

"If only I'd known long ago that to get you home at a decent hour, all I had to do was call my sister," she joked, only she wasn't really joking.

He laughed, however, because he had no idea she knew.

He didn't know the joke was really on him.

Something had to be done.

41

Meg, Now

MEG SAT IN her home, her son, Joey, on her lap.

It had taken her a while to compose herself outside of Gen's apartment, but once she did, she had Ubered right home to Joey.

He chattered about his day at day care, and she hugged and held him tight. His smell would fuel her all of her days... that little-boy-outdoorsy smell.

"I miss you, Mommy," he told her, his eyes large.

"I miss you, too, baby," she answered. "We're just looking for Aunt Nini. I'll be home as soon as we find her."

"Is she playing hide-and-seek?" he asked, because that was his favorite game.

"Yeah, kind of," she said. "But as soon as we find her, I'll be home. And I'll tuck you in every night."

"Except for when Daddy does it," he answered.

"Yeah."

She tucked him in and pulled the sheets up to his chin. "I'll be here when you wake up," she told him, kissing him on the nose. "So sleep deep, little one."

She turned off his light, left the door open a crack and walked down to the living room, then stepped outside for some air. She called Thad.

"They know," she said quietly. "Detective Hawkins knows."

"About?"

"That night."

"And?"

"And I don't know. I haven't seen him since earlier. They're going to think that we did this, Thad. We have to tell them everything."

"No." His answer was abrupt. "I'm not going to risk my career, and you certainly aren't going to, either."

"They're going to figure it out," Meg said firmly. "He's not stupid."

"No, he's not. A one-night stand is one thing. An abduction is another. They can't prove something that isn't true."

Meg hesitated, and there was a pregnant pause.

"You don't believe that I had something to do with this, do you?" Thad asked, incredulous. "I know I've been short lately, and even a bit of an ass, but there's a lot going on, and I can hardly deal with the fact that you didn't choose *me*. In spite of that, you know me better than to think I could hurt anyone. You know I have to separate myself from her. We made the decision to divorce, and I can't open that door again with her."

"You can't pretend to care, you mean," Meg said, and she felt so damn guilty about everything.

"I do care," he said sharply. "You know that. But she and I are over. She made her choices, and I made mine."

"I know," she answered limply. "You know there were a million reasons why I couldn't choose you."

"Yeah, yeah. You've said. It would be too complicated."

Meg stayed silent.

"Anyway. Whatever the detective thinks he knows is fine, but since we didn't have anything to do with this, then I don't see why we have to share information that only makes us look worse."

Meg sighed, and spun slowly around, eyeing the landscape around her house. It felt like she was always looking over her shoulder now, and she didn't like it.

"My gut says otherwise," she finally answered.

"Your gut is mistaken with this," Thad said. "Trust me."

Meg was starting to feel that she couldn't trust anybody, and that wasn't a way to live.

"We've made ourselves look guilty by not telling him."

"We can't change that now," Thad said. "But we don't have to make things worse."

"I'm not promising anything," she finally agreed. "But I'll leave it, for now."

"You'll see that I'm right," he answered. "When all of this is done."

"You mean, when Gen is found?"

"Yes."

But the way he'd said it hadn't felt like that. Did he know where she was?

Damn it. She didn't like anything about this.

"When are you coming back?" he asked her.

"Tomorrow, I think. Unless Hawk tells me otherwise. Joey misses me. I hope it doesn't take long. I just want this to be over. I want Gen home where she belongs, and I want everything to be fine."

"We all want that," Thad told her. "Just tell Hawkins that we had a fling. That it was nothing. That's what you want to believe anyway. I'll tell him the same thing."

She hung up, and her heart felt so heavy. So many things had weighed it down. How long would it stay afloat?

"Things aren't well?" Joe asked from behind her.

She turned, and he was leaning on the house. It annoyed her for a second. After all these many months, he still hovered. Like she hadn't recommitted to him back then, like she hadn't spilled her sins, like he hadn't forgiven her, like she still had some penance to do.

His ever-watchful eyes studied her.

"The detective found out about Thad and me," she said simply.

Joe nodded slowly.

"So, soon, everyone will know," he answered.

"I don't know. I don't know how it works. I don't know who he can tell."

"I don't know, either."

"Thad doesn't want us to say more than we have to."

"Of course he doesn't." Joe was derisive. "He has a lot to lose."

"His career is built on his reputation," Meg pointed out, and it sounded like she was defending him. Joe didn't miss that.

"So is yours," he answered. "Thad is an ambulance chaser. He'll survive. He's like a cockroach after an atomic bomb."

Meg was smart enough not to point out that Thad made a lot of money doing what he did, and that he still had a law degree from Cornell hanging on his wall.

"If it gets out, everyone will look at us differently. They'll look at us like we're monsters, like I'm a monster for what I did, and like you're stupid because you forgave me… They'll look at us all like…" Her voice trailed off, and Joe took a step and then another.

He stood in front her and looked into her eyes.

"What they think shouldn't matter," he told her, kinder than she knew she deserved. "No one knows us. They don't know the situation. They don't know what happened. If they want to judge us, let them."

"But what about Gen?"

"What about her? What happened to her in New York isn't related to you and Thad."

She didn't tell him how her gut twinged when she was talking to Thad, how she was starting to wonder if maybe, just maybe, it *was* related. Somehow.

"Listen, in spite of everything, you love your sister. You know it, I know it, everyone who knows the two of you knows it."

Meg nodded. It was true.

"So everyone else can go to hell," Joe said emphatically. He pulled her close, and rested his chin on the top of her head. They stood still for several minutes, before he pulled away.

"Now, you ready for bed?"

Meg nodded, and they got ready for bed and then climbed in together. It was early enough to watch TV for a while, so Joe clicked through and found something suitable. Meg rested in the crook of his arm easily—he was so familiar, so good. She was asleep before the end of the program—the first good sleep she'd had in days.

In the morning, Joe propped up on an elbow and stared at her.

"I know that things haven't been the same," he said. "But we're a family, Meg. I'll get past what happened, because I know it was a mistake. I know you and he were drunk, and you were both frustrated. I'll get past it because I love you. And you love me. I don't know, though, what Gen will say when she finds out. I wish I could say that she'll forgive you, but I just don't know."

"She'll think that I'm the one he was having an ongoing affair with," Meg said quietly.

"And you swear to God that's not the truth?" Joe asked, his breath catching a bit.

"I swear to God. He and I... We were one night. That was it. It was nothing. Literally nothing."

"It was something," Joe answered. "It almost tore us apart, Meg. I'm only here because you swore to me it would never happen again, and because you came to me and told me. You didn't have to do that, but you did."

"Because I love you," she said simply. "Because I didn't want to lie to you. Because I hated myself for what happened."

"Don't hate yourself," he said softly. "No matter what happens, don't do that."

She pressed a kiss to his lips. "Why are you so good to me?" she asked. "Don't you get weary of this? Of the drama? Of the fact that I hurt you? Of the fact that we're growing apart?"

"Don't say that," he answered. "You're my wife. The past is the past."

With that, he got up and walked down the hall.

42

Meg, Now

MEG STARED DOWN at the buckle on her seat belt. The airplane seat was rigid, and Hawk being next to her didn't make it any less awkward.

The flight attendant did her spiel, and then they were up in the air. Meg settled down into her seat, and Hawk cleared his throat.

She looked up at him. His gunmetal eyes were steely.

"So you never told your sister it was you," he said, and he was judging her with each word. Meg shook her head.

"It would've made things a million times worse."

"For you," he pointed out. She swallowed.

"You can't understand what happened unless you've been in my shoes."

He nodded at that. "No, I can't imagine what it would be like to do something like that to my sister."

Meg looked away. He couldn't help but note that she'd been biting her nails to the quick.

"Does your husband know?"

"I don't think that's your business. But yes, he does."

"So you told him, and Thad was in on it, of course. The three of you knew and you kept Genevieve in the dark? That seems cruel, not protective. At any given moment, one of you could've slipped and revealed something, and she would've found out in a heartless way. Did that ever happen?"

He stared at her, and she returned his gaze. She felt terrible about what she did, but she didn't answer to him about that.

"No," she said firmly. "No one slipped."

"Did you ever plan on telling her?"

Meg paused. "No. I don't think so."

"That's pretty cold."

"Your judgment isn't necessary."

He shrugged. "People just rarely surprise me anymore. You did."

"Glad to be of service." Her voice was cold, and she turned to stare out the window.

"How is your relationship with Joe now?" he asked, apparently not reading her body language.

Her back was turned to him now—she was done talking. He ignored that. "Strained?"

"Why does this matter?" Meg asked, without looking at him. "Do you think Joe is a suspect now, too?"

"Should I? What would be his motive?"

"You're crazy," she muttered. "Joe wouldn't hurt a soul. He loves Gen."

"You guys just keep it in the family, huh?"

Meg's cheeks flushed red. "I didn't mean like that."

"Listen. We're stuck next to each other for another hour and a half. You might as well talk to me. Tell me all of the details, and don't leave anything out. Any little thing could be something important."

Meg stared at the window. She blinked once, then twice.

"How did it start?"

"Sleeping with Thad?" She half turned toward him, gazing over her shoulder. He nodded.

She sighed. "It's complicated."

"I'm sure," he agreed. "Interfamilial romance always is."

Meg glared at him. "If you want me to talk, you might want to stop with the snide remarks."

"Fine." He sat back in his seat and waited.

"I've known Thad a long time. I watched him go through law school, and mature and get more ambitious. Gen has always been wrapped up in her own worlds...all the fictional ones she creates. As her sister, it never bothered me. It was entertaining. But for her husband, it got old, I guess."

"So that is Thad's reasoning. What is yours?" Hawk kept his face impassive. He didn't look away from Meg, even when the flight attendant handed him a soda and he thanked her.

"I don't have a good one," she said. Red mottled her chest, the bit of skin that showed above the neck of her shirt. She was nervous, uncomfortable. "My husband is a good man. I've known him since high school. When I married him, I needed someone stable and secure. I was in med school, and everything was in chaos. Now...everything is stable, and..."

"And?"

"I don't know. I thought I needed more. I thought I needed my mind stimulated."

"Joe doesn't do that for you?"

Meg closed her eyes. She hated talking about it. She shook her head. "No. He's so good and so kind. He just doesn't understand what I do, or how I think. I spent a lot of time at

Gen's and one thing led to another one night when Thad was attending a function with me. We were drunk."

"Did you know Gen hired a private detective?"

"No."

"So I wonder if she figured out about you and Thad?"

"You'd have to ask the private detective. Obviously, she didn't tell me."

"How did she tell Thad that she knew he was cheating?"

"You'll have to ask Thad. I don't want to get something wrong—I wasn't there."

"Surely she told you how it went?"

"She said he was detached, and matter-of-fact. He didn't want divorce to ruin his reputation, so he asked her if they could keep it hush-hush."

"He thought that a divorce would ruin his reputation? This isn't 1970," Hawk pointed out.

"I know. He just worked really hard for his practice and didn't want anything to ruin it."

"And Gen was okay with that? It seems like she'd be too pissed to care."

"She was, at first," Meg conceded. "But I think, and don't quote me on this, but I think he was giving her a one-time payment to compensate her for her cooperation."

"He was paying her to divorce him quietly," Hawk said, his eyebrow lifted.

"Yeah."

"You told me before that you didn't know if Gen would be getting remuneration from Thad."

Meg sighed. "I didn't want you to find out about my involvement with him."

"Has he made the payment?"

"The last I heard, he was to pay it when the divorce was

final. She was dragging her feet with signing the papers, and he thought it might make her sign them faster."

"So, theoretically, if she disappeared, he wouldn't have to pay her," Hawk pointed out.

Meg didn't say anything. It was something that had crossed her mind, but she hadn't wanted to entertain the suspicion.

"How much is the payment?"

"I don't know. You'll have to ask Thad."

"Oh, I will."

When the plane landed, Meg gathered her carry-on and wandered down the LaGuardia corridor. She felt Hawk watching her, but she didn't turn around. She'd never felt so subhuman as she did right now. All she wanted to do was disappear into her hotel room, away from judgment.

Hawk hailed a cab, and called Thad Thibault. He told him to meet him at the station in thirty minutes.

Thad was exactly on time.

When he sat down at Hawk's desk, Thad was perfectly put together, his shirt pressed, his shoes polished, his belt lined up with the seam of his fly.

"So, I spoke with Gen's private investigator," Hawk began. Thad waited, unflinching. "I know about your affair with Meghan."

"It wasn't an affair. It was one night."

"I'd like for you to tell me about it."

"That night? That hardly seems gentlemanly."

Hawk stared at him coldly.

Thad sighed. "What's there to tell? I made a mistake. It caused the end of my marriage, so I've paid for it."

"Not yet you haven't," Hawk answered. "Because the way I understand it, your marriage ended because Gen thought you were having an ongoing affair. And if your night with Meg was only a night, do you care to explain?" As he spoke, he pulled some of the photos from Gen's wall and put them in front of Thad. The ones of him and the other woman, the woman who wasn't Meg or Gen.

Thad sighed again.

"That's my sister, Jody. I'm her caretaker. I never told Gen about it because the circumstances around it are painful."

"So you'd rather have your wife think you were unfaithful than simply tell her about your sister? That hardly makes sense."

"And tell her how I killed my parents and ruined my only sister's life?"

"I think any rational person would understand."

"It's not just a matter of her understanding. Talking about it makes me relive it. I have PTSD from the whole thing. I can't bear to think about it."

Hawk stared at him, not entirely convinced.

"I also knew that if she poked into it far, she'd discover what happened between Meg and me. I didn't want that for Meg."

"So you're an honorable cheat?" Hawk raised an eyebrow, and Thad narrowed his eyes.

"You don't know me."

"I know that you arranged for a one-time payment to Gen if she divorced you quietly. I know that she disappeared before the divorce became final. And I know that you don't pay her until then."

Thad's eyes shifted just a bit.

"How much is that payment supposed to be?" Hawk asked.

Thad's jaw clenched, and he exhaled.

"A million dollars."

Hawk whistled, low and long. "That's quite a bit of money just to keep her quiet about the divorce."

"I wanted to make sure she was taken care of," Thad said defensively. "I fucked up. She shouldn't have to pay for it."

"So you regret what you did?"

"I regret hurting my wife in that way."

"Have you hurt her in any other way?" Hawk was casual. Thad glared again.

"Of course not. Do I need an attorney?"

"That's up to you," Hawk said. "I mean, *you're* an attorney," he pointed out.

"Just ask your questions," Thad snapped.

"How did Gen confront you?"

"She was waiting for me one night when I got home from work. She said she knew I was having an affair, that she didn't have proof, but she knew. I almost denied it, but that seemed like it would cause her more pain, all things considered. So I told her she was right."

"But you wouldn't tell her who it was," Hawk replied.

"Of course not," Thad answered. "There was no need to crush her like that."

"I can't believe the two of you really thought it wouldn't eventually come out," Hawk told him. "This kind of thing doesn't usually stay buried."

"You don't know Gen," Thad answered. "She's got her head in the clouds most of the time. Real life things don't attract her attention."

"So it must've been easy for you to fool her," Hawk said.

Thad stood up. "If you don't have any other questions, I'm done here."

Hawk stood up, as well. "One more question. Do you know where Gen's laptop is?"

Thad's head snapped up. "No. I do not."

Hawk stared, then answered. "Okay. Needless to say, I'm going to need you to stay in the city for now."

Thad nodded curtly and walked out. He tried to call Meg, and she didn't pick up. He swore under his breath, and realized then that their phone calls might be monitored now. He slid his phone back in his pocket.

When he arrived back at the Aristotle, he went straight to Meg's room.

When she answered, her eyes were red and the bed was rumpled.

"It's going to be okay," he told her. He stepped inside without waiting for an invitation.

She didn't respond. Instead, she went to the desk and opened the drawer. Then she pulled out Gen's ring.

"Who put this on my doorstep the other night?" she asked, twisting the ring in the light. "Someone did. Was it you?"

"Why would I do that? How would I have gotten it? I wasn't in New York then, remember. You're not using sense. You told me Gen threw it off the balcony."

"Maybe you were here," she suggested, and her eyes were a bit wild. "Maybe you were following me, and you saw her throw the ring, and you found it. Or maybe you did something to my sister, but still wanted this ring back so you could sell it. It IS expensive, after all."

"Have you been drinking?" Thad demanded. "That's crazy. Even if I was watching your balcony from the street, I couldn't have seen her throw something. It's too high up. You're spiraling, Meg. Take some deep breaths."

"Don't talk to me like I'm Gen," she snapped. "I'm not. And nothing feels right about you now. Not a thing."

"I know what this is about," Thad said suddenly. "It's about the payment. Hawkins got you worked up about it. I know it looks bad, but it's coincidence, Meggie."

"Don't call me that."

"I love you," he told her. "You know that."

"Stop. We were caught up in a situation, and that was all."

"You know that's not true. I love you. You love me."

"No, I don't," she said, and her voice was ever so cold now. "I thought I loved you once. Like a brother, and then that night…it was more, but I made a mistake. No matter what the situation was, we were wrong. I could never be with you now. Not ever."

She tossed the ring at him, the diamond catching the sunlight in the air. Thad caught it neatly.

"Neither Gen nor I want anything to do with you," she said. "Ever again."

"When did this ring turn up on your doorstep?" he asked quietly.

"The other night. With this note." She handed him the scrawled letters on the paper.

She turned her back, and Thad walked away. She heard the door click behind him as he left.

He stepped into the elevator, thinking about the dark handwriting. When he reached the landing, he pulled out his phone and dialed Jody's number.

There was no answer.

43

Gen, Then

GEN HAD FALLEN asleep before Thad arrived home.

When he came to bed, he curled up behind her. "You okay?" he whispered, lightly rubbing her shoulder.

She pulled away from him even in her sleep.

"Okay, then," he muttered. He rolled over, and when he woke up the next morning, Gen was gone. That was unusual, too. She rarely left the house before him.

He called Meg. "Gen went out before I got up. She's acting odd."

"You don't think she..." Meg's voice trailed off, and Thad shook his head.

"No. I don't think so. Has she texted you this morning?"

"No," Meg answered. "But I'll let you know if she does."

They hung up, and Thad got ready for work.

By the time mid-morning rolled around, Thad had forgotten all about his concerns, wrapped up in preparation for a case.

Across town, Gen sat on a quaint wooden bridge in a public park, her feet swinging merrily beneath her. She thought people might be looking at her oddly, but she didn't care. It was almost time to execute her plan, and she was nervous, excited, terrified and ready.

All of the emotion from finding out about her husband's philandering and her sister's participation had pushed her over the edge. She just needed a good morning—one good morning—before she pulled this whole thing off.

She walked for most of the morning, marveling at how good the air smelled. It smelled like rain and freshness. She chatted with strangers and bought street hot dogs, which were the best dogs she'd ever had. She walked past Thad's building, half expecting to find Meg standing outside.

She wasn't.

Gen almost went in.

She didn't.

She sat at the bench in front, where she'd once seen him and Meg, and she wrote in her journal.

She wrote about the pens, and the air, and the colors, and how for the first time this month, anger wasn't consuming her.

The vastness is survivable now, she wrote. *I'll live. I thought I wouldn't, but I will.*

She recorded everything she knew until this point. She scribbled pictures, and doodles, and important words. She thought she'd create a mind map, and write down everything she knew about the whole affair. So she did.

She drew arrows and made a flow chart.

She wrote Meg's name over, and over, and over.

She spent a couple of hours on Michigan Avenue, buying a magnificent outfit, slender winter-white slacks, a winter-white cashmere turtleneck and butter-soft calfskin ankle boots. She walked into a salon and had her hair blown out. She bought a luscious new perfume.

When Thad walked in the door that night, she was waiting.

And she looked amazing.

His eyes flickered over her when he came in, and he saw her. He *truly saw* her. That made her happy. This way, he'd know in this moment what he was going to lose.

"You look nice," he said hesitantly.

She saw him wondering… *Have I forgotten something? Were we supposed to be somewhere?*

"We need to talk," she said, motioning at the couch for him to sit. Thad's eyes narrowed.

"That never ends well," he answered, and he perched on the edge of the sofa. "What's up?"

His fingers drummed a beat on the leather next to him, and for a moment, Gen enjoyed his anxiety. *Welcome to my world*, she thought.

"I know you've been fucking someone else," she said calmly.

She walked to get the wine bottle she'd opened a few minutes earlier and poured a glass. She glanced at Thad, her eyebrow lifted. *Do you want some?*

He hesitantly reached out for the glass she handed him.

"Why would you think that?"

"The fact that you're answering me in such a way just proves to me that I'm right," she told him. "Who is the whore?"

He flinched and tossed back half the glass of wine, then set it on the coffee table.

"You don't understand," he said slowly. "It's not like that."

"Then tell me what it's *like*," she hissed, and now her fury showed, like a set of fangs.

"I don't think that would be productive," he said simply. "You're right. I've been involved with someone else. I hate that I've hurt you. I'm sorry."

To be honest, Gen hadn't been expecting that.

She hadn't expected him to just admit it, like he was admitting to leaving the door unlocked or the toilet seat up. Although, it did irk her that he wouldn't tell her it was Meg. Was he protecting her, or protecting *Meg*?

"Aren't you going to beg me to forgive you, beg me to stay?" She took a drink of wine. "I've never had an unfaithful husband before, but I hear that's what happens."

"Don't get nasty," he cautioned her.

"You don't get to tell me how to be," she snapped. "Not now, and not ever again."

"This is why I'm not begging you to stay," he answered. "You won't want me again. You won't be able to forgive me. And honestly, it just wouldn't be right. I don't think we're right for each other anymore. We're different than we used to be."

She wanted to scream, *And my* sister *is right for you?* But she didn't.

Instead, she calmly crossed and uncrossed her legs.

She drained the rest of the wine.

"Tell me who it is," she demanded.

"No."

"Tell me."

"No," he answered. "Damn it, Gen. Let it go. It doesn't matter. It isn't about her anyway. It's about us. You and me."

"What about us?" she shrieked, her serenity slipping away. "What about till death do us part, Thad? What about through sickness and health, so long as we both shall live?"

"It just got to be too much," he said limply. "You were always in your own worlds. Never in mine."

"You mean my career made you fall out of love with me?"

He stared at her. "I'll sleep in the guest room."

"You will not," she retorted. "You will go to a hotel." She didn't care that she had a fully equipped apartment down the street that she could retreat to. He cheated—*he* could leave.

"Genevieve," he said slowly. "I don't want people to know. Please, I'll sleep in the guest room until we figure out what to do."

"You don't want people to know?" She practically cackled now. "Why ever not? Who the hell cares, Thad? Who cares aside from you and me? For fuck's sake!"

He flinched at her words and drew in a long breath. "Gen, you know how long it took me to build my career. In my world, this could damage me. I want to be able to take care of you, even after all of this. If it damages my career, it will damage your alimony."

"My alimony?" Gen asked, her eyes wide. "What makes you think I want that? I don't. I have a career of my own that I've worked hard to build. I don't need your support."

"You do have a career," he said carefully. "But you've struggled to put out this last book. You've been blocked for ages. I just want to help."

"Are you fucking kidding me? You cheated on me. You don't get to act like you care!" she raged. She felt unhinged, and that was okay. Anyone would be in her position, right? "You're insane. I'm late on this book. It happens. I'm a god-damned artist."

"You are," he agreed, and it annoyed her because he was so clearly trying to calm her down.

"Shut. Up," she told him. "I can't even stand the sound of your voice right now."

Thad surveyed the situation as an attorney would and saw that he would have to do something to change things, and he'd have to act fast.

"I'll pay you to cooperate," he said quickly. "You can have whatever you want. Just please. Can we keep this private?"

Gen wanted to set fire to the goddamned building.

Instead, she contemplated.

Finally, finally, she looked at him.

"You can pay me a million dollars," she said evenly. "And I'll be more cooperative than anyone you've ever seen."

"A million dollars," he repeated. "You know how much the firm made last year, Gen."

"Oh, I know. And I know what it's projected to make this year. You can afford it."

"Barely," he replied.

"But you can."

He was quiet, and stood up, pacing to the windows and looking down at the city.

"You have broken our marriage vows," Gen said to his back. "We stood together in front of God and my parents, and everyone else, and said we would be together always. We would forsake all others. You haven't done that, Thad. You broke your promise."

She cried now. She couldn't help it. Her rage abated into grief, grief that she hadn't allowed herself to feel, in spite of her therapist's warnings.

Her shoulders shook, and when Thad came to try to console her, she threw his arm away.

"Don't ever touch me again," she warned.

He didn't. He sat still, and listened to her cry herself out. It took over an hour. When she was too weary to keep her eyes open, almost too weary to breathe, Thad spoke, quietly in the night.

"Okay. A million dollars."

Gen closed her eyes.

In her mind, she was swimming in a black ocean, far from here.

Thad retreated to the guest room and collapsed on the bed, his head in his hands. He hadn't wanted to hurt her. She was a good person. Hard to handle at times, like most artists were, but good to the bone. He thought back to the beginning, to the good days, and it truly pained his heart that things had come to this end.

He crept down the hall and paused at her door.

He could hear her inside, sobbing quietly.

He stood still as a stone, unsure about what to do.

He waited until she was quiet, and then he softly walked in and sat next to the bed. She slept, her hand curled under her cheek, her hair splayed. He brushed it away from her face, and listened to her even breaths.

Once upon a time, he had loved her more than anything.

Once upon a time, she was the other half to his whole.

Once upon a time, he'd never have thought they'd wind up here.

He sat with her while she slept, and when she finally started to stir, he crept back down to the guest room. She'd never known he'd sat with her all night.

44

Meg, Now

MEG SAT ON the bed in the hotel room, sifting through Gen's bag for the twentieth time. Underwear, a bag of travel-sized toiletries, a pair of blue earbuds. She took each thing and carefully laid it out on Gen's hotel bed. Four shirts, four sets of underwear. It was more than she needed to pack, but Gen had always been that way. Their mother always teased her about trying to pack the kitchen sink whenever she went anywhere.

Nothing seemed unusual or out of place. There was no clue here at all.

Meg slumped against the cushions and stared at the ceiling. She'd never felt so useless in her life. In her head, she ran through a million memories with her sister. Swinging on the tire swing when they were kids, spinning the rope and letting it whirl, their hair streaming around them in blond clouds.

The two of them had stayed outside for hours. Their father could never tell them apart when he'd stood on the porch and called them in, because they were both blonde and skinny.

She'd never known what it was like to be without her sister.

It was a lonely feeling.

Her gut started churning, and she ran to the bathroom, kneeling in front of the toilet, waiting to vomit. Gen had known about Meghan and Thad; she'd known all along.

Meg retched, a hand on each side of the cold porcelain seat.

She couldn't fathom how Gen had contained herself, how she hadn't said a word.

Why had she done that? Why hadn't she said something?

She must've felt so betrayed, so absolutely gutted.

Meg retched again. When she was finished, she sat back and wiped her mouth with her hand. She flushed the toilet as she stood up and quickly brushed her teeth. Her phone was ringing when she walked back into the bedroom.

She grabbed it, seeing her mom's name on the screen.

She groaned, but knew that if she didn't answer, she'd just have to call her back.

"Hi, Mom."

"Meghan, you haven't called me all day. Has there been any news? I'm looking for flights right now. Your dad and I are coming."

Meg recounted what she and Hawk had found in Chicago, the apartment.

"I don't understand," her mother said when Meg was finished, her voice thin. "Had she already moved out of the condo? I thought she was moving back to the country."

"She was," Meg confirmed. "I have no idea about the apartment."

"It doesn't make any sense. I guess she just needed a getaway." She paused, though, and the silence was heavy. Meg and her mother both knew that Gen didn't do well with stress. But she also didn't do well with too much alone time. An apartment where she sat in solitude was probably not a healthy thing for her.

Yet, that's what had happened.

Meg thought of the photo collages, of the many images of her and Thad and the angry red slashes through them. She shuddered.

"Meg?"

She snapped her attention back to the phone call.

"Yes?"

"I'm booking a ticket tonight. We'll be there tomorrow. I'll text you the flight details."

"Okay."

They hung up, and Meg dreaded her mother's arrival. Not because she didn't love her, but because it would complicate everything. Her mom and dad were annoyed with Thad, and they didn't know about the role Meg had played.

If they found out... Her stomach rolled again.

Instead of retching, she picked up her phone again.

She called Hawk.

"I know you're disgusted with me right now," she said instead of saying hello. "But could you meet me for coffee? I really want to discuss something with you."

Hawk was silent.

"Are you still there?" she asked after a few minutes.

"Yes. Just discuss whatever you need to right now."

Meg clenched the phone tight. She deserved this. She had done something heinous. She deserved people treating her this way.

"Detective, please. I would like to see you in person to discuss this."

There was more silence, and then a sigh.

"Fine. I'll meet you at the place by the station."

He hung up without her confirmation.

She grabbed her purse, and within a few minutes, she was in a cab. She stared out the window, at the blurs and the shadows, and she couldn't help herself—she watched for Gen's face.

But that was nothing new. Every place she went, she looked for Gen's face.

The only thing she saw was her own, staring back from windows and mirrors and shiny cars.

Hawk was already at a table when she arrived.

He barely looked at her when she sat across from him. Her stomach clenched.

"Thank you for coming," she told him. He nodded. She noticed that his dark hair was touching his collar. He needed a trim. But he looked good in tousled hair, too.

She took a deep breath. "I know this all puts me in a terrible light," she told him. "I know you probably don't come across many people in this situation."

He snorted.

She paused.

"You did a terrible thing," he acknowledged. "But I've seen people who are far worse. You didn't kill her husband. You slept with him."

Meg wasn't sure it was any better.

"Just tell me what you want," Hawk told her, although he seemed softer now.

"My parents are coming tomorrow," she said. "They don't know about Thad and me."

"So you don't want me to mention it."

"Pretty much."

"I won't cover it up if I need to discuss it," Hawk answered. "If it's relevant to this case, I won't hesitate."

"But you won't bring it up if you don't have to," Meg urged. "Right?"

"Good God. Stop being a child," Hawk snapped. "You fucked up. Face the consequences. That's what adults do."

"I know what adults do," Meg answered. She kept her voice level. "I went through med school, residency, a surgical fellowship, I'm a mother... I know a little something about being an adult."

"Okay," Hawk said. He stretched one leg out, and Meg tried not to look at it. She knew if she did, she'd see the contours of his thigh through his pant leg. It was just a reminder of his masculinity. Of all the things in the world, she didn't need to focus on that right now. But when his steel eyes met hers, in spite of herself, she felt a surge of attraction, and she jolted to life. It was something she hadn't felt in quite some time.

"I'm a good person," she told him. "I really am."

"Usually if someone has to point out what they are, then they aren't," Hawk replied.

He lifted an eyebrow. She rolled her eyes.

"Not in this case. I just know how I must seem."

"Generally, in my line of work, I judge people based on their actions, not their words."

Hawk took a drink.

"And I fucked my brother-in-law."

Hawk didn't even blink at her language.

"Pretty much."

"You don't understand the situation," Meg told him simply. "Nothing is ever black-and-white."

"No, but everything is either right or wrong," Hawk replied.

"Don't you ever wonder about the people you arrest?" she asked suddenly. "Don't you ever wonder if that man who robbed the gas station had starving kids to feed, or if that woman who shot her husband had been abused for a decade?"

"Well, normally, I know all the extenuating circumstances by the time the investigation is complete. And it's not my job to determine the morality of their choices. It's my job to uphold the law."

"There's no room for gray in the law," Meg said quietly.

"No, there's not."

As Meg watched him, she understood. Being a detective wasn't a job to him. It was simply who he was. He must see someone like her as complete scum. There was no point in her being here at all.

"Last night, I dreamed I died," she said, putting her words into the air, not directing them at him. "I was trapped somewhere, in a foggy, ethereal place. My feet were tangled in tree roots, and I couldn't run. I knew I'd been there a while, but I don't know how long. It was dark, misty. And finally, in my dream, I decided to die. I decided I'd had enough of the solitude and the fear, so I sat down, said a prayer and closed my eyes."

"Deep down, you think Gen is dead, and you are powerless to find her," Hawk interpreted her dream.

"My emotions have been all over the place," she admitted. "I'm not myself. I think random thoughts. I'm distracted… I'm just not me."

"Of course you're emotional," Hawk said, and he was kind now. He gestured for another cup of coffee. The waitress came and filled his cup up. Meg shook her head and covered the top of her own. She needed to sleep tonight. "This is emotional. All of it. Have you been to see someone, maybe?"

He watched her, his eyes more gray than blue in this moment.

She realized what he was saying, and startled. "A therapist?"

"It couldn't hurt." He cleared his throat. He almost couldn't believe he was suggesting it himself. Therapists generally annoyed him, with their fascination with blaming everything on the mothers. But this was a cesspool of a situation, and it would take a professional to help figure it out.

"You think I'm crazy," she said, and her voice shifted from serious to laughing.

"I wasn't trying to be funny," he assured her. "I'm not making fun."

"I know." She twisted her mouth, trying to hide her smile. "The irony of life is just funny sometimes. I don't need a therapist. But trust me, I'm a doctor. If I decide I need one, I know a few."

"Good," was all he said. His long fingers messed with his cup, running over the reservoir, the handle. Meg watched. She didn't want to leave, yet she didn't know what else to say.

"My mom will never forgive me," she said, and it was completely unexpected, both to her and to Hawk. She didn't know how the words bubbled out. Hawk sat up a little straighter.

"She's your mother," he pointed out. "She's going to be more concerned about Gen's absence than about anything you did with Thad."

"You don't understand."

"So you keep saying," Hawk said. "I think I deserve more credit."

Meg shook her head with a watery smile. "I mean, it's more complicated than I could convey in one conversation.

My parents always favored Gen, for as long as I can remember. She got away with everything. I got away with nothing."

"Isn't that backward?" Hawk interrupted. "Usually, it's the oldest kid who gets the heavy-handed treatment."

"I know," Meg replied. "Not in this case. Here's an example. One time, Gen and I were outside playing. Our dad had built us this incredibly huge play-town in our backyard. It had several playhouses built to look like an old-fashioned main street. We had a little soda shop, a general store and a post office. At the end, there was a jungle gym with a big slide."

"Sounds nice," Hawk offered.

"It was. Very. But one day, we were out there playing, as we always did. We were fighting over the wooden fruit from the general store, some bananas and oranges. I had them in my basket, and Gen took them from me. I wanted them back, and I snatched them away, and she hit me. You know, as little siblings sometimes do."

Hawk nodded, following.

"My dad, though, he was watching from the back porch. He started hollering and screaming at her, and was coming over to tan her hide. Only...he thought she was me. When he got close enough to see the difference, he stopped. He didn't whip her. He just told us both to straighten up and he went back to the house."

"So he was going to tan your hide, but when he saw it was Gen, he didn't?"

"Exactly. And that was the story of my life."

"But why? Because she was the firstborn and they thought she was perfect?"

Meg laughed. "No. They knew that wasn't true."

"So you think once they find out about you and Thad, they won't forgive you."

"I know they won't."

"If you explain the circumstances, which by the way, you haven't explained to me, maybe it will help."

"Trust me. Nothing will help. I've spent my entire life trying to come out of Gen's shadow. I worked hard in school—I always got straight Λ's. I was captain of the cheerleading squad. I was point guard on the basketball team. They barely noticed. I became a doctor. All that did was give them peace of mind that I'd be able to help Gen out as we got older if she needed it."

"Why would she need it?" Hawk lifted an eyebrow.

Meg sighed. "She's just Gen. She's never focused. She's got that artistic side of her that is ten feet above the ground at all times. She doesn't worry about realistic things like bills, or problems. She just floats above it all."

"That would drive me crazy," he remarked.

Meg laughed. "Sometimes. And sometimes, she's the most fun person in the world. It depends on the day. On her mood. On whatever she's writing. She gets absorbed into the character she's writing. If it's a good one, so is she. If it's a troubled one, so is she. She calls it *method writing*."

"She becomes the character she's writing, like with method acting?"

"To a degree," Meg commented.

"What is she writing right now?"

"I don't know. She rarely talks about her books until they are finished. She feels that it dilutes her creativity."

"I'll be honest with you. I don't understand artists," Hawk told her. His hand was on his thigh, his index finger tapping restlessly.

Meg laughed. "I don't, either. But thank God for them. Otherwise, life would be boring."

"Not in my world," Hawk disagreed.

"Your world is black-and-white," Meg reminded him. "That's pretty simplistic."

"No. It's honest. Honesty is the most entertaining of all."

"Truth is stranger than fiction?" Meg stared at him.

"Exactly." Hawk paused. "Where is her laptop?" he asked.

Meg thought about it. "It's not in the hotel room. She must've left it at the condo."

"Must've. Because it wasn't in her apartment, either. I need to find it."

For the first time, since this whole thing began, Meg agreed with the detective.

45

Jenkins, Then

SIMON JENKINS LOOSENED the top of the bottle of aspirin. He popped six of them into his mouth, far more than the instructions indicated. He rubbed at his temples and studied the chart that Gen had given him for safekeeping.

"I don't know how things will play out," she'd told him that morning. "I don't know if Thad will be decent, or not. He's becoming volatile. I'm afraid he won't keep his word. I'm keeping mine, though. I'm not telling a soul, except for you, what has really happened…that Thad has been sleeping with my sister."

The chart she'd tucked into his hand was startlingly detailed. Each person in her life was listed: Thad, Meg, Joe, her parents, and details about each one. He looked at Thad's name.

Thirty-six, DOB September 12. Medications, Xanax as needed. Dark hair, brown eyes. Six feet. Ring size, ten. Shoe size, eleven. Decent in bed. Funny, superficial, sarcastic, down-to-earth. Ambitious to a fault.

For Meg, she'd written: five-seven. Perfect, too perfect. Shoe size, eight. Pant size, ten. Driven, used to be loyal, sarcastic, pragmatic. Blond hair, blue eyes. Has a secret bank account and trust issues. Probably because she's been cheating on Joe, so she subconsciously thinks he'll do the same. Good at her job.

Mom: busy, gossipy. Loves her kids. Loves her dog.

Dad: stern. Loves me.

Jenkins didn't know what any of this had to do with him.

"Simon, come eat," his wife urged him. "You're not taking care of yourself lately."

He stood and kissed his wife of twenty years on her forehead. "I don't have to, Becky," he said. "You do that for me."

She shook her head in annoyance, but her eyes beamed. She loved him, and it showed. "Come sit," she told him. "I made your favorite."

She bustled around the table and poured him a scotch, setting it next to his plate. She poured it neat, without adding ice. He'd always liked it that way, straight from the bottle like God intended. She sat next to him, and they held hands while she said a short prayer.

Then they ate together, homemade bread and thick beef stew, his mama's recipe.

"This girl bothers me," he admitted to his wife as he buttered his bread. "Her family, they've done her wrong, and she seems so...delicate."

"Fragile?" Becky suggested, and he nodded right away.

"Yeah. That's a better word. She doesn't seem like she belongs to this world, if that makes any sense. Her head's always someplace else. Imma 'fraid they're gonna take advantage of her."

"Not while you're around," Becky said knowingly. She patted her husband on the knee. She knew him, backward, forward and sideways. "You always get sucked in."

"I do not," he announced gruffly, and shoved a bite of meat into his mouth.

"What about that girl last year...the mama of four kids? She couldn't pay you and you took the job anyway. Her husband wasn't going to give her any support at all."

"She does own his Porsche now," Jenkins acknowledged. Becky smiled.

"And his house, and his business."

"Well." Jenkins was indignant. "He should not have been out tomcatting around with his personal trainer."

"That poor girl couldn't compete," Becky said with a shake of her head. "She didn't have a penis."

They chuckled a little, because they could. That "poor girl" had been well taken care of as a result of the evidence Jenkins had gathered, proving her husband was in a secret gay relationship. She was now remarried to a loving accountant who hung on to her every word.

"You'll take care of this one, too," Becky said. "You always do. I love that about you. Your big ol' heart."

Jenkins grunted, but he beamed on the inside. He loved his wife. Her opinion was everything to him, and always would be. That's why he couldn't figure out men like Thad. If they weren't happy at home, they needed to fix it. Not go looking for even more problems.

After Becky had cleared the dinner dishes and wiped off the table, she turned to her husband. "Go get your stuff. I'll help you look through it."

It was their routine; they'd done it with every case.

They sat at their kitchen table, shoulder to shoulder, and

looked through everything he had accumulated. Jenkins couldn't remember how many cases Becky had helped him with.

"You like this as much as I do," he told her as he handed her the files.

She smiled, the tiny wrinkles forming a web at the edge of her eye as she did.

"Perhaps."

She pored over the pictures with him, flinching over some. "I can't believe what blood will do to one another sometimes," she muttered. He agreed.

"Didn't you say she told you about a journal?" she asked, turning to him. He nodded.

"Yeah. She did. She told me where it was hidden in case I ever needed it."

"Well, if your gut is worrying you about this, I'd say you need it."

Jenkins had to agree. His gut was rarely wrong; he'd been doing this too long for that. Something was niggling at him, something persistent. He needed to know what it was.

"So get that journal."

Jenkins waited until Becky went to bed. She retired every evening at 8:00 p.m. ever since she was a grade-school cook and had to get up at 4:00 a.m. every day. Doing that for thirty years had made it an ingrained habit in her. She'd do it until she died.

Jenkins left home and went to Gen's, knocking on her condo door at eight thirty, an excuse at the ready.

He was just checking in to see if she needed anything else for her divorce attorney.

She answered immediately and was delighted to see him.

"Simon!" she exclaimed, and she hugged him. "How are you? Would you like something to drink?"

She let him in and he saw a couple half-empty wineglasses sitting around.

"Did you have company?" he asked curiously, sitting down on the sofa. She shook her head.

"Not since earlier."

She didn't specify who it was, and he didn't want to seem like he was curious.

She seemed a bit tipsy, and she perched in the chair next to him, her legs tucked childlike beneath her. Her eyes were wide and glassy, and her cheeks were flushed pink, as though there was something exciting on the horizon.

"You seem happy," he observed, and she laughed.

"Did you ever think I'd be happy again?" she asked him. "I thought my life would be over. But here I am. I'm thriving, Jenkins. I don't have him holding me down anymore, no more of his rules, no more of his nonsense. I have this place to myself and my life back."

"Your husband had rules for you? You never said." Jenkins lifted an eyebrow. If he ever tried laying down rules with Becky, he didn't even want to venture what would happen.

Gen laughed. "He was a control freak. Meg can have him. They'll fit like two gloves."

"How much did you have to drink tonight?" he asked her.

"Only a bit, Jenks," she answered.

She got up and went over to the glass door that led to the balcony and slid it open and went outside.

Leaning against the balcony railing, Gen looked down.

"The whole world is small," she called back to Jenkins. "Come see."

"Are you drunk?" he said, coming over to tug on her hand. "Come back inside."

"No, no." She shook him free. "I'm part of the stars out here, Jenkins. I'm a comet."

"You're not a comet," he told her. He took a step forward, and she took a step back.

"I want to fly," she announced. "I think I can."

"Gen, are you okay?" He narrowed his eyes. "You're not acting right."

"I'm fine," she insisted, then tilted her head and howled, a long pitch that lifted the hair on Jenkins's arms.

"Let's go back in," he said firmly, and he pulled her arm this time. He was, after all, bigger.

"You don't seem yourself right now. It can happen sometimes in these moments. The emotions are too big to handle. You shouldn't drink when you're feeling bad, Gen. It only makes it worse. It makes the emotions even bigger."

He locked the balcony door and stood in front of it, staring down at his client.

She stared up at him, outraged.

"You need to sleep it off," he instructed her, like a firm father would. "You've mixed alcohol with extreme emotion, and that never ends well."

"I wasn't going to sleep here tonight," she said. "I was going to sleep at the condo. Thad still doesn't know about this place."

"I don't think that's wise. Text him and tell him you're staying overnight with a friend. He doesn't deserve to know the details anymore," he told her.

She lifted her eyebrow.

"Just text him and tell him you won't be home tonight. You're separated. He might be sleeping in your guest room, but you don't owe him any explanations."

"You got that right," Gen agreed cheerfully, pulling out her phone to obey.

"Now go in. I'm going to wait here until you're safely asleep."

"You're like a granddad," she decided. "A big ol' grand-dad."

He rolled his eyes and sat while she got ready for bed. Once she was actually in the bed, he turned off the light to her room and left the door cracked. Like a father would, he had to acknowledge.

He sat in the living room, waiting until her breathing turned deep and even, then he got up, very quietly, and went into her bathroom.

As she'd instructed him earlier, there was a tile above the toilet that slid back. He reached up, tall enough that he didn't have to stand on her toilet. He felt the journal and pulled it out.

Then he sat on the sofa and started reading.

It started out fairly sane, but he could tell when she'd been drinking while she wrote. It made her particularly mercu-rial. She drew pictures, stick figures of her and Meg, one of them in a cage. The other stood on the outside and laughed. He wasn't sure who was who.

Other stick figures showed Thad jumping off a building, or Thad getting hit by a train.

Gen was obviously furious and it showed. This was a jour-nal of revenge, an outlet for her rage. He understood that. It was a private diary; she could write whatever she wanted. He'd seen far worse in his day, and he wouldn't judge her for it.

The thing that bothered him was that she'd said to come get it if he needed it. Why would he need this?

He skimmed through the drawings, getting to pages where she'd written. Some were neat. Some were scrawled. There were red wine droplets on the pages.

She reads to me sometimes. She thinks I don't know, but I do.

She always wanted to be me, Diary, and now she is. She thought my life was gilded, but now she sees the tarnish. Now she sees the cage.

He read through existential musings and dark thoughts.

They think I don't know why they lie to me. They think they don't know it's so they can be alone. Even when we were kids, I never could figure it out, but now I do... Meg has always wanted Thad. Always, always, always, always. Now she can have him. No more locks, I'm free.

It was hard to work through the nonsense. Situations like this were so caustic, so explosive. Mix them with alcohol and they were much more potent, and it showed in this diary.

My sister wants my ring, I can tell. Isn't that weird? Isn't it enough that she has taken my whole life? She told me today that it's the prettiest thing she's ever seen. Who would want someone else's ring? It's cursed. Whoever wears it will be cursed to a life of misery.

This journal was nonsense.

He put it back into the ceiling and went home, sliding into the dark bed, careful not to disturb his wife.

46

Hawkins, Now

NATE HAWKINS LEANED back in his office chair, tipping it, then dropping. Tipping, then dropping. His eyes didn't leave the file on his desk. Meg's face stared back at him in the pictures that Jenkins had taken on surveillance.

These were the photos of Gen's apartment, and the pictures that were plastered on the walls. So, so many of her sister. It was as if Gen were obsessed with Meghan somehow, something different from the affair.

But that wouldn't make sense. Meg was the one who had been in her sister's shadow all these years, not Gen.

But out of 231 photos, 129 were of Meghan.

Did Meg somehow sense this energy focused at her? She and Thad claimed that they hadn't known Gen knew about them, but perhaps they were lying. He didn't know. But he knew the photos made him damned uncomfortable.

His desk phone rang.

"Hawk, you've got some folks here to talk to you. About that missing woman. They say they are her parents."

Damn it. He looked at the clock. It was 3:00 p.m. He was scheduled to meet with Gen and Meg's parents. Time had gotten away from him.

He went to retrieve them, and found a travel-weary older couple in the waiting room. Meg was with them.

"It's good to meet you," Mitch McCready shook his hand firmly.

His daughters had his eyes, Hawk noticed.

"Can you tell us what is happening?" his wife, Ginny, asked. "Meg says there's been no leads and no explanations, and that doesn't make sense at all. You should look at Thad. Are you investigating him? He was cheating on my daughter." Ginny's cheeks flashed hot, and Mitch grasped her shoulders.

"Calm down, Gin," he murmured to her. "The man is trying to help."

"Come on back," Hawk told them. "I'll tell you where we are at."

He guided them back to his office and Meg trailed behind. Her perfume was soft and flowery, a breath of fresh air in the stale police station.

When the McCreadys were seated, he poured them coffee. Meg declined with a grimace.

Dishwater.

The corner of his mouth unwillingly twitched. Meg noticed and smiled. An inside joke, however small.

"Well, Detective," Ginny said, politely now. "Are you looking into Thad? I'm telling you, anyone who would do what he did... He was so coldhearted. I can't begin to fathom it. Anyone who would do that deserves some examination, I think."

She stared at Hawk without flinching, although Meg did. Behind her mother, Meg's face burned hot and red. Thankfully, her father wasn't an observant man, and her mother's back was turned. She exhaled slowly, once, then twice.

Above her mother's head, Meg caught Hawk's eye. *Please don't tell her.* It was as if she were speaking out loud. Her eyes were blue and pleading, and Hawk looked away. He'd already said he wouldn't say anything unless he had to. Jesus.

He found himself hoping, though, that the McCreadys didn't ask.

He didn't want to let her down.

It was a kick to the gut when he realized it.

He didn't want to let Meghan McCready, a suspect in his active missing-persons case, down. His pulse quickened, then raced. This wasn't a complication he needed in his life. This wasn't professional, and he was always, always professional. Black-and-white, neat and tidy.

"Yes, Mrs. McCready. We are currently investigating every avenue, looking at every angle." He was pretty sure Meg flinched again. He continued, "I promise you, I'll do my best to find your daughter."

Ginny searched the detective's eyes, hunting for sincerity. She'd been on this earth for over sixty years, and she knew when smoke was being blown up her ass. It wasn't now. The detective was telling the truth. She relaxed.

"Did Meg tell you everything about Gen?" Ginny hesitated. "Do you have everything you need to know?"

"Mom, yes." Meg was impatient now, annoyed. "I've been here for the past two weeks. I've been through everything with him. You can send him her dental records to examine if you want."

As soon as she said that, everyone froze.

The police often used dental records to identify a body.

Meg blinked and swallowed hard.

"That's not what I meant," she stammered. Her mother looked away pointedly.

"I can have them sent to you," Ginny told him. "But let's hope it's never necessary."

Hawk shook her hand gently. "We're doing everything we can, Mrs. McCready. But I do have an important question."

Meg's stare penetrated deep into his, but he didn't look at her.

"Do you have any idea where Gen's laptop is? It's not at the hotel, it's not at her apartment in Chicago, and Thad says it's not at the condo."

"That's strange. She never went anywhere without it," her mother replied. "Maybe she took it with her."

"No. I was there when she left. She just said she was going out for some fresh air." Meg shook her head. "It was nighttime. She didn't take her laptop. She just grabbed her purse and then my coat when I reminded her it was chilly out."

"Maybe it was in her purse?" Ginny suggested. But Meg was already shaking her head again.

"No. Her purse was small. Way too small."

"Then I don't know what to tell you," Ginny answered. "All I know is, I can't imagine she left that laptop."

"Okay, then. I'll let you know when I know anything more," Hawk assured her, and handed them each a card. He escorted them back to the waiting room and only curtly acknowledged Meg when she said goodbye.

He felt her staring at him, like electricity snaking on top of water. He turned sharply and returned to his desk. When she was gone, he felt alone.

Jesus. He needed to stop.

He sifted through the file again, and as he was halfway through, his phone rang. He answered, and it was an account manager from the Black Heron Insurance Company. Yesterday, when Hawk was going through the Thibaults' joint bank statement, he'd found a couple payments to the insurance company, beginning just two months ago. Since Thad and Gen had both health insurance and life insurance from another company, it caught Hawk's eye. Interested, he'd put a call in.

"Detective Hawkins?" the man on the other end asked.

"Speaking."

"This is James Aberdean over at Black Heron returning your call. I'm sorry for the tardiness, I just had to look up the account information," he said.

And confirm the warrant, Hawk thought, annoyed.

"Anyway, I looked it up. Genevieve Thibault has a life insurance policy through us," James told the detective. "For quite a hefty amount, too."

"How much?"

"Five million dollars."

"Shit. That *is* a lot. When was this policy taken out?"

"Let me see," James said, his fingers clicking on a keyboard. "Two months ago."

Hawk's breathing went quiet. His fingers stopped drumming the desk.

"And the beneficiary?"

"Thaddeus Thibault."

Motherfucker.

Hawk hung up, and he shouldn't have been surprised. *It's always the spouse.* He rolled his eyes, thinking back to the academy and all the years he'd been on the force. Seemed like nine out of ten times it was the spouse.

Which meant…it wasn't Meg, unless they were in on it together.

He wasn't going to reflect on how much that relieved him.

Instead, he grabbed a jacket and headed for the Aristotle.

When he got there, he rode the elevator up directly to Thad's room.

Thad answered almost immediately, dressed in jeans and a black slim sweater, ever snobby.

"Can I come in?" Hawk asked.

Thad nodded and pulled the door open widely.

Hawk strode in, noting the neat hotel room. Stacks of files were on the bed. They appeared to be client files. Hawk looked closer just to make sure—but none of them appeared to be about Gen. Thad wasn't trying to investigate on his own. He wasn't sure if he was surprised or not.

"Can you tell me about the life insurance policy you recently took out on your wife?" Hawk asked stiffly. Thad's head snapped up, his eyebrows knit.

"I don't know what you're talking about," he answered. "I didn't."

"Yet, there is one," Hawk replied. "You're the beneficiary. I just spoke with the insurance agent. In the event of Genevieve's death, you will receive five-million dollars."

"That might be so," Thad answered slowly. "But I don't know anything about it, and I certainly didn't take the policy out."

"Then who did? For a policy so large, the monthly payments were hefty. No one would want to pay that kind of money unless they were invested in the situation. Also, the payments came out of your account."

Thad sat in the chair at the desk, and he stared up at the detective.

"I swear to you, I didn't take that policy out."

"Is there anything else you want to tell me?" Hawk asked him. "Because now would be the time. You're not looking too good, friend."

"There's nothing else to tell you," Thad answered. "I'm not involved in this. I've stayed in New York to answer your questions, and I've done everything you've asked. I'll take a lie-detector test, if you want, although you and I both know it's not admissible in court. But I'll take one anyway. I'm that confident it would be in my favor."

"Fine. Be at the station tomorrow at ten. I'll set it up."

Thad stuttered an agreement, not expecting Hawk to be able to pull it together so quickly. Hawk smirked just a little.

"I'm efficient."

"I guess."

Hawk left, closing the door firmly behind him, walking through the quiet hotel halls. He considered going up the two floors to talk to Meg, but there was no real reason to. So, by the book, he punched the down button.

When the doors opened on the ground floor, he strode through the lobby out the front door and barreled directly into someone.

It was a woman, who had now fallen backward toward the wet ground. He lunged to grab her, but not in time. She made contact, spilling on the sidewalk in a cloud of blond hair.

He knelt to help her up, and Meg's blue eyes stared back at him.

Damn it.

47

Gen, Then

GEN'S AGENT WAS on the phone, her voice pleasant, as always, but there was something else there. Anxiety? Was she worried the book wouldn't get done?

"Don't worry," Gen assuaged. "I'm a professional, Karen. I've changed directions, and I think I might be bridging another genre with this one, but it will be done. Soon."

"Wait. Gen. Another genre?" Karen's voice was thin now, like fragile ice on a newly frozen pond. Any movement and it could break. "We can't just switch genres for a signed book, Gen. Your publisher paid for the book you outlined. The romance."

"This book *has* romance," Gen assured her, pacing circles in the living room. It was her new thing. She loved the comfort of it, the ritualistic feel of monotonous circles. It allowed her mind to run. "It's just darker than usual. Don't worry. You'll love it."

"I'm not worried about me," she said limply. "I love everything you write. I'm worried about *them*."

"They'll love it, too," Gen told her. "Trust me."

They hung up, and Gen paced nearer to her open laptop.

She glanced at the page, at the blinking cursor. It was waiting for her to continue, to figure out new ways to exact revenge.

Her character's name was Melanie, which sounded close enough to Meghan, she thought. And her lover's name was Thomas. Her sister was a sweet girl named Georgia. Melanie, Meghan. Thad, Thomas. Genevieve, Georgia. She singsonged the names in her head as she thought. She had to think of something else to do to them. In the first part of the book, she'd destroyed Thomas's business. He deserved it, really. He was a cad.

Poor Georgia was the victim. It wasn't her fault they'd played her for a fool. So when she'd planted a bug in the ear of Thomas's partner about him stealing from the company, it had snowballed into a giant lawsuit, where at the end Thomas would lose everything. He didn't know it yet, and it certainly wouldn't happen until after he paid sweet Georgia's payoff when the divorce was finalized. Thomas loved his company more than he loved anything else in the world, so when it came down in shambles around him, he would be broken, and justly so.

Because to be fair, the bug in his partner's ear wouldn't mean a thing unless it was based on fact. And last year, in a lapse of judgment, Thomas had withdrawn company funds and hadn't recorded it. It would come back to bite him in just deserts.

Melanie, though. Her revenge took some thought.

Gen had paced for hours upon hours coming up with it.

Melanie was straitlaced when it came to her job. She up-held the rules. She never prescribed things for friends. She never diagnosed things that weren't accurate. There wasn't a thing Gen could think of for that. So, she'd have to think of something else.

It was only fair.

Melanie had committed the ultimate betrayal.

Thomas had broken his wife's heart, but Melanie had gone beyond that. She had shattered blood ties, and that wasn't right. That deserved more than ruining a career.

Gen was still pondering that when Jenkins knocked on her door. She'd been expecting him. They were going to lunch.

She opened the door, and greeted him with a kiss on the cheek. It had become her custom with him. He was like the grandfather she didn't have.

"Jenks!" she said. "I'm famished." She grabbed her purse and pushed past him.

Jenkins hadn't moved, so she turned to him, confused. "Are you coming?"

"As soon as you put on pants," he told her, amused.

Aghast, Gen looked down, and sure enough, she had never put on pants this morning. She was wearing a T-shirt and underwear.

"Shit. In my defense, I'm knee-deep in this book. I've got to turn it in soon, or I'll be in breach of contract. So I've been in fiction-world all morning."

She laughed over her shoulder and hurried to the bedroom to pull on some jeans.

Jenkins didn't seem offended, nor had he looked at her in any way other than fatherly. But he was concerned.

"You're a gentleman, you know that?" she asked him as

she locked her door. "You didn't look at me twice when I was only half-clothed."

"Well, twenty years ago I might've. I'm old now."

"You aren't," she argued. "Where are we eating today?"

"Hot dogs?" Jenkins suggested, knowing full well Gen loved grabbing dogs from the street vendor and eating them in the park. So that's what they did. Once they were seated at a bench, Gen watched joggers flying past and started musing out loud.

"I'm stuck in my plotline," she told Jenkins. "My agent is breathing down my neck to get this book turned in, and I changed it a few months ago, so I'm behind."

"Well, you're a professional," he pointed out. "You can do it."

"I'm just… I'm trying to think of a retaliation plot," she answered. "It's not really my normal jam, so I've had to think hard. Do you have any interesting stories from your years as a PI?"

Jenkins laughed at that. "Gen, the things I've seen would curl your toes."

"Tell me," she urged him, drawing her knees up to her chest as she waited. "I'm in desperate need of some inspiration."

"Oh, Lord," he shook his head. "Let me think. Well, I had a nurse who was claiming that she was injured on the job. Her medical center hired me, and I found out that she was stripping in her free time. So clearly her back wasn't an issue."

"Not if she could wind her body around a stripper's pole," Gen agreed.

"I had another case where a wife thought her husband was stepping out. He came home several times a week smelling like strange perfume."

"And, was he?"

"No. He was taking dance lessons to surprise her with."

"Awww. That's so sweet. I wish more men were like that."

Jenkins humphed at that, seeing how he was a man. Gen glanced at him. "You know you're always excluded from my derision of the male species."

"Okay," Jenkins told her. "I'm not worried about it."

He was accustomed to her anger at men, and in fact, he thought it was normal at this juncture. He'd been around many wronged women, and they always went through an anger phase.

"Gen," he said, casually now. "When will you sign the divorce papers? Thad has sent you several versions, and you keep sending them back."

Gen shrugged. "It annoys him. He wants it all done quickly, and why should I make it easy for him?"

"I thought you were ready to be rid of him?"

"Oh, I am. I just want a little revenge first. I want him to sweat."

"But when you sign, and it's finalized, he's going to pay you a lot of money."

"You're not supposed to know that," she reminded him. "It's part of my settlement with him. I can't tell anyone."

"I won't say anything," Jenkins replied. "You know that."

She did. She trusted him.

"I don't know when I'll sign," she admitted finally. "I just like having the control in this situation. He can't move on until I sign. It serves him right if I drag it on for months. Maybe I'll wait a year."

"Don't do that," Jenkins cautioned. "You need to move on, too. You're too focused on him right now, Gen."

Which was the real reason he kept coming to visit her. She spent her days obsessed with her anger. Her paintings, which she'd hung in her hallway in the apartment, were angry shades of red and black, furious slashes of paint splattering the canvas. He didn't know a thing about art, but even he could see that.

After their hot dogs, they had a little walk, and Gen sucked in the fresh air. If she was to finish this book, she needed her circulation going. She knelt and gave a duck the last bit of her bun. She'd saved it just for this.

"You know, they say nowadays that you're not supposed to feed them bread," Jenkins told her. "It swells up in their bellies, or something. They can't digest it."

Startled, Gen stood up. "Well, damn. I wonder how many ducks I've accidentally killed in my life?"

"I doubt you've killed any," Jenkins assured her.

"God, I hope not." The very thought filled her with panic. She didn't want to hurt a helpless little creature.

They walked back toward Gen's apartment complex, and they paused in front of the doors.

Jenkins looked down at her. "Gen, I think you need to consider signing the papers, and being done with this."

"That's exactly what Meg says." Gen screwed up her face. "She just wants to move on with Thad herself. Poor Joe. I don't know what he's going to do."

"Joe will take care of himself," Jenkins said. "You said their relationship isn't that great anyway."

"It's not. Because of Meg. He deserves wayyyy better than her," Gen told him.

"She's still your sister, you know," Jenkins reminded her.

"Then she should act like it." Annoyed, she leaned up to kiss Jenkins's cheek. "See you soon, Jenks."

As she was turning to go inside, the condo manager noticed her on his way out and stopped.

"Ms. McCready," he said, and Jenkins paused to listen.

"We will be sending a maintenance man in to take care of your hot water heater this afternoon."

"Thank you, Dan," she answered.

The manager smiled and continued on his way, and Gen turned slowly, knowing full well that Jenkins would be waiting.

"I was still Gen McCready when I bought this place years ago. I never changed it."

"It doesn't make much difference, really," Jenkins pointed out.

Once inside the apartment, he looked at the photo of Meg on the wall. "You certainly do look alike," he mused.

Gen smiled. "I'm banking on that."

Jenkins stared at her, and the look on her face was unnerving.

48

Meg, Now

HAWK HELPED MEG to her feet, his hand grasping hers.

"Let's get inside," she said, and she tried to take a step, but faltered. "Ow."

She tried to turn her ankle to test it but winced.

Hawk didn't hesitate. With rain pelting them like hail, he scooped her up and carried her into the building. He set her gently down, and while they dripped onto the marble lobby floor, he examined her foot.

"It's already swelling," he told her. "You need some ice. Let's go."

He wrapped his arm around her shoulders, and she looped hers around his waist. He helped her hobble to the elevator and then limp into her room.

"Sit here." Hawk lowered her onto the bed. "I'll get you some ice packs." Kneeling, he found the extra small trash sacks in the bottom of the trash can by the bed, and went to fill them with ice. He returned a few minutes later.

"Very ingenious," Meg told him, as she pressed them around her throbbing foot.

"I solve problems," he quipped. "It's what I do."

She sucked in a breath as the ice chilled her skin. Hawk winced.

"I'm sorry," he told her sincerely. "I didn't mean to plow into you."

"Well, that's good. Here I was thinking you'd done it on purpose."

Their laughter was almost nervous.

"Are your parents staying here at this hotel, too?"

Meg nodded. "On a lower floor."

"As far from you as possible?" he guessed.

She smiled. "Something like that."

"How are they handling this?" Hawk asked her. "It seems like your father is holding it together."

"Yeah. My dad is an old battle tank. Unflappable. My mother, though…"

"Yeah," Hawk agreed. They laughed again, softer now.

"Hey, about…well, everything. It really bothers me that you might think the worst of me," Meg told him. "I know it looks bad, and I wish I could put into words everything that has led me to this point, but that's impossible. I just really, *really* hope that you're able to see the good in me, as well."

Hawk swallowed hard, because there was no way he was going to let her know what he'd been seeing in her, or how often he'd thought of her.

"I'm very good at seeing through the bullshit to a person's true nature," he told her gruffly instead. "That's my job."

"Okay."

"There's a life insurance policy on Gen. A large one. Thad is the beneficiary. And it was just taken out recently."

"Oh, my God. That's… Oh, my God."

"I just found out that you are a secondary beneficiary."

She froze.

"How… That… It doesn't make sense," she stammered. "I didn't. I have no reason to do that, Hawk. I swear to God."

"So you don't know how you and Thad are beneficiaries on a large life insurance policy. That's a little convenient."

"I think it's a little *too* convenient, Hawk. Both Thad and I are intelligent people. If we'd done this, we'd never have left tracks like that. I've watched enough *NCIS* in my life to know that much."

"Do you know how often someone has told me *if I had done this, I wouldn't have…* Fill in the blank. Intelligent people often say that. As you just said, you and Thad are both intelligent. If you'll excuse me, I have work to do."

Hawk left abruptly, without another word.

Meg sat limply on the bed, her ankle throbbing and pulse racing. Trembling, she picked up the phone to call Thad.

She rattled off to him quickly, and he was silent on the other end.

"I thought you didn't know about it," Thad said stiffly, uncertain.

"I didn't."

"The insurance company needed our social security numbers to list us."

"We know each other's social security number."

"Do I want to ask why?"

"When we were on a road trip with our parents once when we were kids, we spent the time memorizing our numbers," she answered. "Aloud. We were bored."

"Normal kids play the alphabet game, or spot the tag."

"We don't get to claim we're normal at this point," Meg pointed out. "Why did you take out such a large insurance policy? You've been in the process of a divorce for months."

"I didn't."

"That doesn't make sense," Meg answered. "You're the only one who would benefit. I know that I personally didn't do it."

"Well, therein lies the mystery," Thad replied.

Neither of them were comfortable, although this didn't feel like Thad to Meg.

"You sound so cold," she said, and she was truly bewildered. "I don't understand how you're holding it together."

"I'm not cold," he answered. "I'm tired. I'm just bone-fucking weary, Meg. This has been such a long ordeal, and it's ending up just how it started—a mess."

"Your entire marriage wasn't a mess," Meg told him, indignant on her sister's behalf. "Gen was good to you. I can dig out your wedding photos if you want. You were happy in them. You were happy on that day."

"Any situation where the husband loves his sister-in-law is a mess," Thad said, and he did, in fact, sound weary. "Particularly when that husband is a good man deep down."

Meg couldn't argue with that. She did believe he was a good man, which was why the life insurance was messing with her head.

"Did you think she'd kill herself?" she asked, trying to make sense of it. "Is that why you took it out?"

"Meg, first, most insurance policies don't pay out in case of suicide," Thad told her. "Second, I didn't take that policy out. I don't know how many times I need to say it."

"Would she have taken it out herself? Maybe she…maybe she didn't want to live anymore." The words seemed to carve little pieces out of her heart.

"You think we devastated her so much that she wanted to die, and not only that, she wanted to make sure I was rich in the process?"

As Thad said the words out loud, Meg heard how ridiculous they sounded.

"Okay, you're right," she admitted.

"But you're making me think," he said, his tone picking up. "What if she wanted us to turn on each other, as sort of a revenge thing? She wasn't happy, so she would want to make sure we weren't happy, either."

"That would explain why she never confronted us," Meg answered slowly, running the scenario through her mind, scene by scene. "She wanted to take us apart, brick by brick. Revenge."

"You know if she was in her right mind, she wouldn't do that," Thad said. "But she wasn't. She was stretched thin, and this whole thing took a toll." His voice trailed off, as they both thought about the possibility.

"If that's the case, then she ran away," Meg said aloud. "She's somewhere right now, laughing at us."

"It would be devious," Thad said.

"Like you said, she was devastated," Meg answered.

Although they didn't say it aloud, they were both thinking a similar thought: a wounded animal was dangerous.

49

Jenkins, Now

JENKINS POKED HIS hand back up in Gen's bathroom ceiling. When Gen had given him a spare key, he'd guffawed and told her it would never be necessary. But she'd insisted, citing that she might lose her own etc., and he'd finally agreed, in the capacity of her friend, not her private investigator. He was glad of that now.

That New York detective didn't seem to be getting anywhere with Gen's disappearance. He felt he needed to step in and do something.

Gen didn't deserve this. It had dragged on long enough.

He pulled the journal out again and took a seat in the living room.

Her apartment felt so haunted now, her paintings so very sad. The collage she'd made of Thad and Meg was disturbing, or at least it would be if he didn't know Gen. She was the kindest soul in Chicago—he'd stake his life on that.

He skipped over the strange, sad drawings and read through more of the words. Some were neatly printed, but most were scrawled, large and loopy. He could tell from entry to entry which ones she was drinking and which ones she wasn't.

Thad spent a lot of time on his phone tonight. I don't know why, because Meg is away for work. So who was he talking to? Is there someone else?? If so, I'll need to get Jenkins on it.

She'd never said anything, so it must've resolved itself.

Meg lied to my face tonight. She said she was going to a movie with her friends, and I know for a fact that she's with Thad. He's working late again, yet his assistant told me he left early.

Jenkins and I had hot dogs today. Becky sent home chocolate muffins for me, because she knows I love them. They're such good people. I'm so lucky. I wonder if Thad will be home soon?

The next few pages were drawings, and they contained bloody images and a picture of a bullet, then another entry.

Jenkins didn't notice that I took one of his guns out of his closet tonight. We played bridge with Becky. I don't know how to use it, but I'll figure it out. There are probably videos on YouTube. I told him that I'm buying a gun. It just feels like the right thing to do. I'm tired. So tired. I don't want to be this way anymore.

Jenkins's head snapped up, and he called his wife immediately.

"Becky, look in the guest-room closet," he told her quickly. "How many guns are there?"

"Just a minute," she told him and he heard her walking through the house. The floor creaked by the guest-room door, and he heard her open the closet. "Well, let's see. There's a shotgun, your .44 Mag and your Kimber .45."

"What about the Beretta?"

Becky rifled through the boxes of ammunition and head-phones. "No. It's not here."

Gen had taken his 9 mm.

"Thanks," he mumbled to his wife, and hung up.

What had Gen wanted with a gun? Did she run away and use it on herself?

Diary, life is a blur of faces and names. I want to paint it all, but how do you paint a person without a face? The Amish do it, I guess. But I'm not Amish and it feels weird.

Why do I still love Thad? It's crazy, and I'm broken.

I'm not normal.

My sister wants my ring, I can tell. Isn't that weird? Isn't it enough that she has taken my whole life? She told me today that it's the prettiest thing she's ever seen. Who would want someone else's ring? It's cursed. Whoever wears it will be cursed to a life of misery.

Maybe I'll leave it for her, and run far from here, into the ocean, and I'll never look back.

Does dying hurt?

Or do you close your eyes and you wake up in Heaven?

He says he'll do it, but I don't know and I don't trust him. We'll see, I guess. You can't count on anyone.

Damn it. Last time Jenkins had read this journal, he'd read just the one section on this page, the one about Meg want-ing Gen's ring, and had run with it. He'd closed the book without looking further.

He'd been filled with enough agitation toward Meg, enough that when he first heard about Gen's disappearance on the news, he'd tried to call Meg. He'd wanted to offer to help, but when she answered, he couldn't bring himself to speak to her. All he could think about were the photos he'd taken of that woman with Gen's husband.

So, instead, he tracked Meg down. He'd found out she was staying at the Aristotle in New York, which was easy enough to do—she really should have a talk with her staff about confidentiality—and he flew there.

He was just entering the hotel when he saw several staff members combing through the landscaping outside. He listened to their conversation. *Some lady threw her wedding ring off her balcony. It's worth a lot of money. She's missing now!*

Jenkins had been so focused on protecting Gen that he hadn't realized how unhinged she had actually become from this whole divorce thing.

Maybe he should've reached out to Meg long ago, to share his concerns.

Now Gen had his gun. And she was obsessed with revenge.

Nothing good could come out of any of this.

50

Meg, Now

"**MEGHAN DIANE**, I'm not saying you didn't look through Gen's things. I'm just saying that I want to, as well."

Meg sighed in exasperation and pursed her lips. She didn't say another word as her mom disturbed all of the carefully laid out articles Meg had taken from Gen's bag.

"How you girls wear these lacy uncomfortable bras, I don't know," her mom clucked, folding things and putting them back in the bag as she went along.

"Mom, leave it out. Just in case it triggers something. A clue, or a thought, or *something*," Meg told her.

"Your sister's panties are not going to trigger a thing," Ginny answered sternly. "Everyone doesn't need to see them."

"Everyone? Who in the world do you think I have in my room?" Meg demanded. "No one. Just… Fine. Do what you like." Meg rolled her eyes.

Ginny continued looking, and like Meg, she came up without answers.

Her eyes were red as she sat limply, and Meg realized that her mother was being even more annoying than usual because she was scared. She put an arm around Ginny's shoulders.

"It will be okay," she told her mom. Ginny patted her hand.

"I know it will. But your father is worried."

Meg rolled her eyes again. This time because of the tired old routine her mom always did... She worried about everything, and blamed it on her dad.

Your father worries, she always said.

Meg played with the edge of Gen's toiletry kit. It was Burberry, very classy, very expensive. It was also unlike Gen. It was more something that Meg would buy. Gen preferred to be artsy, original. She didn't like to reside inside a box, which was what she considered name brands.

Without thinking, she pulled the zipper open and peered inside. She hadn't looked closely last time, because it was all the usual suspects you'd find in a toiletry bag. Small toothpaste, small mouthwash, travel toothbrush, moisturizer, perfume.

Her gaze shifted back to the perfume bottle.

Her belly in her throat, she turned it over.

Vanilla musk.

Her gaze met her mother's, her heart pounding.

"Gen only wears that perfume when she's upset."

Meg nodded. Yes, she knew. It wasn't unusual. She was upset. They all knew it.

Gen had such an artist's heart. She always had. She'd always succumbed to the maudlin, the darkness. She embraced it. When her heart rained, she wanted her surroundings to rain, too. It had made growing up with her difficult. And being married to her difficult, too. She truly couldn't fault Thad completely.

Yet, he'd known what he was getting into when he married her.

Had it all become too much?

Hawk had gone for a vigorous jog that morning. He was dripping wet when the phone in his armband buzzed with the station's number.

The cop at reception told him that Simon Jenkins was there to see him, and was planning on waiting until Hawk showed up. With a groan, Hawk headed straight for the station. He had a spare set of clothes hanging in his locker, so he'd shower there after.

Traffic was a nightmare, and Hawk's cab got stuck twice, so it was well over an hour before he arrived. He was sweatier now than when he'd started, thanks to a cabbie who didn't believe in air-conditioning.

He strode in, and sure enough, Jenkins was standing near the desk, waiting, and not quietly. The desk cop looked pleadingly at Hawk, and the detective sighed.

"Hello, Mr. Jenkins," he said politely to the older man. He'd seen it before, these washed-up older PIs who got attached to their cases. They lost their edge, and so they got sucked into the emotional aspect.

"It's about time," Jenkins grumbled. "I've got something to give you."

Hawk waited.

"It's *information*," Jenkins told him. "Let's head back to your desk."

Hawk led the way, and Jenkins scrunched up his face.

"You do need a shower," he advised as they entered the bullpen. "In my day, we wore ties to work, too."

"You a retired cop?" Hawk asked, gesturing to the empty seat next to his desk.

"Yes," Jenkins answered without giving details. Instead, he reached into his jacket and pulled out a pink journal.

Hawk took it.

"You told me once to find the answers in a pink journal," he said slowly. "Is this it?"

Jenkins nodded. "Yeah. I figured you'd find it by now."

"You knew where it was the whole time?" Hawk was taken aback, and Jenkins held up his hand.

"Yeah, but I only wanted to make sure you'd do your part to find Gennie. I thought she'd been taken. But now... Well, now I don't know. This journal makes it look like several things were going on, but one of them is... It makes it sound like Gen wanted to run away and hurt herself. She stole one of my guns."

Hawk sucked in a breath, but Jenkins was already shaking his head.

"I didn't know that part before. And I would never have thought she'd run away or hurt herself. I know her. But now there's something else. She wasn't in her right mind. This journal shows a clear progression—she was coming unhinged. I fear an actual mental break. She's prone to dramatics anyway, but all of this... It can take a toll on someone."

Hawk riffled through the pages quickly, and his eyes narrowed at some of the entries.

"It does look like she wanted to hurt herself," Hawk agreed. "She also was extremely angry with her sister."

"That's why I'm here. Wherever she is, I don't think she's safe. She's a danger to herself. Maybe even to Meghan. I don't know."

"Exactly how close were the two of you?" Hawk asked him now, staring at him hard.

"It wasn't like that," Jenkins said quickly. "I have a soft spot for her. My wife does, too. She's like a lost bird."

"I really thought it was abduction," Hawk said aloud. "Someone kept trying to call Meg, and it threw me off."

"That was probably me," Jenkins said, embarrassed. "I didn't have the whole picture. I was taking Gen's word, and then later, I tried to call Meg but hung up. I shouldn't have."

"Jesus, do you understand that you've thrown off this investigation?" Hawk asked incredulously. "As a former cop, you should've known better."

"I let my emotions get the best of me." Jenkins shrugged. "You can lecture me after we find Gen."

"You're not going to help," Hawk told him. "You've proven what your *help* does."

"Good luck trying to shut me out," Jenkins told him cheerfully. "I'm a PI. I'm used to cops not wanting me around."

"You're a PI, all right," Hawk said. "Did you ever figure out that the *other Ms. Thibault* was Thad's sister? He wasn't having an affair with someone else at all."

Jenkins froze. "What?"

"He's a caretaker for his sister. He wasn't having an affair. Maybe you should've dug deeper."

Jenkins's mouth opened, then closed, and his gaze wavered. Then he got up and walked out.

Hawk bristled and texted Meg.

I need to see you. Meet me at the coffee shop.

Meg arrived first this time, and she had coffee waiting for him. It steamed above the cup, and Hawk stared at it as he sat down.

"I've got something."

He slid the journal across the table, and Meg picked it up,

flipping through the pages. Hawk patiently drank his coffee while Meg took her time. He watched her eyes flitting from line to line.

"Son of a bitch," Meg breathed, without taking her eyes from the page.

Hawk stayed quiet.

Meg's fingers moved fast, flip, flip, flipping, and when she finally hit the last of it, she sat back in her seat with a thump.

"She stole his gun?" she asked in a very thin voice. "The PI. Have you talked to him?"

"Yes. He's the one who gave me this journal. He seemed to be under the impression that she would never hurt herself, but that now she's unhinged. He says he watched the progression of her anger turn into something more akin to unbalanced rage. He thought it would be okay, but now he's not so sure."

Meg didn't seem surprised. "My sister has always been mercurial," she said. "Even in the best times. I just... I can't believe she hated me so much. I don't know how she hid it so well. She can't usually."

"She usually tells you when she hates you?" Hawk lifted an eyebrow and Meg rolled her eyes impatiently.

"No. She's never hated me before. I meant, she can't usually hide her feelings that way. She doesn't have the self-control, never has."

"You make her sound like a child," Hawk observed. "Yet, I know you love her."

"I do," Meg agreed.

"So, you think she could've been out of control," Hawk said, urging her. "She's certainly unhinged on these pages. There's no denying that."

"My sister can be very fragile. She's always been that way. My parents spoiled her, but she's just...very dramatic. Very emotional. When she's upset, she immerses herself in it. There's no controlling her."

"So you believe she was out of control," Hawk repeated, not believing what he was hearing. "And you're only just now telling me."

Meg nodded somberly. "Yes. She only wears vanilla perfume when she's very upset. We found it in her bag. I just realized it today."

Hawk stared at her with this newfound knowledge.

Gen might have serious issues, and she was out of control.

This changed everything.

God only knew who was in danger.

51

Gen, Then

GENEVIEVE'S CELL PHONE RANG, and she paused while peeling an orange. It was the therapist Lila's office. *Again.* Jesus, when would they stop calling?

She answered it.

"Yes?"

"Mrs. Thibault?" The voice on the other end was uncertain. Gen laughed.

"Yes."

"Well, um, I'm calling for Lila Bernstein."

"Okay."

"Yes. She...uh, wanted me to call and see if you could please come back in. She was very concerned at your last session and definitely wants to see you again. Have you found another doctor?"

Genevieve took the easy road. "Yes, I've found a psychiatrist," she lied, throwing most of the orange away. "My husband and I are getting divorced, and I want a completely new start. I'm moving away, and so, I had to find another doctor. I know that I'm in a bad place, and I figure I need a doctor, not a therapist."

"Oh." The person sounded relieved, and Gen rolled her eyes. "Good. Okay. Well, we wish you the best of luck, Mrs. Thibault."

"Thank you." Genevieve hung up and chewed on her pen. What-the-fuck-ever. Fucking therapists. They kept you coming back for more, more, more so they could pad their bank accounts, and nothing ever changed. They were all money-grubbers who worked for insurance companies. She should know. Thad had her seeing one years ago.

Fuck them all.

She perched on the counter, her bare toes hanging off the edge. She was wearing a nightgown that she'd been wearing for days. Jenkins had come yesterday, but she hadn't answered the door.

He was starting to act like a babysitter.

She'd had enough.

It was time.

She just needed to figure out how she would do it and when, and it would all be over.

She was so goddamned tired.

She closed her eyes and felt the beat of the music. She'd been playing this same album from The Doors over and over, feeling the bass, feeling the deep tones of Jim Morrison's voice all the way in her core.

Life was pain. Jim understood that.

She rocked and rocked, and then hopped down and painted. She used her fingers, and used red paint as the medium. It was red like blood, red like rubies. She wished it glittered.

She didn't know what made it pop into her mind, but she was tracing the outline of a giant red eye when it occurred to her.

She should be receiving the newest set of divorce papers today. Thad had texted last night. They'd be delivered to the condo.

With a sigh, she wiped her hands on her nightgown, streaking it with red.

Blood red.

Without getting dressed, she grabbed her purse, and meandered down the street to the condo. People stared at her, but she didn't notice. She didn't realize her blond hair was stringy, and she looked like she'd been in an accident.

In fact, at one street corner, someone approached her.

"Ma'am, are you all right?" the woman asked hesitantly.

Gen smiled widely. "Yes, I'm perfect."

She sang a Doors song the rest of the way. "Hello, I Love You."

When the doorman at the condominium opened the door for her, she crooned a lyric of the song at him.

He gawked. She was oblivious.

She'd only been in the condo for thirty minutes when there was a knock.

Peering through the peephole, she saw a delivery guy in a uniform. Perfect.

Genevieve tipped the courier and set the certified letter on the coffee table.

She knew what it was. She'd been waiting for it for almost a week.

Every day, she'd wondered, *Will it be today?*

And each day it wasn't.

Until today. Never mind that she had sent it back five times before. This was the one. This was the time.

Nervous energy buzzed through her fingers and toes, tingling through her veins, like ants scurrying in a thousand directions. She paced for a minute, stopping at the floor-to-ceiling windows, staring at the magnificent cityscape lining the horizon. Buildings burst through the hazy pollution, their tips scraping the clouds.

People far below her were bustling here and there, quick to walk, slow to linger. They had things to do, places to be, and she didn't.

Not anymore.

She ripped open the envelope, pulling the banded documents out, scanning through the words, hunting for the official stamps and signatures that declared this an official act of the court.

They were all there.

This was real.

It was finally happening.

She focused her gaze on the words before her.

The black-and-whiteness of them was stark and startling. There were no gray areas, no areas open to interpretation.

They reduced the last ten years of her life into a handful of legal phrases and technical terms. *Incompatible differences associated with adultery, marriage dissolution* and *absolute divorce*.

She stared at the words.

Soon, she would be *absolutely divorced*.

It had only taken six months of her life to iron out the details. To separate all of their worldly possessions into two camps, his and hers, to figure out who got what. Divorcing a lawyer was the only thing worse than being married to one. Regardless that he was the one in err, because he repeatedly fucked someone else, he was out for blood and it took months to sort it all out.

But thank God no children were involved.

That's what people kept saying, like it was a good thing or a blessing.

But if she'd had a child, she wouldn't be all alone, and someone would still love her.

Fuck Thad, and fuck Meg. Fuck them both. Fuck them sideways. Fuck the other woman. Fuck them all.

She felt like she was floundering. For so long, she'd put all of her energy into a man who hadn't deemed her worthy to stay faithful to. That had done something to her self-confidence. Plus, he'd kept telling her she needed medication, and wanted her to change.

What kind of person wanted his wife to change?

She was perfect as she was.

Wasn't that what all the self-help books preached? *Love yourself. You are perfect.*

She wasn't Genevieve Thibault anymore, one half of a whole. She was Genevieve McCready again. She shared a last name with her liar of a sister again. Damn it. Why the hell couldn't Meg have taken her husband's name?

Ah, well. It wouldn't matter soon.

Nothing would.

She had a plan and it was time.

She just had to have the courage to do it.

She went into the kitchen, rinsed her coffee cup and picked up the phone and called Meghan.

"Meg, I'm moving home."

Her sister paused. "Home as in...?"

"Cedarburg." There was a long pause now.

"Um. Why would you want to move back to Wisconsin? You haven't lived there in..."

"In eighteen years. Since I left for college. Yes."

"But...why?"

"I don't know," Gen lied. "I just feel a need to get back to my roots. I love Chicago, but the traffic and the noise..."

I need to run. Why doesn't anyone understand? She stared out from her twentieth floor windows again. Even from up here, even though the vehicles looked like Matchbox cars, she could still hear the honking. "This feels like Thad. I want to feel like *me*."

"There's nothing there," Meg said carefully. "Nothing but fields and cold and—"

"And friendly people," Gen interrupted. "And our parents, and familiarity, and open spaces, and distance from Thad."

"But I won't be there," Meg reminded her. "I'm not moving back. I think you need to be near me, Gen. You need a support system. Divorce is no joke."

"I know that," Gen said patiently. "I'm the one living it. You're still with your Prince Charming and point five children living the American Dream, and I'm the one sitting in an empty condo."

And you have my husband, too, you cheating whore, she thought. *Fuck you.*

"I'll tell Joey that you're counting him as a point five," Meg chuckled.

"Well, he's only five, so it's fitting. I mean, honestly. He's not a whole person yet."

They laughed, and then Meg sobered up.

"Is this really something you want to do?"

Gen nodded. "Yeah. I think so."

Meg took a big breath. "Well, let's do it, then. I'll help you with your condo, and finding a moving company, and looking online for a house there, and hell's bells, we've got a lot to do!"

She was all abuzz, and Gen could feel her energy from here. *You just want my stuff. You want to sell my condo for the most possible money so you can have it. You already have my husband. You want my stuff, too.*

"But first, you promised to go to my convention with me," Meg reminded her.

Gen hesitated, as though she had forgotten. She hadn't.

"Don't tell me you forgot. New York City? Spa days, shopping—you need a new wardrobe, sis—and nights on the town. *You promised.*"

Gen paused again, on purpose, and Meghan cajoled. "Pleasssse. We need this. You need this. It can be your divorce party."

"Okay," Gen said purposely, as though she'd just decided, as though this wasn't her plan all along, as though she wasn't prepared. "Fine. I'll still come."

Her sister squealed and Gen hung up before Meg could get too excited. She was moving away from everything she'd known for over a decade. Even though the world seemed unsettled and uncertain, for the first time in at least five years, she felt at peace.

She changed her clothes because she did smell, and she sprayed herself down with perfume. She loved a good rich vanilla scent when her emotions were heightened. It grounded her, and it was time to calm down, to get collected, to be focused.

She waited until dark, and then she took a cab to a bad part of Chicago and waited for the man she'd found on Craigslist. She chose a back booth, and she shrunk down in the seat.

The man came, finally, wearing a black hoodie and a chain looped from his wallet to his pocket.

She reached out to touch it and he shoved her hand away.

"I'm ready," she said. "It's time."

"There's no turning back," he told her, his face hidden by his hood.

"I know," she agreed. "You said you would do it. Will you?" He nodded.

It would be done.

"You've paid. We're good. It will be done."

She nodded and sang a Doors song.

52

Meg, Now

HAWK WAS PACING his office, while Meg looked through the journal yet again.

"My sister can't seem to control herself when she drops into a bad funk. She's such a character writer that there are times when her depression gets bad."

"Like, how bad?"

"Like not showering for days, like not speaking to anyone."

"And she's always been this way?"

"Definitely, since she was a young teenager. Fourteen, maybe. But my family... We always knew she was a bit different, even before that."

"And Thad? He knew about this side of her when they got married?" Hawk asked.

Meg nodded. "Yeah. He always said life with her wasn't boring. But she was more controlled back then. It was only when she started really embracing her life as an author and deciding that she was a *character writer* that it got terrible. It almost gave her permission, so to speak. It seemed to have gotten better."

"You *thought*."

"Yes. I thought."

"Why didn't anyone tell me about this?" Hawk demanded. "Didn't you think it was pertinent information?"

Meg looked pained. "I'm so sorry. We were afraid that you wouldn't take it seriously if you knew. You'd just think she ran away."

"And it's looking like that's exactly what she did," Hawk snapped. "If so, this hasn't been a good use of New York tax money. This is the same as feeding me false information, you know."

"I'm sorry," Meg whispered. "I just wanted you to find my sister. It's been such a terrible few years. She's been so... God. You can't possibly understand. I'm sorry."

Hawk looked away, annoyed, yet sympathetic. How, he didn't know.

"I don't even know what to say right now," he said limply.

A phone buzzing against wood interrupted his train of thought, and he looked at his desk to find Gen's phone lit up. He'd had it plugged in, and was monitoring it just in case of any activity.

This was the first time it had rung.

"Hello?" he answered it.

"Could I speak with Genevieve Thibault?"

"She's unavailable right now, but I can give her a message."

"Okay, thank you. This is Rita calling from Delta Air Lines. Mrs. Thibault left her laptop on her recent flight. It was turned in by a flight attendant and has been unclaimed for the past few weeks in our lost and found."

"How can we get it?" Hawk asked quickly.

"Just come to the baggage-claims window. Bring the claims ticket that was attached to her boarding pass."

"Thank you." Hawk hung up and turned to Meg.

"Was Gen's boarding pass among her things in the hotel room?"

"No," Meg answered. "But it's in the pocket of my pink coat. She was wearing it that evening…she must've stuck it in there for some reason. God only knows what was going through her mind."

"We need it."

Meg nodded, and they traveled to the hotel together.

They were quiet in the cab and quiet as they walked up to Meg's room. She pulled open the closet door and fished out the ticket. The claims tab was there.

"Bingo," Hawk said triumphantly.

They climbed into another cab and headed for the Delta terminal at LaGuardia.

"This really, really wasn't like her," Meg said as she stared out the window at the dingy New York streets. "She never forgot her laptop. Even on her worst days."

"Well, she did this time."

They pulled up to the Delta sign and got out of the cab. They wove their way through the busy terminal and eventually found their way to the baggage-claims window, handing the ticket to the clerk.

Within a few minutes, they had the lost laptop in their hands.

They carried it to a lounge area, and Hawk booted it up.

Then he clicked into the text messages that fed into her laptop.

"Just some to you," he said, looking through them. "And a couple to Thad. One to your mother, from the night she disappeared. There's a picture of the two of you in the back of a cab."

He turned the laptop toward Meg and showed her the picture of their pink-cheeked faces.

"You both look happy," he observed, examining the photo closely. "Gen's arm is around you. She's smiling. I really don't get it."

Meg sighed. "She can be like that. She's able to compartmentalize. It's hard to say what she believed in that moment. But we actually had fun that evening. We drank, we laughed."

"I'm not an expert, but isn't drinking when you're that upset a bad idea?"

Meg nodded. "Yes. But this was supposed to be a getaway weekend to celebrate her freedom. On the surface, Gen seemed fine."

"So she immersed herself in her story lines so much that she could easily detach from reality. And no one ever thought that was unusual?"

"Have you ever known a writer?" Gen asked dubiously. "They're unusual. When she was deeply immersed, she would get obsessed with particular things. Especially music. When she was feeling dark, she loved The Doors."

"The music group?"

Meg nodded.

"She didn't like them when she was in a good mood. She thought they were too dark, too moody."

"But they suited her when she was dark and moody herself, or writing a dark and moody character," Hawk guessed.

"Bingo."

He pulled her phone out of his pocket and clicked into the music app, then looked into Recently Played.

Every song was The Doors, with "Hello, I Love You" a hundred times in a row.

"She listened to it on repeat," Meg said, not surprised. "It seems like it suited her mood."

Hawk continued to look through her laptop. He was in her emails now.

"This one time, she was writing a book about someone who was having a mental breakdown. She took it to heart."

Hawk looked up

"How so?"

"One time, she showed up on my doorstep at two a.m. She was scraped and bloody, and Thad never even heard her get out of bed. We never did find out what happened to her, or how she made it several miles without her car."

"Did she get like that frequently?"

"Yes. And it was exhausting trying to keep track of her moods."

Hawk pulled up Word and went to Open Recent. The laptop opened the book she was currently working on.

He started skimming it, to get a feel for how she'd been thinking.

"Thad and I… We just understood each other when no one else did," Meg said defensively. "Joe didn't get it. He's a good man, but we got married too young, and we're not right for each other. I think that if this whole mess has shown me anything, it's that."

Hawk wanted to ask about that but couldn't, because he was noticing the characters' names.

"Melanie, Thomas, Georgia," he said out loud. "Do those sound similar to Meghan, Thad and Genevieve to you?"

Meg froze and scooted closer to Hawk so they could read together.

They ignored the noises around them and the voices on the intercom as they lost themselves in the story Gen had created.

"It's about a crumbling marriage," Meg murmured aloud twenty minutes later. "It's reality-based fiction. That does make sense. She's always been a method writer."

"You're Melanie," Hawk pointed out. He read aloud a sentence. "'Melanie wanted everything Georgia had. She couldn't begin to know how to be her own person, because she'd never had to be.'" He looked up at Meg. "Harsh."

"And untrue," she snapped. "Entirely untrue. I didn't want my sister's life."

"No, just her marriage," the detective agreed.

Meg grunted and shook her head. "I didn't want her marriage, either. Thad and I had a connection when the two of us needed it the most. It's lonely when you're dealing with someone who isn't based in reality."

"Wasn't it a bad idea to allow her to have a career in fiction, when in real life, she was detached from reality?"

"*Allow* her to have a career?" Meg reared her head back. "You don't know a lot about Gen, do you? We couldn't *allow* or *disallow* anything."

"Okay, noted," Hawk said calmly. "I didn't mean any offense."

"I know you didn't," she answered. "Gen is just an unusual person. I love her, but she can be difficult. And no one can understand unless they've seen it."

"Well, you're a doctor, so you do have an advantage."

"True."

They kept reading, about how Georgia was the victim, and Thomas and Melanie were plotting against her. It was very apparent that they were the villains in her story.

"That's normal," Meg said aloud. "She was lashing out.

This story was her catharsis, the way she handled her pain. Artists frequently do that."

Hawk started to read aloud.

"'Georgia kept to herself, growing more and more isolated. What was this life? Was madness, in fact, freedom? Behind her back, her husband and sister cavorted in sin, as Georgia whiled away in silence.'"

"Now she's getting ridiculous," Meg muttered. "She was never silent."

"'Her bedroom was a tomb, quiet and dead. She tread in it alone, with only her own madness to accompany her.'"

They continued to read, shoulder to shoulder.

Melanie combed her hair and waited for Thomas to join her. They laughed about Georgia's naivete while they readied to climb into bed together. Down the hall, Georgia slept, blissfully unaware.

"You are the love of my life," he whispered to Melanie as he climbed in beside her.

"As you are mine," she murmured, her lips on his throat. They clutched each other, as they rode waves of ecstasy, over and over throughout the night. By morning, Thomas's member was wet and limp, thoroughly used.

"I forgot she wrote romance," Hawk said ruefully. Meg didn't answer, as she was absorbing the fact that her sister was writing about her and Thad's lovemaking.

In the morning light, Georgia crept from her own bed and stood in the doorway, gazing at her sister and her husband.

Her sister's face was beautiful in the light. They had gotten their good looks from their father, the same blond hair and blue eyes, although they inherited the cleft in their chins from their mother.

She loved them both. She hated them both.

She would rather die than stand in their way, would rather die than watch them live happily ever after together. There was only one thing to do at this point.

She had to kill her sister.

Hawk and Meg reached this point at the same time and looked at each other.

"In the journal, she wrote that *someone agreed to do it.* I thought it was gibberish, along with the rest of that page, but I think she might've been talking about the abductor," Hawk said slowly.

"My coat," Meg said, and her voice shook. "She took my pink coat that night. She was wearing it. Hawk, we look enough alike to be twins."

Hawk stared into Meg's pale face, and the truth dawned on him like the sun.

"It was supposed to be you."

53

Gen, Then

GEN GRABBED MEG'S pink coat and slung it around her waist. She fluttered her fingers at the doorman, and brushed him off when he cautioned her about New York at night.

Of course, she knew.

She was drunk, not a child.

The stars twinkled at her like fairy lights and she waved back, dipping and flouncing along the sidewalk. The lights blurred and followed her like snakes, and her cheeks were flushed.

She stopped at the chipped yellow fire hydrant to adjust her shoe. Then she threw her head back and twirled in the night.

She'd never felt anything so magnificent as the night air on her skin right now.

"Meghan," a voice whispered from behind.

She paused, and for a split second, she remembered what she had done, what she had set up, and that someone was mistaking her for her sister right now.

But there was a pain in her head, and then nothing.

It was the buzz that woke her.

Before she was really awake, she felt her body being jarred, vibrated.

Her head throbbed, and she opened her eyes. It took a moment for her eyes to focus—everything was so blurry.

Two red eyes burned in front of her. She started to thrash and kick, but her hands were bound. She was in a dragon's belly, she decided. She would die here, and become part of it. She would be its soul. Maybe that wouldn't be so bad.

But her head.

It throbbed, and she tried to clutch at it with her bound hands.

The dragon eyes blinked, then they closed.

She was in the dark. She was drunk. She kicked and kicked, and then the dragon's mouth opened.

Someone leaned in.

A man in a hood. The pain in her head was so bad, she almost couldn't see.

"No," she tried to say, when he called her Meghan again. *I'm not Meghan. I'm Genevieve.*

But he didn't listen, and her tongue didn't work. Her mouth seemed to be sewn closed. She wiggled her lips, and they worked against glue.

The man hefted her out of the dragon, and her legs banged against metal.

"I'm sorry that your sister doesn't love you," he told her, and she was indignant at that.

"She does," she tried to say. "She always has."

She could hear water, crashing and lapping, and she didn't

know where she was. The stars mocked her now instead of danced, and she cursed them. The water started singing to her, though, and she sang with it. *Hello, I love you, won't you tell me your name.*

"You're fucking batshit nuts," the man said as he was dragging her.

Her shoes caught on rocks, and it should've hurt but it didn't.

She was focused instead on the moon's yellow belly, hanging full in the night.

He lost his grip and tugged at her hair, and she tried to kick him.

He laughed. She'd never forget the maniacal sound of it. He was soulless.

He was part of the dragon, she realized, with drunken logic. He needed her soul. She fought harder, then harder, and still he laughed. She was a tiny insect, and he was the spider.

He threw her on the ground, onto her knees.

She looked at the ground, at the pebbles and the sand. Dead grass floated in bits around them, patchy and sparse. *Where are we?* she wondered, and then she didn't care. She felt warmer than she had in a decade. *I'm floating. I'm sinking. I'm water.*

She hummed and the man kicked at her.

"You're crazy," he decided, certain now.

He shoved her head down, so she could only see the pebbles beneath her. There was a jagged gray one. *It would be a good marble*, she thought. *I'll get it for Thad. He'll like it.* She tried to reach for it, but her hands were bound. She'd forgotten.

"Do you know why you're here?" the man demanded. "You slept with your sister's husband. She's making it right with this. Do you hear? You brought this on your own head. She wanted you to know that."

Something cold was shoved into Gen's neck, right where it met her shoulders. She bucked at it, but it resisted.

Her fingers scratched at the ground as she tried to get the pebble for Thad.

She was startled when the man abruptly fell in front of her, facedown on the wet earth, his gun skittering away from them.

A woman stood behind him, a rock in her hands. Gen could see only her eyes—the rest of her face was covered with a hood—but it was clear that she had struck the man in the head.

"You saved me," Gen told her. "Why?"

"That was a bad man," Jody answered. "I followed you here. I have to take you somewhere safe. Somewhere you can't take Thad away from me."

She used the rock again, this time on Gen.

When Gen woke again, she was in a utility shed alone. She was alive.

54

Gen, Now

"LET ME GO," Gen begged Jody. "I swear, no one will know. You'll never see me again. You can have Thad, and you'll all be happy."

Jody considered that.

"How do I know you're telling me the truth?" she asked. "Thad says I can never tell."

"I will swear to it," Gen told her. "I don't want to be here. You have my word."

"They'll know what I did," Jody said. "And Thad will be so mad at me."

An idea came to Gen, and her eyes lit up. Her plan had been foiled, but there was still something she could do. A way she could escape.

"I just thought of something," she said. "Listen."

So Jody did, and when Gen was finished talking, they were on the same page. They would both benefit.

Jody untaped Gen and picked up the phone to call her brother.

"Thad, can you come get me? I came to find you."

Gen ducked out of the shed without a backward glance.

Seven days later, Meg stood with Hawk on the shores of the Hudson River while divers hunted for Genevieve.

Meg pressed her hand to her mouth, and turned into Hawk's chest to hide her eyes as the divers came up empty-handed time and time again.

"You're sure Jody said she was here?"

"Yes. She said Gen wanted to die and walked into the water and never came out. She had a plan to frame you and Thad for her death, to make sure you paid for hurting her. But she came to her senses and thought better of it. Jody unknowingly saved Gen from the abductor Gen had hired to grab you."

"You mean, the man Gen paid to kill me," Meg corrected.

Hawk looked away.

"Jody knocked him out," he said. "Only Gen didn't want to be saved."

"She wasn't a bad person," Meg said simply.

Hawk wasn't sure whom she was talking to. Maybe herself, maybe him.

"She was a lost soul, I think. She was out of her mind with rage. She loved me."

"She needed help," Hawk said matter-of-factly. Without thought, his hand stroked Meg's shoulder in comfort.

"You didn't know her," Meg answered softly. "She was delicate. Her mind was so brilliant, yet so fragile."

She didn't watch as the coroner's office van waited nearby for a body. They didn't find one, though. Her body was gone.

"She tried to have you killed," Hawk reminded her.

"She wasn't herself."

Meg pulled away and straightened her shirt, and wiped at her eye makeup. She lifted her chin.

"When is Joe arriving?"

"He's not. I'll see him at home."

Hawk didn't ask for details, and Meg didn't offer. She knew what she had to do, and that was her business.

"How are your parents?"

"Mom wanted to be here, but Dad wouldn't let her."

"Good."

"We still just can't believe this. We're in shock. We feel guilty... We feel so many things."

"You're not guilty," Hawk answered, turning to her. "You didn't do this. Thad didn't do this. No one did this. It's just a tragic situation."

"A waste of New York tax money," Meg threw his words from a while ago back at him.

"Sometimes I'm a dick," Hawk acknowledged. "I'm working on it." He paused. "What will you do now?"

"Go back to work, I guess. My partner has had to cover for me long enough. It's time for me to deal with my life. All parts of it."

Meg got into the cab alone and headed back to her hotel room, the one she was supposed to have been sharing with Gen.

She sat on the bed, surrounded by Gen's things, and tried to imagine what Gen had felt like there at the end. She'd known about the affair and hadn't had anyone to talk to about it.

Only the private investigator.

Before she could decide otherwise, Meg called him.

"Dr. McCready," he answered.

"Hello, Mr. Jenkins."

"What can I do for you? I was very sorry to hear about your sister."

Jenkins was somber, and Meg did believe he was genuinely sorry.

"I know my sister paid you a lot of money," she started. "But were you also friends? It kills me to think that she didn't have anyone to talk to there at the end."

"I was her friend," he agreed. "Maybe the only one she had."

"That's not fair," Meg told him. "You haven't been through everything for years, the ups and the downs and the struggles. You've only known her for a period of months."

"She was a good girl, and her family failed her," Jenkins said firmly. "You'll never get me to believe otherwise."

"I don't know why I care what you think, but I do. I'll be arriving back in Chicago tonight. Can you meet me? I have something to show you."

Jenkins agreed, and Meg texted him the address.

She packed up Gen's things, her belly clenching with every item. An hour or so later, her mother rapped on her door. Her eyes were red. Her face was pale.

"Are you almost ready? Our flight leaves in two hours."

"We've got time, Mom," Meg assured her.

"I don't want to be late. I just want to be gone from this wretched place. You never should've brought her here."

Meg stared at her mom. "Mom, you realize that it wouldn't have mattered where we were. Gen was going to do what Gen was going to do. She tried to have me killed."

"And now she's dead," her mother snapped. "I think that's punishment enough."

Tears streaked her cheeks, and she wiped furiously at them. "Damn it. I thought I didn't have any tears left."

"You lost your daughter," Meg told her gently. "Your emotions will be all over the place for a long time. But you'll be okay. We'll get through this."

Meg didn't say out loud what she was thinking, that a little compassion for *her* wouldn't hurt anything.

She felt resentment coming from her mother, and it stabbed her.

"Even now, you're finding fault with me," she said slowly. "What is it about me, Mom? Why have you always blamed me, never Gen?"

"Good grief, Meghan," her mother snapped, and picked up one of Gen's shirts. She held it to her nose and inhaled it. "Gen always needed more attention than you did. Surely, as a doctor, you can understand."

"I understand that you always resented me for being healthy, I think. And since Gen wasn't, she got every latitude imaginable. Even now, she tried to have me killed, and you're angry with *me*."

"You aren't the victim here," her mother answered.

"Only because a mistake was made," Meg tossed back. "Otherwise, I would be the one lying at the bottom of the river right now. And I didn't do a thing to deserve it."

"You slept with your sister's husband!"

Meg froze, unaware that her mother knew.

Ginny eyed her, her eyes bright. "Oh, yes. I knew. Your sister knew, too. Did you think no one would figure it out?"

"You've known this whole time?"

"I suspected. How could you?"

"It was a mistake. People make them."

"Your father and I haven't been unfaithful even one time

in our entire marriage," her mother said. "It's really not that hard."

Meg decided not to reply. Her mother was overwhelmed, and even in death Gen was her priority. She would overlook it for now—her mother was grieving.

"I'll meet you in the lobby," she told her mom, signaling it was time for her to go.

She finished packing, and as she did, she threw Gen's vanilla perfume in the trash. That scent evoked periods in life she desperately wanted to forget.

In fact, there was so much of the past couple of years that she wanted to erase.

She was on her way to the airport, sitting silently with her parents when she realized something.

She hadn't allowed herself to cry yet.

55

JENKINS STOOD AT the window in his living room, and his wife watched from the sofa, where she was knitting a baby blanket for their grandson. She started to say something but, from years of experience, knew better. So she kept silent until he decided he wanted to talk.

It didn't take too long.

"I failed that girl," Jenkins said, his shoulders slumped. "She needed someone. And I let her down."

"You did not," Becky argued, and she was ready for this. She'd known it was coming. "You did everything in your power to help her. You were a friend when she needed it the most."

"She's still dead, Beck," he said, and he felt so very sad. His chest felt hollow when he pictured Gen's face. "She was troubled. And no one could fix her."

"There!" she announced. "You said it. No one could fix her. You couldn't, her husband couldn't, her family couldn't. It's tragic and it's god-awful, but you couldn't make it right, Simon. No one could."

Jenkins sat next to her, trying to relax, but his fingers drummed a rhythm on the arm of the sofa. "Her sister wants to meet with me tonight. I don't know what she wants."

"It's hard to say," Becky said carefully. "But no matter what you think of her, please remember that you only got Gen's side of things. And now we know…her view wasn't always, um, accurate."

Jenkins started to protest, but Becky wouldn't hear it.

"Besides, no matter what else, that girl just lost her sister."

Jenkins couldn't argue with that, and Becky knew it.

"So be compassionate," his wife added. "As I know you will be."

"Well, I'd better git," he said, standing up. "May as well get this over with."

He met Meg at the coffee shop, and to his surprise, Thad was there, as well. He almost turned around and left, but something in Meg's sad eyes stopped him. He hesitated, then sighed.

He sat at the table.

"I'm sorry for your loss," he told Thad. Thad looked like he hadn't slept in days. Dark circles rimmed his eyes, which were red in the corners.

Thad nodded. "It *is* a loss," he replied. "I know you probably think I don't feel like it is, but I do."

"I'm not here to judge," Jenkins told him. "I'm here because Meghan asked me to come. I don't know why I'm here."

"I know that Gen hired you to investigate my affair," Thad

told him. He almost physically winced, as though the words were poison. "It's something I'll never be proud of, but also something I can't take back. The past haunts us like that."

"That it does," Jenkins agreed.

"But Meg wants you to know, and I guess I do, too, that my marriage to Gen was over long ago."

Jenkins stared at him hard. "Then why were you still sharing a condo with her? Why did she think she was married to you?"

"Because she was," Thad said. "We are still technically married. Well, I guess I'm a widower now. I just... It'd been a long time since we really connected."

"She would often call me and tell me about amazing nights she'd spent with Thad," Meg said, staring out the window, but Jenkins could tell she was seeing the past instead. "And Thad would confirm that none of it was real. Their marriage was empty—but yet, she'd imagine passionate nights and marital bliss."

"It was her writer's mind," Thad added. "She imagined the life she wanted, and then she believed it, rather than just confront what our life actually was."

"If she wasn't happy, why didn't she just fix it or leave?" Jenkins asked, confused.

Meg shrugged. "She didn't know how, I guess."

"So you're wanting me to not judge you for your affair," Jenkins said. "Okay. It's not my business. Although, I should point out that your marriage to Joe seems quite real, yet you stepped out on him."

Meg swallowed.

"Yeah. I did. I'm not proud of that."

"But that's between Meg and Joe," Thad interrupted. "We're here to tell you the truth about me and Gen."

"I don't understand why you weren't forthcoming about all of this from the get-go," Jenkins said. "It doesn't make sense."

"I didn't want to hurt Gen," Thad said. "I worked such long hours anyway that staying in a marriage that wasn't awful wasn't really a hardship. It wasn't awful. It just wasn't good. But to her, it was wonderful. In her mind. So I went along with it."

"Gen forced his hand, though. She found out about the affair, and she demanded a divorce. Thad gave her everything she wanted, even offered her money, but in her journals, she concocted an elaborate scheme to drag things out. We think that deep down she didn't want the divorce, but she also didn't want to stay."

"So she concocted the whole thing to make herself less culpable about having a failed marriage?" Jenkins postulated. Meg shrugged.

"We'll never know."

"We've read through the book she was working on," Thad said. "And there's a lot of parallels there, between real life and this book. One of them was a character named Jinx."

"She called me Jenks," Jenkins said. Thad nodded.

"In her book, she loved Jinx a great deal," Meg told the older man. "Jinx made a great impact on her. He touched her deeply. All the while, he never tried to take advantage of her. She said, in fact, that sometimes people took advantage of his kindness. He apparently worked for abused women who couldn't afford to pay him."

Jenkins listened without acknowledging.

Meghan took out her phone and read a few passages. "'Jinx's house was small and tidy, but it was apparent that many of his well-loved treasures had seen better days. Georgia itched to help him, but she knew he was too proud to accept it. She loved him with her whole heart. He was one of the few who had ever looked at her for who she *was*, instead of who her disease defined her to be.'"

Jenkins cleared his throat and looked away. Meg touched his hand.

"My sister loved you."

He nodded, unable to speak. He didn't trust his voice not to crack.

"As you know, in Gen's delusions, she was trying to frame Meg and me for a few things. She wanted to make it appear that I took out a life insurance policy on her. The thing is, that policy is actually in effect, and I am still the beneficiary. Normally, in the event of a suicide, insurance does not pay out. But Gen wasn't in her right mind, so we've appealed. When that money comes in, I'm going to send two million of it to you."

Jenkins choked now.

"She'd want you to have it, so that you can take even more cases on, for the women who can't help themselves, for the women who can't pay."

A tear slipped down Jenkins's face now, and he didn't even try to hide it.

"I'm going to use the rest to fund research for mental illness," Thad said. "What we overlooked as mercurial and dramatic was something far more. We just didn't know it. My wife was a beautiful soul. She didn't mean for any of this to happen."

Jenkins nodded, and his eyes were still welled. They all stood up, and Meg stepped forward.

"May I hug you?" she asked softly. He nodded once, and she wrapped her arms around him. "Thank you for loving my sister," she whispered.

He nodded and turned, thinking they wouldn't see the rampant tears. They did.

Meg smiled softly, watching him go.

"I'll miss you," Thad said quietly. His hand was on Meg's arm.

She looked up at him. "I'll miss you, too."

Thad walked out of the coffee shop and into the breeze. He lifted his face and stood still on the sidewalk for a moment before he walked away.

Meg walked away without looking back.

When she opened the door to her home, she walked straight to Joey's bedroom, where he was napping peacefully. She stood over him, watching him rest, so very thankful for him. Joe loomed in the doorway, and he smiled at her, ever so slightly. There was sadness in that smile.

"Can we talk?" he asked her.

She dreaded it, she yearned for it, she was terrified of it. But it needed to be done, so she nodded. They sat in the living room, inches apart, and Joe held one of her hands.

"We tried," he said simply. "We really did. You tried. I tried. But it's never going to be the same now, Meggie."

He looked deep into her eyes, and his were so kind. She cupped his cheek with her hand, and he leaned into it.

"I love you," she told him. "I am so very sorry."

"I'm sorry, too," Joe answered. He wasn't angry. He was resigned. "I love you."

They sat still for the longest time.

"I'll move somewhere close," Joe said. "We'll split time with Joey equally. We'll be good co-parents. I respect you, and you respect me. We'll make it work."

He smiled bravely. Meg smiled back.

"We'll make it work."

They leaned their heads together and sat for the longest time.

56

One year later

"JOEY!" MEG CALLED, leaning out the back door. "Come inside!"

Her son bounded indoors, kicking off his shoes by the door. Meg kissed his cheek.

"Go wash the playground off your face. Your dad's here."

Joey trotted off obediently, while Joe stepped into the kitchen. "Do you want me to fix that gutter for you on my way out? It's hanging down on the corner."

Meg smiled. "You already spent an hour fixing the air-conditioning filter last night. It's okay, Joe. I'll just call someone."

He met her gaze, and he knew she was saying that *she was okay.*

He smiled at her, and then jogged after Joey, who was already running out the door.

"Love you, Mama," the little boy called over his shoulder. Meg shook her head. He was a mile-a-minute.

"Good luck!" she called to Joey.

He stuck his tongue out at her as he got into the car.

She was still laughing when she went back inside. She and Joe had settled into a comfortable rhythm—a set of good friends who shared a son. After all that had happened, they were surprisingly healthy.

She sat down at her desk to work on the bills. Joe had always taken care of that before since Meg worked such long hours, but it didn't bother her at all to take care of it now.

She clicked into the bank website, paid a few things, then drifted into her email.

There was one from her mother.

Meg,

We're leaving for the cruise in the morning, so I wanted to tell you a couple of things: the extra key is in the metal turtle by the back door, and our wills are in the fireproof safe in the closet. I'm sure you won't need them, but I want to be prepared. Also, just as I always do, I wrote a letter for you to open *only* in the unlikely event that something happens to us. You know the rules—no opening it unless I'm gone. Also, I found a good picture of you and Gen I thought you might like. It's attached.

Have a good week,

Love,

Mom

The corners of Meg's mouth tilted a bit. Her mother always did this when they traveled. So melodramatic, yet so prepared. And she was completely lying—she meant for

Meg to read the letter now. She always did, and Meg would comply, and they would just both pretend that it didn't exist and go back to pretending that Ginny didn't have feelings. It was their thing.

She clicked open the document.

Dear Meghan,
My beautiful baby.

If you're reading this, I'm gone. I want you to know that I love you. I hate that you doubt that, that you think that we loved Gen more. We never did, baby girl. Gen needed our attention. She couldn't function like you could. You were so perfect, so efficient, always. You were born being able to ride a bike, I think. Haha.

When Gen died, I thought my world ended. I never thought I'd really live again, because the part of me where Gen resided was gone. What I didn't understand is that she's not gone. She's still there. She's still there when I read a book or examine a butterfly. She's still there when we dream, because that's where she always existed—in dreams.

I know you messed up. You and Thad made a bad decision, but know that I forgive you. And no, you don't need my forgiveness, but my point is, I forgive you and I know Gen would, too. She knows the situation, honey. Wherever she is now, she knows. She knows that you spent your life protecting her. She forgives you.

You, my love, are my pragmatic genius. You're whom I turn to when I need levity, when I need depth, when I need life-altering decisions. I trust you with that. You are the very best of me, and the very best work God ever did. I love you, a million times.

Please forgive me for not always making you feel that way.

All my love,

Your mom

Damn it. Meg reached for a tissue and dabbed at her eyes. She hadn't realized how much she'd needed to hear those words. She'd spent the past year trying to forgive herself for everything, for every bad choice, and now, in this moment, she decided that maybe she had.

Maybe she didn't need to hate herself anymore.

She opened the picture her mother had attached to find her and Gen when they were around twelve and thirteen. They had their arms wrapped around each other while they stood on the beach. They had skinny arms and chicken legs, tanned from the sun. Their smiles were wide, their faces innocent.

In that moment, neither of them knew what the future would bring. She wondered what they'd have done differently, if they could've done anything at all.

Her cell phone, her modern-day tether, buzzed and she answered it, expecting the hospital since she was on call.

She didn't expect to hear Hawk's deep voice.

"Meg?"

Her stomach dropped and butterflies spilled from their cages in her belly.

She'd thought about him a million times during the past year, had reached for the phone a hundred times to call him. But she was sure he looked down on her, that he thought she was a monster.

"Yes. Hello," she managed to say. "How are you?"

"I've been okay. I'm sorry I haven't checked in on you. I should've. How are you?"

"I'm fine," she told him honestly. "Better than I thought I would be."

"Have you heard from Thad at all?"

"Not for a few months. He's handling it as well as can be expected. His sister is in a group home now, where she has a bunch of friends and is supervised."

"That's good," Hawk said.

There was an awkward silence.

"I haven't been able to get you out of my head," Hawk confessed quickly, before he changed his mind. "I kept thinking it would pass, and it didn't."

Meg's mouth went dry.

"And I was wondering if you'd let me buy you dinner? Maybe we can start off on a normal foot, one where I'm not investigating you for a crime."

Meg laughed, nervous. "That would be lovely. But I'm not planning on being in New York anytime soon."

"That's okay, because I'm in Chicago," he said, and Meg's heart took off like a rocket. "For the weekend. I had a business thing."

"I'd love to," Meg answered quickly. "We'll be just like normal people."

"Or as much as we can be," Hawk amended. "Seven o'clock. Tonight?"

"It's a date," Meg replied.

It's a date, she repeated in her head as she hung up. She was going on a date with the detective who'd investigated her. Life was weird.

She looked at the photo again, at Gen's sweet young face. Her eyes sparked with life, her muscles were flexed in strength and her smile was her armor against the world that would eventually hurt her.

Meg couldn't mend the past. But, going forward, she could

do everything possible to be a better person, the kind of person Gen would've wanted her to be.

"Sisters forever," she whispered.

It seemed as though Gen watched her from the photo, and Meg remembered a line from Gen's book, a book that had since been published and the proceeds were going to women's shelters.

Was madness, in fact, freedom?

Meg wasn't sure. Probably. But it was also the exact opposite. Gen's madness had lied to her, made her believe things that weren't true, and those things kept her in anguish. Because of that, her madness was also a prison.

Meg hoped she was free now.

EPILOGUE

Madrid, Spain

A WOMAN SAT in the corner of the restaurant, sipping her drink and laughing at the music that surrounded her. Madrid suited her. Everyone ate late, stayed up late and loved all through the night. She could unleash her emotions and no one noticed, no one cared.

She had a notepad with her, and she scribbled a book idea. She had a new name now, so she had to establish a whole new fan base, but her talent showed through, no matter what name she used.

Her latest book was about a woman who staged her own death.

It was something she had experience with.

She thought of her old life sometimes, of her parents, her sister, her husband. She missed Meg. She missed her parents.

And sometimes, she even missed Thad. He'd loved her, and she had loved him. For a while.

She had forgiven them for what they had done.

She knew she wasn't an easy person. She knew she could be a challenge.

But she also knew that she deserved to be happy. She deserved to not have anyone stare at her in pity, or lust after her husband.

She could possibly find that here.

She could rebuild. She could become the person that she always wanted to be. No one would ever know who she used to be.

That woman was dead.

And that was okay with her.

She did wonder about Jenkins from time to time, but she searched for him online, and it seemed that he had expanded his practice and was helping more women than ever. He had a soft heart, regardless of his crusty exterior.

The woman didn't miss the person she used to be. In fact, she was even grateful for everything, for the jagged path that had led her to this moment.

Sometimes, beauty came from pain. Beginnings came from endings. And new lives came from old ones that had come to an end. Her old life had taught her so many things. She would treasure them as she lived her new one.

Getting up, she paid her check, downed the rest of her drink and disappeared into the dark night, her flowery perfume trailing behind her.

★ ★ ★ ★ ★

L